INTENTIONAL ACTS

a novel

12/12/04

ISBN: 0-923568-60-3

Special thanks to M&D Investments and Whitford Chiropractic, both in Mt. Pleasant, Michigan.

For further information, please contact:

Chris Zimmerman
P.O. Box 180
Shepherd, MI 48883

INTENTIONAL ACTS

Chris Zimmerman

One

I WOKE UP before the alarm clock had the chance to blare, smelling the aroma of freshly brewed coffee and fried bacon mixed with the pungent, dank odor of Gerry Buchanan's old cabin. He was in the kitchen preparing breakfast and was probably halfway through lunch, too. Mess, his chocolate Labrador retriever, was busy lapping at his water and nibbling the kernels of food Gerry put in his bowl. I rolled over, and heard the old bed ping from the stress. What a great feeling it is to wake up in a strange place and wonder what grand adventures lie ahead.

Gerry's cabin was tucked away in the east end of Michigan's Upper Peninsula, on the edge of the St. Mary's River, on the cusp of Munuscong Bay—one of the best marshes for duck hunting in Michigan. Built in the early 1900s, the cabin was made from white pine logs, purged from the lot where ospreys nested and red squirrels once chattered. Now only Gerry's cabin, and rows of others just like it, stand guard over the freighters that pass up and down the river.

The wind had the storm windows in the old cabin rattling, which is always a good harbinger if you're a duck hunter. Wind keeps the ducks anxious. Ducks rest when the winds are calm and the skies are sunny. They race south on gusty winds and scudding skies, dodging decoys and hunters along the way. The forecast couldn't have been better for hunter or hunted. I heard it the night before on the weather-band radio Gerry keeps behind the rickety cabin door—strong southeast winds, turning to northwest by afternoon with falling temperatures. On paper, we had the makings of a terrific day for a duck hunt.

If only Scott Husted wasn't along. He was our District Coordinator for the insurance company we represented, Surety Guarantee. His job was to police the agents, motivate us for bigger and better sales, and recruit new agents to one day become successful like Gerry and myself.

Scott was one of those bosses that liked to take credit for the efforts of the people who worked for him. He was the kind of guy to be first in line at the buffet table, and the last to leave at a party just as long as the bar was still open. While Gerry and I were good agents, we weren't as good as Scott when he was an agent. He made us feel second best, like we could do more, like we were on the verge of going into the "insurance agent's hall of fame" if there is such a place.

He made a career out of being aggressive, assertive; some would call it pushy, which was hardly our style. He invited himself to the cabin, then made himself at home. If it was my cabin, I would have turned down Scott's plea for an invitation, but Gerry caved in and let him join us. If Gerry had a fault, it was that he was a bit of a pushover.

As much as I disliked Scott, I never wished him any bad luck or ill harm. We were honest businessmen scattered across northern Michigan. Some of us were leaders in our communities, the "big fish in our little ponds," as Gerry used to say. All we ever wanted was a decent insurance product to sell. Our clients trusted us. They respected us, and the advice we gave them. When they had a fire in their house, or were involved in a car accident, we were the ones that helped them out. We were the heroes—the people that came through on the promise to take care of them when they needed us most.

Scott swung open the door and walked into our bedroom, turning on the overhead light bulb. I pretended to be sleeping as he pulled his long underwear and woolen socks from his overnight bag. It was his first duck hunt, so I was confident he'd overdress. Rookies always overdress, for some reason. The bunk heaved slightly as he sat on the lower level and put on his socks. The smell of the bacon was stronger now, and by the sounds of the gurgling coffee pot, breakfast must have been close to ready. Scott disappeared from the bedroom and I heard him laughing hysterically in the kitchen, although I couldn't imagine what could have been so funny at five a.m.

I hopped out of the upper berth and made it to the bathroom, where the five-gallon bucket of water Gerry kept at the toilet's side was empty. Gerry turned the cabin's water off just after Labor Day so he wouldn't have to worry about frozen pipes later in the season. We flushed the toilet and did the dishes by well water, which was no big deal because an artesian well flowed just a few paces away from the cabin's door. Scott must have forgotten the courtesy about filling up the bucket for the next guy.

I quickly dressed and took the tall buckets to the well. It was warm for the end of October, with temperatures in the upper 50s. We had plenty of wind and it whistled around me as I filled the buckets.

"Morning, Larry." Scott greeted me at the door when I returned, grinning as if we were long-lost buddies.

"Morning," I said, straining from the weight of both sloshing buckets. "Thank you," I continued, as he held the rickety door open, "kinda warm out there."

"That's okay, I brought enough warm clothes to last a week," he said, laughing hysterically. I made it to the bathroom and flushed the toilet, then poured a small amount from the bucket into a bowl, where I brushed my teeth and washed my face. I finished getting dressed, then checked in on Gerry, who was scooping up fried eggs with a slotted spatula.

Duck hunting has its roots in ritual. You wake up early, prepare meals, and don warm clothing. You plan ahead, and use tools, equipment, and supplies throughout the day. Gerry and I have our own little jobs, our own ritual. He always cooked the meals while I prepared the gear. "Morning, sir."

"Morning to you, too."

"Where are the keys to the Explorer? I'll get the boat hooked up and ready to go."

"Behind the front door, but grab a plate and eat first."

"Thank you," I said. "Turkey bacon?"

"Yup."

"Still on that cholesterol kick?"

"I wanna get it below 200 by New Year's."

I walked, paper plate in hand, to the back of the door and turned up the volume on the weather radio. Then I sat down on the threadbare couch under the print of canvasback ducks swooping over a vacant blind.

The monotone weather-band voice rambled on and on about regions west of the cabin: *"Water temperature at Whitefish Point 45 degrees."* I took a bite of the bacon, then opened the door for Scott, who was outside in his Chrysler 300m, checking messages on his cell phone. *"For the Algoma region of Ontario..."*

"Got your gear ready to go?" I asked him.

"I threw all I have into the boat. Hope that's where you guys want it." He laughed again, even though there was hardly anything funny about his remarks.

"Sure, that's fine, as long as it won't blow out on the way there."

"Nope. Made sure of that." He walked toward the kitchen to get some breakfast.

"For the east end of the Upper Peninsula..." I quit chewing my toast and listened to the monotone forecast. *"Falling temperatures this afternoon, highs in the middle 50s, lows in the upper 20s. Small-craft advisory will be in effect this afternoon..."* This was good. It was a classic late fall weather pattern that would have every duck in North America on their horse and headed south. I put a piece of bacon on the second piece of toast, added a fried egg, then folded the toast in half. It made a nice little sandwich.

Ten minutes later we were in Gerry's Explorer heading north to the west end of the Sault locks, where a boat launch made the upper St. Mary's River available to sportsmen. On the way there, Scott had to tell us all about his new gun, and how much it cost. That was his style. He liked to brag, even though Gerry and I weren't impressed. When we arrived, Gerry threw the Explorer in park as the tip of his big outboard touched the water's surface. We piled out and tossed the rest of our gear into the boat: shotguns, ammunition batteries, a small cooler flush with sandwiches, and the burlap tarps to complete our steel façade. Instead of hunting in the traditional marshes around Sault Ste. Marie or Munuscong Bay, we decided to hunt the upper St. Mary's River at the end of one of the piers that separates each lock. The piers are made of steel, now in varying degrees of decay that have a collage-like appearance. Our canvas tarps would make our boat look like an extension of the pier.

Gerry parked the Explorer in the lot, then met us at the dock. Scott jumped aboard without being asked, while I held onto the gunnels so the boat wouldn't drift away. Gerry's boat wasn't especially big or seaworthy, but at 18 feet long and six feet wide, we could tackle substantial seas. Then again, we had never had three men in the boat loaded with all our gear. Our outings had always been a two-man, one-dog affair. An extra 180 pounds of man and gear couldn't have been that much of a burden…

Gerry primed the 90-horse outboard motor on the back of the boat, adjusting the throttle, then the choke. The motor whined and whined until it caught, only to die over and over again. Gerry cursed under his breath, "Come on, you," repeating the combination of choke, throttle, choke until the motor sparked to life. "I gotta change those plugs," he lamented, revving the motor. Finally it caught. Gerry gave it more gas and it roared like a caged mustang. As he backed off the throttle, he turned on the on-board electronics, including the Global Positioning System and the ship-to-shore radio.

From there, he lifted the hood on his seat and found the stainless steel pole with the light on one end. He plugged the other end into the boat's transom, and the cockpit took on a warm glow. I still held the boat to the dock until Gerry gave me the nod to climb aboard.

The three of us disappeared into the inky darkness of Mosquito Bay until we neared the row of rocks that separates the "power canal" from the thoroughfares the freighters use to navigate the locks. The power canal is a mile-and-a-half river of its own that traverses the locks on the American side and the rapids on the Canadian side. At the opposite end of the power canal lies the Edison Sault hydroelectric plant, where columns of water fall 30 feet over dozens of turbines.

We were at the upper end of the canal, where a sign illuminated by several floodlights read "*Danger: Swift Current.*" Scott read the sign and asked for a life jacket.

"What do you want one of those for?" Gerry asked.

"Think of it as my own little insurance policy. I'd rather be safe than sorry…"

"We don't wear life jackets on my boat," Gerry advised him. "Haven't you heard of the 'good hands people'?" Scott grinned, then laughed hysterically, looking two or three times at the sign as it slowly passed. Mess noticed it too, from his perch on the bow, amid the stacks of decoys with long cords wrapped around their midriffs. It was true; Gerry and I hardly ever wore life jackets, figuring that if we did end up in the drink, we'd expire before the other could turn the boat around for a rescue. But there really wasn't much need for a life jacket—the howling wind was warm, offshore, and hadn't the reach to kick up substantial waves.

I had a twinge of guilt settling for Scott. He was plainly nervous on his first duck hunt, and I didn't want to have him vomiting or something from a jittery stomach. So I broke the ice with a little conversation. "How many boxes of shells did you bring?"

"Three," he said.

"Good, you won't run out. I guess you *could* run out if you don't shoot very well."

"Don't bet against me. The last things I shot were tin cans in the junk yard, and they didn't fly very fast." He laughed again, nervously.

"You can do it. Swing the gun barrel as you find the bird lined up with the bead on the end of your barrel. When you see the duck's bill just ahead of the bead, squeeze the trigger, but keep swinging the gun, or you'll shoot behind it every time." My arm was wrapped around my torso, so that he'd understand the concept of following through. "It's kind of like a golf swing. Follow through."

"Okay, okay. I can do this. I like golf. I mean, I didn't win three letters in high school for being a lousy golfer. The coach loved me." Laughter. Gerry pushed the throttle down and Mess found his feet as the bow lunged skyward.

"Oh, and one other thing," I yelled over the motor's roar. "You want to keep at least a box of shells in your pockets."

"Sure, sure…" He flipped open the lid under his on-board seat, and stuffed two boxes in his jacket—one on each side of his front pockets. They weighed a couple pounds apiece, I guessed, and now his oversized jacket drooped in the front.

"That way, when the action gets hot and heavy, you're not fumbling around for fresh loads." He nodded, but had a blank stare on his face. "Sometimes you don't kill a duck in the air. They hit the water and they're still alive. Shoot them again, until they're dead, okay?" Again he nodded. That would be it for our lesson. I was sure Gerry would have some pointers when the decoys were set and legal shooting hours began.

A few minutes later we pulled up to the longest of the steel piers. Gerry made a wide pass, cut the motor and let us drift. Mess jumped off the bow and into the cockpit, wagging his tail. Gerry yelled at him, and he jumped back to his post. "All right men, let's get those decoys out." We scrambled, grabbing the decoys by the heads and tossing the anchors off the downwind side of the boat. The decoys made a nice little "plunk" when they hit the water. It was dawn now, with the eastern horizon a smear of tangerine jelly aside from the lights of the city not far away. *Red sky at morning, sailors take warning.* At least 18 decoys were set in a straight line away from the pierhead, making the "tail" of our set. The idea behind the plan was to imitate a bunch of ducks, and the way they feed in the wild. Birds at the end of the tail leapfrog their brethren to reach the head of the flock, so that they don't miss out on any tasty morsels. The "head" of our set would be within a few yards of the boat, and we could throw out those decoys after we tied the boat to the steel wall.

The wind was behind us, blowing into the low-pressure system somewhere over Lake Superior. Gerry reached under his seat and pulled out a pair of plastic bumpers that would keep the boat from banging against the wall. I found the canvas tarps, and draped them over the edge of the boat, but made sure to attach the grommets to something sturdy inside the boat. The pier was 30 feet wide and made from iron pilings. Four feet over our heads was the cement pier, which enabled the dockhands to help handle the mighty freighters. In no time at all we were tied to the pier, had bumpers up to keep us from banging into it, and had positioned the tarps to make us look like a part of the pier. Gerry sat with us and announced the rules of the boat. "Scott, you sit down in the stern and shoot anything that comes in from that side, and Larry, you cover the bow. I'll sit in the captain's chair and shoot both right and left." He laughed.

By then it was close to legal shooting hours, we figured. Gerry looked at his watch and asked rhetorically, "What are the legal shooting hours?"

Scott took the lead and reached into his jacket to pull out the guidelines published by the Department of Natural Resources. He unfolded the papers and laid them on his knee.

Gerry was already scanning the horizon for incoming birds. Without squinting, Scott pronounced that shooting hours started at "6:54 a.m." I watched him fold the paper regulations and tuck them away. Strange, when Scott wanted to read something he didn't need glasses or contacts, but when he didn't want to read something, his misplaced glasses were a convenient excuse.

I looked at my watch, the one with Surety's logo across the face, but it was wrong. "Deader than a doornail," as Gerry used to say. I hoped it was just the batteries.

Gerry announced that we were legal. We loaded our guns and set them against the inside of the boat. Gerry plucked a pair of bufflehead ducks out of the horizon, headed in our direction. We crouched behind the canvas façade, so that only our eyes were above the rail. They veered north to the Canadian side and disappeared behind our pier. Gerry gave them one of his patented three quack "hello" calls, but they were out of our line of vision. Our eyes turned to the horizon too soon, because an instant later they were in the decoys with a small *swoosh* of landing gear sluicing through the surface. They came in from our blind spot at Scott's end of the boat. Scott and Gerry stood just as the diminutive ducks realized something was awry and began flapping their wings like mad. Mess recognized the commotion and began his annoying routine of whining. The guns roared, and both ducks were on their backs, peddling imaginary unicycles. Mess had tough duty, as the wind was quickly carrying them away.

I'm not sure who actually shot the birds—Gerry or Scott. They had shot spattered on the water's surface all around the birds. The ducks didn't have a chance, but it was a quick start to our day, and you don't complain when that happens. Scott was beaming. It was his first duck and it came in short order.

He kept laughing and laughing, an unusual reaction, I thought. Most guys smile, and give their buddies a high five or a handshake. But by and large, the first bird you shoot you hold in your hand and stroke its feathers. Some guys put their nose in the bird's breast feathers, close their eyes, and take a whiff. There's a little bit of reverence paid to the bird, if you're a seasoned sportsman or a greenhorn. Scott didn't seem to have it. He just wanted to kill. He just wanted another plaque for the wall.

Mess brought back both birds in one trip. He was huffing and puffing by the time he made it back. Gerry dropped the swim ladder behind Scott's seat and grabbed the birds from Mess's mouth. Mess needed a little yank on his collar to complete the boarding. Once there, he shook himself silly, sending a shower of water over everything in the cockpit. Gerry gave Mess an approving pat on the head, and turned to look for a small milk bone from under the center seat. Mess took the opportunity to lick the two small ducks on the floor of the boat. He was notorious for that. He didn't bite or chew them, just licked them.

Gerry found the treat and lured Mess to the prow, where the Lab forgot all about the dead ducks. He munched on it for several seconds before watching a seagull whip over our heads on gusty winds. Gerry carefully put the birds under Scott's seat.

We were in a nice spot. Any bird that strafed the bay we were hunting had to give us a look; we were right in the way of their migration. It wasn't the traditional place for duck hunting—like a marsh setting—but sometimes duck hunters are rewarded for taking chances or experimenting with new setups. Sometimes duck hunters take too many chances, and venture out in water that is too rough in boats that are too small. It seems that once a year, sometimes twice, one or two or three duck hunters die or disappear while duck hunting. It's really dumb. You've got to respect the power of the weather, and not get caught in it.

As we looked west, we could make out the lights and smokestack of a downriver-bound freighter. No doubt, it kicked up our two buffleheads, and it was stirring up more. Small bundles of ducks were wheeling this way and that. Gerry's call was singing, and we had birds coming close. A pair of good-sized ducks rounded the point of Mosquito Bay and was steaming their way toward us—seemingly taking the same path that we did. I hit the deck, and so did Gerry and Scott. Gerry sounded the call but he really didn't need to; they saw the decoys and were on their way right in front of me. Gerry muttered "redheads." Just as they reached the decoys, I heard Gerry say "take 'em." I rose to my feet, but before I could whip off a shot, they were skittering across the water's surface, dead.

"All right, I got the first one," Scott cried with laughter. He shot my duck. He shot my duck. And worse, he ignored Gerry's instructions.

I lowered my gun in disbelief. I couldn't believe he shot my duck. Hell, it was more than that; he stepped on my toes one more time. He walked all over me again. What a jackass.

Gerry knew what Scott had done, but elected not to say anything. Gerry could be cowardly at times and he tried to avoid confrontation at all costs. I should have piped up, but was afraid that if I started an argument, Scott would say something that would have tripped my trigger, literally.

Some years ago, while taking a hunter's safety course, I saw a hunter's safety video in which the teacher is in a boat with a make believe "buddy". The buddy is actually a vertically positioned watermelon atop a sawhorse. The sawhorse is covered with a green parka, so with a little imagination, it could be a fellow hunter in the boat. With excitement, the instructor stands to look at a fictitious pair of ducks. He narrates that the pair didn't come in to the decoys, but as he sits down, he tells the young people and the camera that he forgot to flip his safety back to the "safe" position. In the blink of an eye, he inadvertently points his gun at the watermelon's head and squeezes the trigger. The watermelon imploded as if it were hit with a sledgehammer. The image was fantastic. The hunter shot his "buddy" from point blank range, and there wasn't much doubt of the outcome. "Now, young sportsmen, you must be safe with your gun. Watch where you're pointing it, or your buddy will end up like that melon."

I thought about Scott's head for an instant imploding like that melon. But what a ghastly, horrific mess. I couldn't do that, even if he deserved it. Gerry would kill me for making a mess of his boat, too. Gerry wouldn't understand. He didn't like what the company was doing, but he didn't have as much at stake as I did. His goals weren't as big as mine; his dreams weren't as lofty, so the disappointment wasn't as acute. Gerry would never go along with my "accidental shooting" alibi. Gerry was a long way from cracking.

Not me. Maybe I was closer to cracking than I admitted. When all you can do is hope that things get better and they never do, you look for people to blame. When our insurance rates become so high that it borders on criminal, you try to put a face on it, and for me the face was Scott. As a cog in the gears of big business, you get tired of being used. Cogs sometimes break off and sabotage the whole operation. A cog can only take so much stress, so much time in the furnace. I really disliked Scott. I hated him. I hated the way he lied to us, I hated the way he misled us. I hated the notion that his primary job was to recruit new people—so they could help promulgate the increases, while they suffered in a career that was hardly anything as advertised. Some men could kill for less; some men wouldn't kill for anything. Gerry would never kill; I wasn't so sure I'd pass up the chance, if one came along.

I didn't have time to wallow in my redhead anguish. A drake mallard made the mistake of flying over our heads and all three of us took long shots. Somebody hit it, and it splashed down just outside the decoys. Instead of dying, it kept its head up until Gerry finished him off on the water. Our duck didn't have a chance to dive, and that's how it should be. No waste of game.

A bundle of bluebills charged in, and Scott and Gerry had their fun, with Scott laughing hysterically. I seemed to be stuck in the bow without any shooting. That was okay; I was waiting for my chance.

The pride of Oglebay-Norton's steamship line, *Reserve,* was now chugging her way slowly toward the locks. When she got closer to us, it was clear that she had been in rough seas. The front railing was caked with ice, and so was the entire bow. Several crew members at the *Reserve's* stern looked down at us. Beneath the hard hats and woolen coveralls were cheeks as red as cherubs. They had been in some rough weather, and it was coming our way.

Scott was the first to notice the temperature change. He put on his gloves and a scarf. The wind direction had changed, and the decoy's butts were now facing the blind instead of their heads. The surf had yet to build, as it takes some time for the waves to catch up to the blow. We'd have an hour or two before the waves became too big to hunt safely.

Gerry seized the lull from the freighter's passing to break

out the sandwiches. It was 10 a.m., well past lunch hour if you've been up since five. The ham and cheese sandwiches were wrapped in wax paper that flapped in the ever-increasing chill. We passed around the last of the coffee, and shared a few chocolate chip cookies. Mess sat at Gerry's feet, drooling. Gerry flipped a crust his way, and he snared it.

Then Scott started in. "You know, we must be the luckiest guys alive. Here we are on a weekday, out chasing ducks. This has been great. I can see myself coming back this year and trying it again. We are so lucky to have chosen the insurance business, to have Surety Guarantee on our side. I don't see any other company's agents out here. Heck, if they only knew how lucky we have it.

"And now that we've got mutual funds—I tell you, we can really make a lot of money at this. You guys can do it. The days of selling just auto and home insurance are over. We agents have to adapt to change or we're through."

"I thought we came out here to get away from the office," Gerry said.

"I'm sorry, but I'm just too excited about the future."

"You know, Scott, there's nothing wrong with selling auto and home insurance," I chimed.

"There is if you want to make it as a Surety Guarantee agent. You'll starve. Surety Guarantee wants to get out of the property and casualty business, and get into the securities market."

"So you're asking us to throw away 10 years in the auto and home insurance business to be stockbrokers?"

"You can do it. There's no future in auto and home anyway. The Internet will make all property and casualty agents obsolete. You guys are dinosaurs unless you start selling mutual funds."

I looked away, and spotted a duck steaming down the pike. "I know, I know. I'll have to get after that, but I just can't believe that you think auto and home agents will be obsolete. Who told you that, anyway?"

"When I visited the home office last month, Mr. Phidler himself told us about it at a District Coordinator convention. He's really a smart man, and what a leader. I mean, this guy is poised to lead us into the new millennium of Surety Guarantee."

The duck kept coming and I didn't point out its approach. Gerry and Scott were seated with their backs to the wind, their faces to the pier. I had my back to the pier, my face to the wind. Scott continued, "If you don't sit for the exam soon, I'll make sure you never have a rate to sell auto and home insurance."

Gerry looked at me from behind his hood, and then flipped Mess a wedge of cookie. I threw my gun to my shoulder and fired. Gerry stood up quickly and screamed "Holy shit, you idiot! What the hell are you doing, man?" He must have thought I blasted Scott across the length of the boat. He had probably seen the same hunter's safety video.

"I'm duck hunting, you idiot…and on the cement pier over our heads, you'll find a very mature, very dead canvasback. It came right up the pike, and I shot it almost overhead."

"Bullshit!" Gerry bit his tongue. I knew he thought I was being reckless with my gun, and that was taboo in our circle.

"Try me. Mess's about ready for a potty break, let's send him up there."

"Why didn't you say something?"

"Because you two dickheads have had all the shooting this morning, including the ducks on my side of the boat."

The two of them were silent. Although Gerry had every right to shoot the birds on either end of the boat, Scott surely didn't. Scott didn't apologize, but I never would have expected it from that jerk. I didn't mean to admonish Gerry, but he should have said something to keep Scott from firing on my side. After all, it was his boat, and the captain calls the shots.

Gerry screwed the lid on the thermos and put it away with the cookies. He rubbed his hands together, flicking the crumbs from his palms. Mess seemed to lose interest in the treats, and hadn't seen my duck fall. Gerry grabbed him by the collar and gestured to help him up the iron wall. I set my gun down and gave Mess a shove in the wriggling backside. He disappeared for several minutes.

Silence continued in the boat. The BBs that weren't lodged in the canvasback came falling out of the sky. They hit the water around us like pebbles falling from above. Gerry knew what made that sound, but Scott didn't have a clue. He asked what it was, but we ignored him. Scott wasn't bluffing about his insurance threat, and there would be no changing him to our way of thinking. Gerry and I were on our own. He wouldn't help us get a competitive rate in auto and home insurance. What good was he to us?

Mess reappeared a few minutes later with a gorgeous drake canvasback in his mouth. We all praised Mess for his fine retrieve, even though it was probably the easiest one of the day. And what a nice duck. It had a chestnut-colored head, dark breast and bill, and those wonderful whitish sides and back. Gerry handed it to me and we both helped Mess off the pier. I stuffed my bird into the deep pockets of my jacket.

By then the temperature was really starting to plummet. Gerry put the earflaps down on his hat, and put on his big leather mittens called "choppers." We had whitecaps rolling in and the boat banged against the bumpers. It was good shooting for a while, but we only needed a few more ducks to fill our limits. Scott didn't fall out of line and didn't shoot anything on my side. We had an excellent day of hunting, but we were on our own when it came to business at our offices. Scott would be no help. At least we knew the score.

At 4 p.m., with the wind howling and our little live-well filled with dead ducks, Gerry suggested that we call it a day. No one argued. It was time to go. In no time we had the boat unhooked, the blind down and stowed, and the decoys packed in neat rows between the center console and the prow's deck. Gerry pulled up his hood and tied it over his earflaps. I pulled my hood up too, and stood next to Gerry at the helm. Mess was at his post, and Scott was somewhere behind us. Gerry zoomed ahead, but in the process, he sent a huge bucket of spray over the bow. It came back and splashed our faces. Gerry kept the bow quartered into the waves, but the boat heaved. Even Mess stumbled once or twice on the bow. During the next 15 minutes we had quite a bit of water over the bow. It was sloshing around the stern at Scott's feet.

"When was the last time we were out in surf like this?" I yelled.

"Probably the last time we hunted the piers," Gerry screamed.

"Oh sure. That was something. Did we get any canvasbacks then?"

"No. Remember? The season was closed on them that year."

"I've still got that big bull in my pocket. I'll be right back." I turned to the boat's stern and asked Scott if I could throw the canvasback in the live-well, which was under his seat. We were nearing the mouth of the power canal, the illuminated sign. Scott nodded.

He stood, spun around, facing the little live-well box, and lifted the lid. I reached into my pocket and felt the soft feathers, then the thick, chestnut-colored neck. The boat heaved, and Scott bobbed my way; his forearm nudged against my bicep. A gigantic wave pushed the boat into a swell, and his weight shifted toward the railing. He reached for my hand, but missed. I stretched, but his hand kept moving farther and farther away. It felt like slow motion. His hand. My hand. They drifted apart. I saw the look on his face as he headed over the railing. He was scared. He felt betrayed, by the sea, his sea legs, by the storm, by me, too. I lunged for his waders but it was too late. He plunged headfirst into the stormy, frigid surf—shot shells in his pockets pulling him down like pig iron.

He righted himself, choking in the wash. Fumbling, floundering. He was begging for help. All I could do was watch him struggle. I felt like I should help him, but for some reason, I didn't know how. I watched him flail behind the boat in waves that had manes like wolves. He was in peril, and I wanted him to suffer like I had, but I never wanted him to die. My mind raced in the storm's fury until I turned to Gerry and screamed, "Man overboard!"

Gerry cursed. He doubled back in a panic. We screamed and hollered for him but it was too late. The current swept him away, and had him halfway to the powerhouse. By the time we called the police, his body was making the 30-foot drop over the cement embankment and through the turbines. If there were sport fishermen behind the powerhouse they probably never noticed the sudden surge of debris ground into oblivion. But his corpse wouldn't get by the season's last seagulls; they would swoop and soar above the carrion—as if they were munching on mayflies during the hatch. It was horrible. All I could do was think of him—floundering, flailing, screaming for a life ring but getting none. It was an accident that he fell; it was no accident that I stood there watching him suffer. I was paralyzed by the quandary. Help the man I hated so much, or let him die as if he was my worst enemy?

I hoped the police would believe our story.

Two

SIX MONTHS EARLIER, at the District Office, 25 agents in the district were seated at folding tables, staring at the television and a canned speech by the top dog at Surety Guarantee. Gerry was there, scratching his beard, rubbing the sleepers out of his eyes. He had driven a long way for the meeting from Sault Ste. Marie in the Upper Peninsula to Saginaw in the Lower.

Allison Kline was there as well. She always brought back pleasant memories from our week of training at the regional office, where we learned all about Surety Guarantee's brand of life insurance, and how to sell it to our clients. The managers lined us up into teams; they called them "small groups," for role-playing. I always thought that kind of scenario was awkward. I mean, how do you imagine objections when you don't have any? It seemed to be better suited for the comedians in an improvisational setting. Though I tried to sound sincere, I had Allison laughing hysterically after each encounter. The managers weren't overly impressed, but it wasn't like I tried to make her laugh. I just had witty objections to her proposals. And the laughter didn't stop when our training ended. She sat next to me at the evening functions, nibbling on appetizers, sipping her chardonnay and twirling her silky locks of auburn hair. My mind drifted back to her in the swimming pool before dinner. She was really nice to look at. I couldn't help but notice how much more curvy she was in a swimsuit instead of a business suit. I thought that maybe she was checking me out, too. Anyway, I thought we were becoming fast friends until the last night of the conference when she put her hand on my knee as we sat around the elevated bar tables. I thought nothing of it, since there were five or six of us jammed around the table. But gradually, her hand moved farther and farther up my thigh, until it distracted me from the conversation. So, I asked her to dance, and then I asked what she was doing.

"What do you mean?" she quipped.

"Allison...what's up with the patty cake?"

"Is that what we were playing?"

"Bake me a cake as fast as you can?" she giggled, then pulled herself close.

"I'm not so sure that would be such a good idea."

"Oh, come on, we're both adults here, far, far from home." Her eyes were burning a hole through me, and she gradually pushed her knee between mine. She closed her eyes and bowed her head to my chest. I felt her squeeze me, and it felt good...

Gerry had a plaque and an award on the pile of papers that was in front of his seat, as did several other agents. I received a watch with the Surety Guarantee's logo across the face—an anniversary present for 10 years of service. The other awards were for profitability, lapse ratio, and sales growth.

"Ladies and gentlemen, it is my pleasure to stand before you today. I am so thankful for the opportunity, so gracious for the chance to serve you. This great company was founded by hard-working people, and that remains the backbone of our success 60 years later. We have so much to be thankful for, so much to be proud of. We've made great strides over the years. We take pride in the gains we've made.

"While other companies are laying off staff and cutting jobs, we continue to grow. I can honestly tell you that I've never had to lay anyone off. While other companies are cutting claims service, we continue to make strides. Our expenses are down, our service is up, and I couldn't be more excited about the future."

Allison leaned back in her chair, and crossed her arms under those pleasantly round breasts. She looked my way and I smiled, thinking of her in my arms, swaying to the music, far, far from home. When the song ended, she suggested a little more than "baking me a cake as fast as you can."

"What did you have in mind?"

"I can't tell you here....Let's just say that I'd like to have a little life insurance review, just the two of us. I need some clarification on elevating my dividends and I can show you the penalties for early withdrawal."

"My, my. Sounds intriguing."

"Don't make wait. This offer is good for a limited time only. Room 455."

My attention turned back to the television. "Let me read to you a letter from a satisfied customer of ours. I received this two weeks after the events of September 11th.

Dear Mr. Phidler,

My name is Dorothy Hilts from Hobokin, Kansas, and I want to tell you about my claims experience with Surety Guarantee Insurance. I bought a policy from my local Surety Guarantee agent Jim Gooding several years ago for my 1997 Ford Taurus. On the morning of September 11th, I was on my way to school, when somebody ran a stop sign and collided with the passenger side of my car. After speaking to Mr. Gooding, I realized that he was on top of things and would take care of me. Later that day an adjuster called and told me that he would take a look at the car, which would then be followed up by a check in the mail. True to his word, a check arrived in the mail several days later, and there was even an extra hundred dollars to cover the rental car bill. The events of 9-11 didn't affect your claims service, and I was completely satisfied. With service like that, I'll be a Surety Guarantee client for many years to come.

Sincerely, Dorothy Hilts.

"You see, ladies and gentlemen, we all take a role in providing excellent claims service to our customers. From the agent to the adjusters. From the computer programmers to the claims supervisors. From the mail clerks to the actuaries, we all take a role in delivering a promise to be there for our customers. We all take solace in the fact that every day we make good on what makes this company the best in the industry…"

The speech went on for another 20 minutes. Our fearless leader, our CEO, our commander in chief was at the helm, rallying the troops. All of five foot nine, he wore an expensive dark blue suit with a snappy speckled tie. Cheeks slightly dimpled, hair coifed magnificently, he had the moxie of a CEO. Poised, confident, and in charge, he had everyone believing that this great insurance company had everything going its way. Who were we to doubt, who were we to second-guess?

Richard Phidler climbed the corporate ladder and didn't get there by accident. After getting his M.B.A from an Ivy League school, he was hired by Surety Guarantee in the marketing department. But that assignment didn't last long. He had stints in claims, actuarial, advertising, and research & development. He worked hard. He got ahead. You can't blame a guy for that.

Part of his training was to visit the home office in Newark, New Jersey. There, he met the top executives of the day, saw where they worked, smelled the buffed wax floors, and caught a glimpse of where the successful men plied their trades. He went to fancy restaurants while training—on the company—and dreamed of the someday when he'd swim in the lap of luxury. That was his motivation for working hard, settling claims, setting the rates, and working late. Before long he was racking up the accolades from his supervisors and satisfied customers. He quickly became a supervisor, then a manager. There'd be relocations along the way, but that was a minor price to pay for the glory that would eventually be his.

Mr. Phidler, we heard, was paid a salary plus a bonus based on the value of Surety's stock. He seemed larger than the company. He embodied it, or so it appeared. With an incentive plan based on the stock price, his decisions must have been based on short-term benefits, rather than the long-term health of the company.

The agents, seated around tables with folding legs, quickly became bored with the canned videotape. Some of them had their heads on their hands while others passed notes to each other that induced modest smiles. They had heard the rhetoric before, seen the pomp and pageantry all wrapped up in the diminutive public relations guru. The speech was sincerely given, but the message was abhorrently hollow.

I never did go to Allison's room that night at the regional office, although every time I see her I think about what might have been. She never did mention our encounter, but I got the impression that she thought it was my loss, not hers.

The company was only in great shape from the standpoint of shareholders, because the price of the stock had a steady-but-sure increase year after year. It attracted mutual fund managers that wanted a financial flavoring to their blue-chip portfolio. The premiums kept rolling in, but the policies in force were dwindling. They raised the rates over and over again. What was once a large, clumsy insurance company based on fairness in pricing and excellent claims service became a top-heavy, greedy operation. When they gouged prices they got a classic case of "adverse selection," which means that the only people they insured were the folks who nobody else wanted. Instead of targeting a group of people with rates to match the risk, they ended up with an unprofitable book of business.

Surety Guarantee had the poor drivers that live in run-down houses and have plenty of claims. Their underwriting losses became worse, and the result was even higher rates.

The consequences of their pricing were disastrous. When policyholders opened their bills and noticed that their homeowner's and auto premiums went up 40, 50, 60 percent, they become irritated. The first person they called was their agent, who, after being deluged with repeated calls of complaints, became beleaguered. The agent's job became nothing more than back-peddling, excuse-making, and proclaiming false hope that every other company would be going through the same thing.

The promises were cultivated from the lips of the agents' District Coordinator, whose job was to maintain the agents in the district, train new agents, address profitability, make sales quotas, and above all else, hire new agents. Some District Coordinators were millionaires. If they had a big stable of agents under their direction who generated thousands and thousands of dollars in premiums every month, they couldn't help but reap the benefits of huge overrides. The agents heard rumors of District Coordinators who pulled down monthly checks of $100,000 or more.

Our District Coordinator, Scott, was a former agent who came to Michigan by way of several stops on the eastern seaboard, where he started out as an agent, then promoted to District Coordinator. He was a good agent in many respects, because of his productivity. If he wasn't the state's top producer, he wasn't far from it. When he was hired as a District Coordinator, he brought the same level of competitiveness. Some would say that he bent the rules to get ahead. One of his favorite ways to recruit new agents was to contact agents from other companies who were retiring. He appointed them agents with Surety Guarantee where the new agent would roll their retirement funds into Surety's brand of annuities. The new agent would collect the five percent commission on their investment plus the 4.5% interest rate on the annuity. Scott would get the override, and then the agent would quit, collecting an additional sum based on the company's formulated "book value." So in other words, the new agent would come out ahead because of the giant return on their investment, and Scott would benefit in the eyes of the company for putting on a new agent.

Scott seemed to stay one step ahead of the company, often asking for a transfer to a new territory, a new state, before the company caught on to his little strategy. But that wasn't all he had to avoid. Many agents in his former districts hated him because of the way he could tweak the rates without justification. Unprofitable agents had dramatic increases, often putting them out of business. New, promising agents in unproven territories got favorable rates so they could have a chance at reaching the sales quotas that were required to stay afloat.

I wondered if the rumors we heard about Scott were true—that he could help us or destroy us. I wondered if there really was a Dorothy Hilts from Hobokin, Kansas. But more immediately, I had other concerns. Surety Guarantee unveiled their special "Dealer's Discount" on their auto insurance program. It was designed to target a select group of drivers who had clean records and prior insurance, whether or not they were employed. Nearly everyone qualified for the program, and received a slight discount for doing so. The problem was that at the same time, the company decided to raise its rates. The agent had to physically go to the computer and add the discount to those that qualified, but the discount didn't make up for the rate increase. It made the agents even madder, even more distrustful of the company.

After the district meeting, several agents got together at a local watering hole to discuss our predicament and the plight of the company. Things were bad, but they could get worse. After all, some of us were making 10 or 15 thousand dollars a month—more than enough to support our staff, the rent, computer costs, and the other expenditures needed to stay afloat. Some of us sold enough insurance, in the right lines, to be named to a prestigious group of agents. "Commander's Club" was for the cream of the crop, the best of the best. The Commander's Club was held at a city or a resort. The company paid for the lodging, meals, and entertainment, but the agents had to pay for the expense of getting there. I always thought that was cheap.

But what really frustrated the agents was what could have

been. Hope is what motivates agents. Opportunity is why we became agents, with all the lure of future gains.

"I dunno, fellas. This company seems to be in a tailspin," one of the agents lamented after the meeting.

"Yeah, but weren't you moved by that speech from our fearless leader?"

"Ha! Our leader is concerned only with lining his pockets. He's never been an agent. I'd have as much credibility telling him how to run the company as he would telling me how to run my agency." We ordered another round of drinks and hot wings.

Then Scott appeared in the bar. Jack Jenkins, an agent from Petoskey, waved him over. The conversation dimmed, and arms were crossed. Scott couldn't help himself. He sang the praises of the company and what a great decision he made in becoming a District Coordinator: "I really think that this company is headed in the right direction. We have our share of problems, that's for sure, but I know we can make it." He laughed and laughed.

We become bored again, and he knew it. He clammed up, and the agents sitting around the table took over the conversation.

"Scott, the company is putting us out of business. We have nothing left to sell. We used to be able to count on selling auto and home insurance, but that's gone now."

Michigan had its own set of problems. Hardly ever, if ever, was homeowner's insurance profitable in the state, the company alleged. We received memos and statements from the company that were lavished with doom and gloom. Each agent received quarterly operating statements showing the number of policies in force and the losses paid.

Scott's response to the comments about staying in the auto

and home insurance business was pathetic. "We've got to change gears. In a few years you won't see any insurers selling just auto and home insurance. They've got to adapt to change, or they will go under." He was the king of redundancy. "Adapt to change" was one of his favorites, so was "discuss out" and "past history."

"We've really got to recommit ourselves to the profession of being the industry's best trained, most devoted professionals. I'm excited about selling securities, and making all kinds of money. You guys can do it, and I know we'll all be rich."

What he was referring to was the latest in a series of schemes designed to increase the company's profits. The company, in all its wisdom, thought that just because the agents could sell property and casualty policies, they would be successful at selling mutual funds, variable annuities, and other interest sensitive products. The company didn't count on two major pitfalls: one, the agents weren't qualified even if they passed the licensing exam, and two, the company's product and software were woefully inadequate. Surety Guarantee underestimated both.

Oh sure, there were a few agents that picked up the ball and ran with it, but they usually had another sideline business such as an accounting service, home inspection service, or appraisal company. They had been selling mutual funds to their clients through another brokerage house for years. Most of the agents realized that the type of clientele they had in their agencies didn't have any money to invest. They had more important priorities: mufflers for their old vehicles and septic fields for their old mobile homes.

Jack Jenkins raised an outstretched finger from the edge of his vodka tonic and interrupted. "Yeah, but Scott, we're not bankers, and we never wanted to be bankers. I came to Surety

Guarantee because they were good at auto and home insurance, and that's what I wanted to sell. Now you're telling us to go change gears and go to war with sticks and stones for ammunition. I had a lady come into my office this week whose homeowner's rate went from $400 to $752. She had tears in her eyes, and I felt like I was the one raising her rates. There's no reason we need to take that kind of increase. What in high heaven are we doing? When are we going to get back in the property and casualty business?"

"We never got out of it, we're just changing gears. We need the property and casualty business to develop the relationships that open the doors for the financial business. Besides, we have "dealer's discounts" coming out soon that I know will get us back in the property & casualty business."

"And what's that?" Jack asked.

"It's for select groups of people—union members, lawyers, and federal employees. We're looking at more right now. The good part is the group discount gets stacked, in addition to the member's program that's already in place."

"When's that set for rollout?"

"In October."

"This October or next?"

We all laughed at the expense of the company. Scott barely smiled. We all had experience with the company and their false promises. We had been sold a bill of goods before, and were reluctant to believe anything that they said. When you get your hopes up, only to have them dashed, you tend to be a little gun-shy. Not Scott, he kept up the vigil, blindly, even though the company put him in those precarious predicaments. He had egg on his face more than once.

The conversation turned to sports, our cute waitress, and politics. Scott was awkward talking about anything other than

Surety Guarantee. The only other topic he would discuss was duck hunting. I'm not sure if he talked about it because he knew some of us were duck hunters, or if he really wanted to go. He was annoying, and I couldn't stand to be near him. For a man that could influence my livelihood, I was developing a hatred for him. It was all I could do to sit across the table from the annoying twerp.

I pushed away from the table, said my farewells, and drove back to the office. The other agents stayed for a while before they left too.

The next morning I got on the computer and went to work. The stacks of phone messages on my desk would have to wait. I recognized most of the names as people whose policies were up for renewal soon. They probably received our letter, explaining with apologies that the rates were going up again. I entered the state code for Kansas, then "Hilts," and finally "automobile." No matches.

From there, I accessed the claims log. Nothing again.

My last straw was the agency force. There were two agents in that county, but both of them denied knowing the Hilts family, any Hilts family, or even an agent named Jim Gooding. They said that I was the second agent to call them with the same inquiry. I smelled a rat, but so did some other agent somewhere in the company. But even if there was no such person as Dorothy Hilts from Hobokin, Kansas, what would it prove? That the CEO of Surety Guarantee was too foolish to use a real name for a fictitious person? If it was a fake, why use a name? If it was real, why was I so distrustful?

The company continually lied to us, and didn't think anything of it.

Three

When I first graduated from college and was looking for work, I started out as a salesman for a car dealership. I didn't make many sales, but it wasn't bad work until I could find a better job. One of the manager's fathers was a branch claims manager for an insurance company. He came into the shop quite often, and the more we talked, the more he took a shine to me. The next thing I knew, he asked if I wanted to apply for a job. Of course I did. One thing led to another, and before long I was learning the ropes—studying the Michigan Insurance Code and Surety Guarantee's claims manual.

I met fellow claims adjusters who had been with the company from three years to twenty. They were nice folks, honest workers who were responsible for the way the company's money was spent. Sometime in the spring of my first year, they received profit sharing checks from the company. I watched their reaction as they opened the envelopes, because I wasn't with the company long enough to get one of my own. They didn't feel bad about getting a bonus, but I had to wonder why the company was sending out bonuses when they were supposedly losing so much money. All I ever heard from the company was how much money they lost, and yet they were passing out profits? I never could figure that out, but I had enough on my plate so early in my career.

Part of my liability claims training was to visit the home office in Newark. Like Mr. Phidler, I saw how the top executives operated. I saw those busy New Jersey highways and all the traffic. For this Midwesterner, New Jersey was a whole different planet, and one I hoped I'd never see again.

Like many young people right out of school, I wanted to get ahead and make lots of money. The claims kept pouring across my desk, and I tried my best to settle them as quickly as I could. Slip-and-falls and car accidents were regular occurrences. I started out settling relatively minor casualty claims like soft tissue aches, then gradually moved on to broken arms and legs. When our stolen vehicle adjuster went on vacation, I filled in for him. Those claims were fun, because they were notoriously laden with fraud. After digging into a claimant's story, through title searches and speaking to the agent, I often discovered that the vehicles were purchased only a week or so before they came up missing. The agent never saw the vehicles when they wrote the policy. Sometimes the vehicles were purchased for $500 because they had been in a previous wreck, but hadn't been fixed. Still other times the insured was behind on his payments or way over on his mileage allotment, so instead of figuring out a way to make it right, he had the vehicle stolen or burned. "Chop shops" dismantled stolen cars, then resold them to body shops, who told insurance adjusters they were purchased from legitimate sources.

"Soft tissue" claims were harder to settle, because a manual or an estimate couldn't determine their value. Most people realized that their soft tissue injuries would eventually heal.

Most of them did heal, but it was my job to contact them before they contacted a lawyer. Lawyers drive up the cost of the claim by means of the contingency fees they collect, and the doctors they recommend for their clients. Lawyers know the game, and they know how to play it. So, even if I knew that the claimants' injuries were minimal, I tried to give them some money for the sole purpose of having them sign a release. It was better than the alternative—lawyers start the soft tissue negotiations at $10,000, 18 months after the incident happens. If I could close the case in a month for $1,500, I wouldn't have to see that file ever again.

It didn't take long before my caseload began to swell. I had claimants that I thought would never go to a lawyer, but did. One incident came back to haunt me. It involved a "good Christian family" whose mother sustained minor whiplash (soft tissue) when her vehicle was rear-ended by our policyholder. When I saw her several days later, her car was still parked in the driveway. The taillights weren't even broken, and aside from a small crease in her bumper, it was hard to tell she was involved in any incident at all. Still, I took a photo and put it in her file. She wore a padded collar but seemed to be handling her injuries quite well. She had no trouble doting on me and her husband, getting coffee and cookies. They had many religious artifacts on the walls and card tables, as if they had to be reminded that they were a "good Christian family." I should have known something was awry. She didn't want anything for her injuries except her deductible for the damage to her car.

"Are you sure you're okay?"

"Oh yes, I'm fine."

"I could give you an extra $500 to settle your injury claim."

"Oh, that's not necessary. The Lord will provide for us."

I thought about asking her for a tape-recorded statement, but it seemed that would show that I didn't trust her. So, I let it go. Two months later, our office had to pull the file and match it to her attorney's letter of retention. Apparently, she changed her tune, and Bible verse, to "God helps those who help themselves."

Once I had a soft tissue case with a prominent lawyer in town. I knew it was a baloney case, and I knew the lawyer's reputation for settling claims rather than taking them to trial. After trying to settle it for over a month, my boss asked for the file one morning just before lunch. I gave it to him as he headed out of the office, and into a big black Cadillac. He returned an hour and a half later, with the file, and on it was a note to write a check for $2,900. I didn't ask any questions but I made a copy of his note and kept it in a file at home.

When I became an agent, I learned that work didn't come across my desk as it had when I settled claims. If I was to survive, I had to go out and make it happen. The renewals were nice, but if I wanted to make a killing, I had to get out there and work for it.

Successful insurance sales are a mix of effort, a good company, and salesmanship. All three ingredients are intertwined. If you don't have a good company behind you, it quashes all the effort, and you never get to demonstrate your salesmanship. If you have the company, but don't have the effort or salesmanship, you're dead. Salesmanship is something that has to be nurtured or cultivated. I knew how claims were going to be settled, but that really didn't help. When I called people to give them a quote, at all came down to the almighty buck. If my prices were cheaper than what they currently were paying, I had a very good chance of selling them a policy. The good clients were the multiple policies—three or four autos, a home, and toys like snowmobiles, four-wheelers and boats. The more the premiums I sold, the more money I made.

The trick, I realized, was getting my name in front of people when they were ready to pay their insurance bills. I advertised on television, hired telephone solicitors, used direct mail, and hooked up with bankers and real estate agents for referrals. I learned how to market, how to develop contacts, and gradually, how to "pivot." In the sales world, you have to overcome objections, show your worth, and demonstrate how you'll bring value to their world. "Pivoting" is the way accomplished salesmen turn objections into opportunities, cost into value, and claims into real life tragedies. Insurance is all about a promise, a promise to take care of their customers when they need it most. The best insurance salesmen convince their customers that they can deliver on that promise better than anyone else. The best of the best agents convince their prospects that they are worth paying more money. In any event, I was lucky enough to be considered one of the better agents in our little district.

As part of my marketing strategy, I convinced the editor of our local newspaper to let me write a hunting and fishing column. At first, I didn't get paid for it, but gradually they agreed to a paltry sum. I did it for fun, and it was good for publicity. It also helped at tax time—now I could legitimately write off my trips to Gerry's cabin, guns, ammunition, and even more mileage. Just in case I pissed someone off in my column, I made sure that I had "broad form liability" on my policy at the office. Surety Guarantee would cover me for libel, slander, and defamation of character. I also took out a rider for sexual harassment, just in case one of the women I hired got the idea to sue me. Not that I'd ever plan on getting sued for it, I just couldn't afford to hire a lawyer in case someone actually did. Most of the other guys in our district added the same riders to their policy for the same reasons.

In the insurance world, there are what's called "captive" agents and independent agents. Captives only represent one company, while independent agents represent as many as they want. Captive policies develop a "book value" based on the number of policies in force, and the volume of premiums under the agent's control. Independent agents sign contracts too, but their book value is determined on the open market. The independent agent can sell their "book" for one, two, or three times its annual gross commission rate—whatever the market can bear.

Both independents and captive agents have to deal with the marketing committee, who are typically company men who know a lot about the policies their company sells, but have little experience selling them. I'm not sure if marketing committee members don't have the desire to sell insurance on their own, or are more comfortable with the notion of drawing a salary instead of commission. For some marketing committee members their position is a springboard to more lofty positions within the company, or a lifeboat for a floundering career. Some marketing personnel are grateful for the opportunity, while others resent the demotion.

We had a string of horrible marketing committee members overseeing our district. They liked to throw their weight around. We used to call them The Gestapo, because of their strict adherence to the company's rules. When times are good, they intimidate agents by monitoring the way they rate policies. When times are bad, they hover over their agents for more serious breaches of contract—like placing business with another company, and missing or short premium accounts. They're the ones that fire agents when they're naughty and sign the contracts after the District Coordinators recruit prospective agents.

Our "district" was not unlike many other districts in the state. We had about 25 agents spread out across the northern half of the Lower Peninsula and the entire Upper Peninsula of Michigan. The eight or ten other districts in the state were much smaller in geographical size, but had just as many agents in them because they were located in more populated areas of southern Michigan.

In our district, we had a third of the agents who were on the downside of their careers, another third who were reliable producers, and the last third who kicked ass. The group of agents who were on the backside of their careers kept their agencies afloat because the income the policies developed was like a monthly annuity check. The agents cut way back on their expenses—often converting the attached garages in their homes to half-assed offices. They play golf a lot in the summer, spend several months in Florida in the winter, and take long lunch breaks during the week. They don't sell much, but then again, they don't need to. All they want to do is maintain what they have.

The middle tier of agents couldn't sell insurance if they had to. They are nice people, but don't have the salesmanship skills. These are the excuse makers of the world. The rates the company charges are always way too high. The computer system is so antiquated that it makes them unproductive. Commission schedules compared to other companies are uncompetitive. The truth is that the mediocre agents don't have the work ethic, time management skills, or salesmanship to get ahead. In any organization, there are employees with varying degrees of productivity.

The last third of our agents were the ones that succeeded

in spite of the company's incompetence. They figured out ways to sell insurance despite being much more expensive than the competition. They didn't sell price; they sold themselves. Many agents owned businesses before they became insurance agents, and were lured to insurance by the prospects of independence, renewal income, and the predetermined value of their book. These agents are the risk takers, a confident bunch. But, with confidence comes criticism, and they are masters at criticizing the company. It's a rueful paradox for the company—they love their best agents, but hate the baggage that goes with them.

Jack Jenkins was one of those good agents. He was our best producer, and the anointed spokesmen for our district. Eloquent, yet poignant, he insulted the company personnel without them knowing it. He owned his own construction company in the Grand Rapids area before moving north to the tourist-rich destination of Petoskey. What was really impressive about Jack was his guts. He started out with barely any policies, but it didn't take long until he was racking up substantial sales. In his third month of being an agent, he sold 75 polices that netted $5,000 in commission. Not bad for the new kid on the block.

Jack was funny, too. He was a master of imitating the people in our district, and the folks who were supposed to watch over us. His humor wasn't in canned, punch-line-style jokes, but the crazy one-liners and brazen comebacks that nobody else had the guts to pull off. He was a 20-year-old trapped in a 50-year-old's body.

In the summer months, Jack took Thursday afternoons off to spend time on his 35-foot sailboat moored at the understated, yet refined, Petoskey Yacht Club. His idea of a good time was sipping vodka tonics, laughing with his friends, and watching the skirts as they paraded down the dock. Thursday evenings were the yacht races, which seemed like a good excuse for the members to get together and drink. Jack's boat was built for pleasure, not speed. The cockpit and cabin were decked out with teak wood and plush cushions. The instruments were lined in brass, and there were several unnecessary gadgets. But the most apparent reason Jack's boat wasn't built for racing was the jib sail, which was wound up in a sleeve on the bow's rigging. All Jack had to do was pull on the rope, like a giant lampshade, and the sail unfurled. Although convenient, that baggy edge cutting the wind added time and took away speed. But that was fine with Jack, convenience was better than speed, the end justified the means.

When Jack was Commodore of the club, he changed its stodgy image all in one night. At the club's annual "fun race" Jack organized the festivities afterward. Instead of having a four-piece brass set at the club like the Commodores before him, Jack rented a five-acre island from the city of Petoskey. The island was in the middle of Little Traverse Bay, and embraced by the city commissioners as part nature preserve, part gem of the North Country. Therefore, there could not be any loud parties, and the island was treated with care. The club's reputation supported Jack's petition, and he scored the island for one night. He got the most out of it. A reggae band was brought in from Chicago, along with some special chefs who made jerk chicken and served margaritas until dawn. "Man, I dunno how we made it out to the island, we had three generators and four guys in dreadlocks on the deck of my boat. Come to think of it, I dunno how we made it home, either."

Everyone loved Jack.

Like many of the districts, we had some agents who were terminated because they took advantage of the trust the company gave us. One agent was caught overriding the computer's rating system. He'd input the vehicle's identification number incorrectly, so the computer would bounce it. Then, he'd plug in a completely different vehicle's identification number that had a lower insurance rate. The client enjoyed a lower premium, and the agent benefited from the commission he collected. If the client ever had a claim on the vehicle, the agent merely sent the company a memo requesting a vehicle change. He "backdated" the coverage to the day before the accident happened. It became habit to send the claims department a copy of the memo at the same time he called in the "report of claim" form.

The agent's success in manipulating the auto insurance world motivated him to venture into the life insurance arena. After all, there was better commission in life insurance than auto insurance. His technique wasn't brilliant, but it was gutsy. We weren't exactly sure how he pulled it off, but we did glean a few details of his operation. He would write small—$5,000 or $10,000—life insurance policies on people who had a terminal illness. He forged their signatures, and made himself the primary beneficiary. The underwriters never did much underwriting because the policies were so small. They trusted the agent to make sure the person was in good health. When the client died and the company looked into the matter, they never suggested that the agent might be crooked. Since the policies were so small, it didn't make much sense to battle the agent. They didn't doubt his integrity, because the sales force was composed of fiduciary agents, "agents of special trust." They paid the claims, and the agent reaped the rewards.

When that worked, he took his strategy one more step. He waited until a client died, then backdated the life application to the day before it happened. But to throw off the company and the family of the deceased, he waited several months to turn in a claim. That way, the family wouldn't remember their beloved's schedule to deny the application's authenticity. The client always paid the agent in cash, quarterly payments, so the paper trail was harder for the company to piece together. From the company's standpoint, it was cheaper to pay off the claim than get into a legal battle with the agent. It was the agent's word against the company's, whose star witness was six feet under.

On the east side of the state were two other agents who were big shooters—Dan Rowe and Allison Klein, both from Oscoda. Both sold plenty of insurance, but in completely different ways. Allison seemed a little ahead of her time, especially for northern Michigan. In the rough-and-tumble world of insurance sales, she excelled. The men that dominated it didn't intimidate her. In fact, she understood that she could deliver something that her male counterparts couldn't: an attractive woman in a short skirt who was a wealth of insurance knowledge. She took pride in her looks and usually wore something that enhanced her long legs and curvaceous profile. Her Lincoln Navigator turned heads, which is precisely why she owned it. Some of her female clients didn't like their husbands' reactions to her presentation. The husbands couldn't help themselves and would steal a glance. She was pushy, gaudy, and good at selling insurance.

Dan Rowe was a Surety Guarantee agent slightly longer than Allison. Rowe used to work at the butcher shop, where he gained a reputation for being a nice guy and an encyclopedia of information. Dan would have been happy to work at the butcher shop for the rest of his life if he didn't have two kids. He knew that they'd be going to college in a few years, and he knew that he could never afford to send them on busman's wages. So he started selling insurance—autos, homes, life insurance and commercial, "the gravy."

But Rowe's book never was profitable. He wrote questionable homes and "forgot" to rate drivers in the household. Young drivers were buried in order to keep the rates down. When the young drivers got in accidents, he added them to the policy, telling the clients that the "first claim was for free, the second one we gotta account for it." None of us approved of that kind of field underwriting, but that wasn't half of the tricks he had in his repertoire. Postal workers were given the company's "ultra pleasure" rate—designed for drivers that drove less than 5,000 miles annually. Of course, they drove a hell of a lot more than that, and should have been in a different rate class, and therefore a more expensive premium. Dan cheated the company, his clients, and himself. Those huge rate reductions and poor field underwriting amounted to cutting off his nose to spite his face. Dan didn't see it that way. He only thought of today, and if he got caught, the company would slap his hands, which happened more than once.

But despite his misgivings, I really liked Dan. He liked to hunt and fish and so did I. He was an avid duck hunter, which is quite an accomplishment for someone in his late 50s. Duck hunting is hard work. You wake up early, pay your dues, and take joy in seeing the sunrise over a secluded marsh. Most guys start duck hunting in their early 20s, then burn out by the time they have families of their own. Not Dan. He is still going strong, in fact "Duck Hunter Dan" is the only guy I know who routinely shoots a "Scotch double" (two birds with one shot) at least once a year, when the flights are in and the gunning is good. It's those doubles that always take him one bird over his daily limit. Imagine that.

Gerry Buchanan from the Sault was another duck hunter

who fit into the cream of the crop of our agents. He had never taken a Scotch double in all his years of hunting. Gerry wasn't flashy or flamboyant, but he sold a lot of insurance because of his reputation as being a nice guy—quick with a smile and a wise crack. He didn't work especially hard, or do a lot of advertising; he simply knew a lot of people, and a lot of people knew the family he married into. Gerry's brother-in-law was a cop, the chief of police in Sault Ste Marie. Gradually, over time, Gerry built his book of business. Gradually, he learned to take more and more time off during duck season to pursue his passion.

The last of the best agents was Ted Buxton, who was the caboose of our bunch. He worked hard, and was well connected in the community, but there was always something that kept him from achieving his goals. Ted let the small stuff get in the way.

Ted's brother-in-law owned the bar in downtown Mt. Pleasant, just a block from the courthouse. It was called "The Judge's Chambers." The previous owners, the Chambers family, thought the name was perfect; Ted's brother-in-law thought the name might lure some of the legal eagles through his doors after a hard day of work.

Ted took over a book of business that belonged to a 30-year veteran, Jim Cripsaw. He had 1,500 auto policies, 500 home policies, and a handful of commercial accounts that netted $125,000 in annual commissions. Ted's book was about the same size, so overnight, Ted doubled his agency and walked into a gold mine.

Ted was pushing 50, smoked a pack of Camel cigarettes a day, and laughed at almost everything. He had a thin build and flowing white hair, stained a smoky yellow. He laughed at his good fortune, and his bad luck. He laughed at the bombastic computer system Surety Guarantee employed, but laughed at the expense of an alternative. That's why his clients liked him—his laughter made them feel at ease. But the most identifiable thing about Ted was his bitterness. He hated Surety Guarantee for the way they jacked up rates, causing his clients to leave. He hated our District Coordinator, Scott, because of the way he continually lied to us, and for never acknowledging our concerns. He hated the company executives because they always had an alibi for not giving us a competitive product to sell. But above all else, he hated the direction the company was going so close to his retirement. Ted wanted to ride out the wave, absorb Jim's book into his own, and retire on a handsome dollar.

Ted, Jack, and I met at the Petoskey Yacht Club for steaks, beer and a sailboat ride one summer afternoon.

And that's when all the trouble began.

Four

JUNE IN NORTHERN Michigan can be fickle. Although the calendar says summer, June is merely an extension of spring, where storms can whip up winds of 50, 60, 70 miles per hour. It is usually a wet month too—the kind of every-other-day rains that farmers and cherry producers dream about. In June, the alfalfa fields in Petoskey grow an inch or two a day, and the orchards blossom into an undulating sea of white and pink.

Jack, Ted and I met at the yacht club at about noon on a Tuesday. We were the three amigos of the district, not because we had the same interests, but because we were so diverse. Jack had never been hunting, but Ted and I hadn't much interest in sailing. Jack had a cabin up north, but had never been fishing. What brought us together was the innovative ways we could complain about the company.

When we arrived, several yacht club members were leaving, having just moored their boats in the harbor down the boardwalk. They all knew Jack, smiling approvingly of his presence. Everybody liked Jack.

Jack lit the grill that was in the courtyard, while Ted opened the trunk of his oversized Buick and pulled out a small cooler. He met us in the courtyard, and in minutes, had a beer in his hand and a white paper package resting on the grill's shelf. Jack had three plates on a metal wicker table not far away. Baked potatoes were resting on the plates next to a mound of leafy green salad. The napkins under the silverware flitted at the corners; the wind inside the courtyard was strong. On the big water of Little Traverse Bay, we'd really have our hands full on Jack's boat.

"Hanson, you ready for a beer?" Ted gestured my way. "Hanson" was my nickname, short for my surname, Johanson.

"Thanks, Ted. Red label, huh?"

"Yep, good old Budweiser. Hey, cook, you want a beer?"

"No thanks, I've got myself a little vodka tonic. How'd you like your steaks?" Jack asked as he jabbed a long-tined fork into the first of three chunky rib eyes. The grill sizzled.

"Make mine red," Ted said, patting his belly. He followed that with, "I'd like to get a head start on that colon cancer." He lit up another cigarette, which he called "coffin nails."

"I like mine medium…I thought Surety Guarantee was going to kill you before the cancer does."

"No kidding, those damned idiots running that operation ought to be hung up by their thumbnails and left to die. I've never seen such incompetence…." He laughed, we all did, another diatribe.

I winked at Jack—he knew that I was trying to get Ted going and it worked. Ted loved to criticize the company, and he seemed to concoct new and tortuous ways to seal their fate. Today it was "thumbnails," but last week it was "nose hairs." He was very bitter.

"Ted, okay, we're trying to have fun out here, get off your soapbox, will ya? You're preaching to the choir. Hanson and I know that they're lying, cheating jackasses, but what are you going to do for a living? I mean, look at us, here on a Tuesday afternoon in northern Michigan. We didn't ask our bosses to make it here today. We're our own bosses, and if we want to take the day off to go sailing, we just do it. How many people do you know that can get away with that?"

"Sure, but just think how much better we could be doing if we had a better company standing behind us."

"I know, Ted. It's scary to think about. That's what's so frustrating. I lost a client here yesterday that came in with tears in her eyes, because her husband said that they had to leave me because my rates were too high. I couldn't blame her; they were going to save $500 a year by going somewhere else. What could I say? I'm not worth that much extra."

Then it was my turn. "Jack, I thought we left our soapboxes at home today. We've got that meeting coming up to announce the new auto rates. They'll take care of us. You watch. What are the odds of finding some steak sauce in the kitchen?"

"Go look, and on your way back pour me another vodka tonic. Better yet, you watch the steaks and I'll chase up a drink." Jack handed me the steak fork and his big apron, and disappeared into the clubhouse. The steaks were already flipped, and when I pressed the fork on them, they bled heartily. Ted looked over my shoulder and told me to move his to the top shelf. He wanted his steak bloody, to go along with his third beer.

Jack returned a second later with salt and pepper shakers, steak sauce, and a large tumbler tingling with ice. I handed him his utensils, then waited for the rebuff that was sure to follow.

"They'll take care of us, all right. Just like they did the last time, and the time before that. Those jackasses only know how to do one thing—raise the rates. They don't have a clue what they're doing."

"Ted, you heard what Scott's told us. This time around we've got the profitability numbers to warrant a lowering of the rates, or at the very least, avoiding another increase. He's talking about the nicer cars getting a substantial rate decrease, too. He even said that the company will approve towing coverage for cars that carry liability only."

"That slimy dirtball has lied to us before, and he'll do it again. Lemme tell you something. If they don't get their head out of their asses, I'm leaving."

"Ted, you've said that before. I dare you to leave," I said.

"What would you do anyway?" Jack asked.

"I don't know. But there's got to be something better than this."

Jack pulled the steaks and put them on the plates. He turned off the grill and sat at the table. "But what could be better than this?"

"I've got something going, but I can't tell you about it right now. Pass me some of that steak sauce." He took the napkin off his lap and wiped his brow, folded it in half, then wiped his brow again. Ted had a huge forehead under his thick, curly head of white hair. His thin frame and narrow shoulders made him look like an oversized Q-tip. We let his feint go.

"Good steaks. Ted. Where did you get them?"

"Some Amish butcher down by Clare. Got a pretty good deal going. Doesn't believe in insurance, or work comp, so he keeps his overhead low. Doesn't have to pay his family members either. They eat pretty well, though."

"Did you ask him about his insurance plan?"

"Sure, but I didn't get far. They figure that if one of their members has a big fire, whether it's in his barn or in his butcher shop, the other members pass the hat and make him right. I guess they pass the hat for fires and accidents from as far away as Ohio and Pennsylvania. In a way, they pay voluntary premiums, unlike the system we now have with Surety Guarantee. Those cheatin' bastards. God, if they had a clue of what direction they were going, we might have a chance."

"We would have a chance."

After cleaning up the dishes and loading the cooler with more ice and refreshments, we jumped aboard Jack's sailboat. A few minutes later, the dock lines were tossed, and we were underway. When we cleared the break-wall, the wind hit us. Jack smiled, pulling on the long rope that operated the lampshade-like sail on the bow. The motor died, Jack turned the wheel, and the craft lunged silently into the watery oblivion of Little Traverse Bay.

When the sails were set and we were cruising along, I brought up the latest round of corporate executives who were busted for one crime or another. The recurring theme in all the cases was greed. They didn't care who or what stood in their way. They trashed the company in order to pad their own pockets. They took the long-term sacrifices the company made and turned it into instant cash. They had no scruples, no loyalty to the people who made the company great. The executives at the top of Surety Guarantee seemed to be doing the same thing.

Jack had a way of breaking the tension. He said he was going to open an insurance office with scantily clad female employees. "It would be great. I'd have a uniform for the girls—short-shorts and tight tank tops. Of course, I'd have to interview the applicants to look over their qualifications. They'd have to be good at the computer, good with the customers, and know a little about insurance. I can see this thing catching on; guys would come in every month to pay their premiums. Wives would be happy to do away with the burden of paying the insurance, and the husbands couldn't resist some nice looking dish in a sexy little outfit..."

We all laughed until Ted said that he was having trouble with his secretary, Sarah. "She's claiming that I've already started doing that already."

"Hey, that was my idea first. I'll patent it if I have to." Jack let it drop, changed gears, and brought up the meeting on the horizon and its impact on our agencies, our livelihoods, and our clientele. Everything in our careers seemed to be pointing toward the meeting and whether or not we would be getting relief. Ted was at his wit's end. He needed some sort of hope that Surety Guarantee was going to turn things around. He needed something to sink his teeth into, otherwise he'd quit, or so he threatened.

"Maybe I'll start sailing professionally," he laughed.

We never thought that Ted would have the guts to leave Surety Guarantee. But then again, we never thought that some of the other agents would leave either. They did. A few of the mediocre left—tired of seeing their book of business shrink, seeing their clients leave in droves.

In a week's time we had our meeting, and no one was surprised when the rate relief wasn't there. Hope for the future was dashed again. Scott didn't know how to deliver the news, but he toed the company line, like a good foot soldier. He didn't apologize or make excuses. He had egg all over his face again. He was pathetic. Ted called him a "mealy-mouthed, good-for-nothing little idiot." It seemed like Scott actually believed the company would deliver on the rate relief. I really thought that the state executives had a good plan for selling it to the home office actuarial department. But that didn't happen. Surety Guarantee raised the rates 12 percent across the board, which usually meant that the net increase would be somewhere in the range of 20 percent after the smoke had cleared. That's how the company operated—they'd say one thing and it would come back another. That's how the executives thought—keep raising the rates, padding their pockets, gouging the customers, and screwing the small-town agents like us.

After 10 years as a Surety Guarantee agent, Ted turned in his resignation the following morning.

Five

WE COULDN'T BELIEVE that Ted was actually on his way. How could he do this? Things were bad, but were they so bad that he would really throw 10 years as an agent out the window? And what was he going to do?

Nobody in the district could believe it. Rumors swirled about his career move. Even more swirled about the second round of "sweepstakes." First it was Jim's retirement, now Ted's.

The Peligrini boys were the heirs apparent, since they had an office down the street from Ted's. But the Peligrinis also had their baggage. One brother was a Certified Public Accountant by trade, and the other was a real estate agent. While one brother was filing tax returns, the other brother was out selling homes. They didn't hire any staff to help them out, which could have freed up time for sales. All in all, they didn't make much of an effort to sell insurance; it was merely a sideline business.

At first, I didn't want anything to do with Ted's office, or the theoretical windfall it represented. I knew Ted too well. I knew that he was going to go after his old clients, despite what his contract said about not competing for a year. I knew that he had an axe to grind with Scott and the executives that supposedly tried to screw him out of a living. I knew that there'd be no talking to him. But still, the carrot at the end of the stick dangled there… It was an easy $7000 a month in renewals, with the possibility of turning it into $14,000 within a half year. Renewal commission is where the money is, and Ted's Mt. Pleasant office had a nice little bundle. The money Ted's book generated would be on top of the monthly income my own book produced. Between the two offices, I could probably clear $200,000 a year—not bad for a misfit without a MBA, a workaholic's long hours, or a stipend from a rich uncle.

Ted's office wasn't much to look at, but it was established, and the clients were used to it. It was a brick home off the main drag in Mt. Pleasant, where other businesses converted similar homes into beauty parlors, accounting services, and even a dog grooming operation. Outside the front door stood a large balsam tree that shaded the entryway. It looked like a cottage. Inside, the walls had a dingy, yellow cast—the result of several hundred cartons of Camel cigarettes being smoked there. The florescent light bulbs had no covers on them, and the place looked like it had been milked, and milked hard, which is exactly what had happened since Jim was an agent there 30 years ago. Nobody poured money back into the building; there wasn't any money to spare, no spirit of hope. I think Jim was eager to get rid of the building, rid of the hassle of renting it to others. Scott made him an offer, and he took it.

Surety Guarantee had rules about taking over a book of business. The first rule is that the acquiring agent gets paid half the commission until he writes an additional line of insurance in the household. At that time, the agent collects the full amount of commission, and the policies add to the agent's book value. Until then, the agent collects half of the normal commission.

Trouble arises if the policies leave the agency; then the new agent has to pay back the commission to the company. And if enough clients leave the company, there was is no guarantee that the commission would be enough to cover the expenses required to keep the doors open. Any way I looked at it, taking over the Mt. Pleasant office was a gamble. Risk and reward. The risks were substantial, but so was the reward.

And so, I decided to roll the dice and go for it. I had built a nice agency in Big Rapids, a half hour west of Ted's office, and I also had a staff in place that was extremely capable of running the office without me.

All that stood in the way of my taking over the Mt. Pleasant office was the blessing of that little twerp, Scott. He was the guy who assigned abandoned policies; he was the fellow who cut the deals with agents. In a way, it was like striking a deal with the devil, and I hated the thought of it.

After looking over a profile of the agency's commission base and its policyholder data, I put together a business plan. It didn't have to be elaborate or extreme. It just had to be a little better than a part-time insurance agent's business plan, and that shouldn't have been hard at all. After an hour at the computer I had it done, all five pages. One of the concessions I had to make was agreeing to get my Series 6 and 63 licenses. Those allowed me to sell Surety Guarantee's brand of mutual funds, variable annuities, and variable life insurance. I knew that the deal was contingent upon that, so I agreed. If nothing else, I could sit for the exams. If I failed, I failed, but at least I still had the policies. I could lie to Scott if I had to; I could fake my desire to sell something of which I had no intent.

Scott liked my presentation, as I knew he would. I covered all the bases: marketing, contacting the clients, keeping the office open, periodic reviews, life insurance sales, and of course, the securities license. He wouldn't let that one pass. The company put the pressure on the District Coordinators for agents with the securities license, and the DCs in turn did the same to the agents. They had to have the agents selling this stuff, because it made the company more money.

The next day I learned that I got the job. Scott made me feel like it was a close call, and somehow I owed him something for the honor. In reality, he didn't have much of a choice. Getting the policies was a bittersweet feeling. Now I was in bed with the devil, and I hadn't yet dealt with my old buddy Ted. We had to sign over the lease, get him to sign off on the phone numbers, and I had to purchase equipment. The contract we all had with the company stipulated that the office space and the phone number would be made available to the company once the agent left and received payment for the policies.

Ted was reluctant to do either, and frankly, I couldn't blame him. He was expected to give up his only bargaining chip based on the promise of a couple of company men that had a suspect reputation when it came to integrity. His check was in the mail, or so they wanted him to believe.

I met Ted for lunch at one of the local eateries to iron out some of the details of the takeover. It was about three weeks after our sailing outing. He told me all about the agency where he was going to work, and the cut he would receive for the policies he sold there. Apparently the owner of the agency liked Ted, and they played golf at the same private club. Surprisingly, Ted didn't have a beer with lunch. I figured that was his usual routine, but he said that he never had done that. I asked him about Sarah, his assistant, if she'd like to fill out an employment application. "I doubt if she would be interested. That girl is bad news. You don't want any part of her."

"What? She's been there with you for four or five years. She knows her way around the computer and all. I thought she was really good."

"She did a fine job, but lately, she's kinda lost her marbles. Besides, she might come and work for me." By judging Ted's reaction, I got the feeling that he didn't want me talking to Sarah, and that was fine.

After I paid the lunch check, Ted lit up a Camel and pushed back his chair. I waited until his cigarette was halfway finished before I looked him in the eye and told him to keep his hands off the policies for a year. "Aw, come on, these people are leaving anyway. Surety Guarantee is so high-priced that the clients can find it cheaper every place else. I can't keep them from looking me up."

"Ted, give me a year. Or I'll turn you in to the company."

"You would not."

"Are you willing to bet a lawsuit that I won't?"

"I'm telling you that they're leaving anyway."

"I need a year."

Back and forth we went. I tried rationalizing with him, but that didn't go so well. He was hell-bent on all but admitting that he would be rolling the policies. I gave up and let Scott and the marketing middle manager, Don Tadrick, take over.

After a week or two of bickering and backstabbing, they hashed things out. Ted got his first of three book value payments, and I got the office, the phone numbers, and a dingy office in need of a makeover. Scott and I hired a lawyer to draw up the paperwork for our arrangement. Scott bought the building and I'd pay him rent, $100 more a month than the going rate in the neighborhood. He told me he needed the extra $100 a month to "make it worthwhile." But he didn't stop there, "Hey, I made $200,000 last year, and it wasn't because I gave it away." I wasn't worried about the extra $100 a month, because I could always find new office space once the dust settled. For now, my goal was to get acquainted with the new clients and preserve what I could of the commission.

Before Ted departed for his new company, he sent a letter to his old clients. I figured that he'd want to send out a farewell letter, and it really wasn't that bad. It read:

> *Dear Friends,*
> *After 10 years as your Surety Guarantee agent, I have decided to retire from the agency force. I'll still be in the insurance business, but I cannot handle your insurance for 12 months because of the non-compete provisions in my contract. I can, however, help your friends, neighbors and relatives with their insurance. Please have them call me at the number listed below. I regret the price increases and rate changes that you experienced while you were with Surety Guarantee. It was frustrating experience for me, and I'm sure for you too. If you know of anyone who might need my services, please have them give me a call.*
> *Sincerely, Ted*

I'm not sure who gave me a copy of the letter, but it really didn't matter. Eventually someone would have brought it in, as if they were turning in a pop bottle for a 10-cent deposit. There's always a snitch in every group.

I handed the letter over to Scott, who in turn gave it to Don Tadrick, Scott's boss. They'd think that the letter was a veiled solicitation and grounds for a lawsuit. Ted's contract with Surety Guarantee prevented him from soliciting Surety Guarantee's policyholders for a year. Scott seemed genuinely disappointed in Ted's letter, but anything Scott tried to do "honestly" was a challenge.

Not long after I moved into the office, I realized that Ted was making hay. He was rolling business from his old office to his new. What were once Surety Guarantee clients were now insured at his new agency with a host of smaller, regional type companies. When people called to cancel their policies, I made it difficult. They had to come in and sign the request to cancel, and they had to write down their new agent's name. Most left to go to Ted, who apparently forgot all about my warning.

Tadrick and Scott were building a case against Ted, but first Tadrick sent him a warning letter. It read something about how soliciting former clients was a violation of his contract, and not only could he lose the remaining two-thirds of his book value, but also face damages payable to the company. Ted kept writing his former clients' policies, and before long he forced the company's hand.

Tadrick and Scott paid me a visit one morning a month after I was in Mt. Pleasant. They wanted to know how things were going. I sat behind a card table in a folding chair. I could only offer one of them a seat, because the other chairs held up my fax machine and portable copier. So with as much muster as I could, I tried to toe the company line, yet paint the picture that a traitor was hosing me. It worked. Tadrick took the bait. "We're talking to a lawyer now, and he should be served within a week or so."

"You mean a lawsuit?"

"Well, the first thing to hit him is an order to cease and

desist. Next comes an injunction, and then the lawsuit."

"Oh good. I'm getting clobbered here! Every day it seems I get hit with a dozen cancelled policies. He's not getting all of them, but the lion's share. You gotta help me here."

"I thought you two were friends."

"We were friends, but I told Ted to keep his hands off the policies. If he had done that, we'd still be friends. But I have no use for the guy now. He's stealing from me and I've had enough of it."

"He'll get his due, believe me."

"I hope it doesn't take too long. At this rate, I won't have enough to keep the doors open."

"What do you mean?"

"Don, I need at least five grand a month to keep this office open. Rent is $500, and my new assistant works part time, but still draws $1,500 a month. Add postage, phone, and you've got a pretty big nut to crack."

"He'll get his due. What kind of mailings have you done?"

"Well, I sent out a letter last week to everyone stating that I'm their new agent. Kind of generic, but it's been hard to gauge its success. You don't want to come on too strong or anything. I can say this, not everyone liked Ted. They didn't like his smoking, and his secretary made a lot of people mad." Scott let Don do all the talking but I could tell he was getting restless, looking for a spot to jump in and take over the conversation.

"Really?"

"Oh yeah, I thought everyone liked her too, but apparently she kind of got an attitude at the end."

Scott had his opening: "I had a lot of personnel problems at my office, in Maryland. I had this one girl who stole a bunch of money, but we couldn't prove it," I tried to pretend

I was interested. Don did the same. "She had a buddy that worked at the bank, and pocketed deposits that were made after hours..." Scott blabbed on *ad nauseam* while I sized up Don. Just like every other time I saw him, he wore a cheap sport coat and slacks. The sport coat looked to be off the rack, over the counter. Today it was tawny green, but other times it was burgundy or taupe. Small, round pill balls clung to the undersides of his sleeves and lapels. His trousers bowed in the front, where his round belly protruded beyond his belt. "But I overcame a lot to make it to Commander's Club all those years," Scott finally concluded.

You phony moron, I thought.

"Who told you about Ted's secretary?" Don asked.

"Ted. He said that she was acting really weird. I'm not sure what he meant, but I guess it's water under the bridge now." The conversation lulled for an awkward minute or two. The phone rang, and I had to answer it; my new assistant was at lunch. Scott and Don stepped away from the card table and wandered across the room to the other makeshift desk. They trampled over the drop-cloth that the painters left. I kept an eye on them as I scribbled information about the billing error the caller had. I put on an extra layer of courtesy and sympathy, more for the benefit of the men in my office than the person on the telephone. When I hung up, they acted like they had just finished a conference at the pitcher's mound.

"I do want to tell you that I am sending out another letter," I said, opening a box of copy paper under my card table. As I shuffled through the folders, I told them about my discovery that some of the policies in Ted's book didn't have the "member" discount, which could have saved the clients hundreds of dollars a year. The member discount was the predecessor to the dealer's discount. It was available to clients in select groups, such as the teacher's union, labor unions, accountants, and so on. If the client didn't work in one of the groups, it was a widely accepted practice of agents to facilitate their membership in the cheapest group available. In Ted's case, he didn't take the initiative and find those deals for his clients. Some would call it laziness; I thought it was a gamble on Ted's part. If the clients stayed with him, he collected more premiums, and therefore, more commission.

But my motivation was different. I wanted to save my new clients as much money as I could. If I did that, I'd have more credibility with them. I had to make my letter strongly written, so it would motivate them to call us. So I pulled two copies of a letter out of the folder and slid it across the card table. They each picked up a copy, and were silent again. My letter read:

> *Hello again folks!*
>
> *I hope you and your families are doing well. It has been three short weeks since I've been in the Mt. Pleasant office, and there's a lot going on. The office is undergoing a facelift, so there won't be that smoky odor any more.*
>
> *We have a new office manager now. Her name is Jamie, and she and her family live in Mt. Pleasant. Her two sons go to grammar school at Pike Elementary on the south end of town. Be sure to ask Jamie about her sons' baseball team.*
>
> *After reviewing most of the policies I took over, I discovered that almost all the clients were missing our most generous discounts. Your old agent could have given you the discounts if he wanted, but for some*

reason he did not. It could have cost you hundreds of dollars a year.

Please give me a call, or stop by the office today. Meet your new Surety Guarantee agent, and Jamie, the new boss in town. We'll do our best to save you a lot of money.

Sincerely, Larry Johanson

Scott finished first, but seemed to wait for Don. Scott didn't have the guts to voice his opinion first, for fear that it didn't jive with the company line. Neither wanted to speak. But finally, Don said it was okay. "It's not a bad letter. Friendly, yet motivating. I can read between the lines, and hopefully the clients will too."

"What do you mean, 'between the lines'?"

"Well, you kind of allude to the saving money part, and that Ted should have done a better job for them, but you really stated the obvious, too, in that Ted overcharged them."

"So it's okay to send?"

"Sure, you know what we want. We want to save as many clients as possible, and as long as you have good judgment, send whatever you want." He set the paper down, and so did Scott, approvingly.

"Okay," I gestured to a stack of addressed envelopes a foot high on the counter across the room. "They're all set to go."

Just then the back door opened, and in strolled Jamie, like a breath of fresh air. She had shoulder-length blonde hair, wonderful green eyes and a pleasing, feminine physique. But she possessed more than an attractive face; she carried herself with confidence, with style, and with an air that any man or woman would envy.

Don licked his chops. He pulled up his sagging belt while

she scribbled notes at the answering machine. Even a dumpy middle manager in a $69 sport coat could appreciate beauty in his midst.

Don introduced himself, as did Scott. They asked about her sons' baseball team, just to break the ice. They quickly had their minds on other things when I asked them about the latest rate debacle. They wanted to go outside to finish our conversation, but I didn't let them squirm.

"Well, you know we've got a pretty bad loss ratio in auto."

"Everything Scott's showed us has been pretty good," I countered.

Scott jumped to his own defense, and admitted that he didn't have the whole loss ratio picture. "Yeah, but pure loss ratio is different than adjusted loss ratio, and we seem to have a good one here." He was pathetic. He sold us out at the first hint of controversy. The company always had both sides of the sword when it was to their benefit. "Statewide, though, it's horrible."

"Do out-state agents help subsidize the losses in the metro areas?"

Don squirmed. That question hit a little too close to home. He wanted to get out of there, but he really liked the view across the room. "Look, we know our rates are horrible. We know that our policyholders are paying way more than they could, but we believe in our agents. We believe in you, and that's why we gave you Ted's policies."

"Do you know how much higher our rates are than everyone else's?"

"No."

"They're 30, 40, 50 percent higher than the competition. Am I wrong for thinking that the company is trying to pay for that acquisition earlier this year? Or is there some other reason we have to be so much higher than everyone else?"

Don didn't want to hear that, either. The acquisition of a smaller, financial services company was soft-pedaled by Surety Guarantee. I was beginning to get under Tadrick's skin, which wasn't my intent. I wanted him to warm up to me, to earn his confidence. I apologized. He paused, looked at Jamie, and leaned over the card table. In a low, stern voice he said: "Look, we know that we're taking advantage of our clients, but that's what upper management wanted to do. It's only temporary. We'll keep the clients that really want to keep us, and that's why we need agents like you." He stood, hoisted his belt again, and looked Jamie's way one last time. Without hesitation, he smiled and cried out, "Now you keep an eye on this guy! Nice to meet you, Jamie. Bye, Larry, and good luck." They both waved, halfheartedly. Scott mimicked whatever Don did. He was putting on a clinic of how to butter up to the boss. He was a spineless coward, and my contempt for him was growing stronger every time we spoke.

When the door slammed and the smoke had settled, Jamie asked me who those men were. "Those two work for the company. They call the shots. They're the ones that hand out the rates from the home office, and split up the policies when an agent leaves or gets terminated. Come to think of it, the plump guy, Don, is the one that does the terminating."

"Oh, okay."

"We'll probably want to give that guy a wide berth."

"No problem."

"Remind me to tell you about his story...and what he did to the women he worked with at his previous assignment."

"I'm not sure I want to know."

"No, you've got to hear it—for your own good."

Six

THE NEXT TWO weeks were busy. I was getting accustomed to the drive from Big Rapids to Mt. Pleasant. Occasionally Caroline, my assistant from the "home office," went with me to Mt. Pleasant to train Jamie. Caroline was a good assistant. She learned to anticipate any issues that came up, and knew ways to fend off the glitches of the Surety Guarantee computer system. It was hard to teach Jamie all the little nuances, because the Surety Guarantee computer system defied logic. Discounts were mysteriously removed from clients' policies, rate classes suddenly changed, and premium payments astonishingly disappeared into the company abyss. Caroline had to do her work over and over again, but when we mentioned the flaws to the company executives, they didn't do anything about it. They fell short of saying it was the agent's problem, but they refused to correct it, either. So not only was their computer system an aberration, but their reluctance to fix the problem was nothing short of idiotic.

There were other problems too. Adjusters took a week or more to contact claimants, when it should have been done in a day, at the most. But I could hardly blame them; they were assigned 10 or more new claims a day. A supervisor at the claims office hired a marine surveyor to inspect a $400 boat claim. The surveyor drove from Columbus to northern Michigan, which cost the company $1,800 after his fees, photos and report was completed. The surveyor said that the damage to the boat motor was the result of "wear and tear," which is excluded under most policies. The client said that he hit a stump. The claims supervisor denied the claim.

Every day, it seemed, more cancellations arrived. Some came through the mail. Others walked in with a smug gait, as if they were walking in to personally collect the money that they saved by changing to Ted's agency. I saved the forms they signed, and faxed them directly to Tadrick's home fax machine. I made sure that they wrote that Ted was their new agent. Sometimes I went along with their joy—"Ted is a friend of yours? Oh, good. I've got a few of those clients too, so I understand." It seemed to make the people feel better about making the change.

I couldn't blame them for leaving Surety Guarantee, or hooking up with Ted. Surety Guarantee charged too much for their insurance, and Ted had developed a personal relationship with them. Still, Ted broke his covenant with the company and disregarded my warning. My contempt grew stronger, and my resolve for revenge more determined. I wanted to avenge his actions, and if that meant helping the company with their lawsuit, then so be it. I wasn't about to give up the opportunity without a fight.

My letters to the clients became more and more poignant. They became less friendly and more surly. I sent letters to folks that cancelled their Surety Guarantee policies and went to Ted's office. I sent letters to my clients that called to complain about their rates.

I figured that if the letters were strongly written, the clients would be more apt to come in and give me the opportunity to save them money. The folks that got letters and came in to the office seemed to like my aggressive style. Still, there were a lot of people that didn't respond, and I wondered how they felt about the letters. I thought they were good letters, and they were necessary to stop the hemorrhaging in my agency.

I liked the letter that I sent to people that defected to Ted. Tadrick never responded to it after I faxed it to the machine he kept in his office.

> *Hello again,*
>
> *We recently processed your request to cancel your Surety Guarantee policy. I would hope that you'd get your refund check (if there's any unearned premium due) within a few weeks.*
>
> *I regret that we never had the opportunity to handle your insurance personally. We have made a name for ourselves in Big Rapids by offering excellent customer service to thousands of customers just like you. They have grown to like our friendly staff and our reliable answers to their questions.*
>
> *If you left our agency because of price, you may have your old agent to blame. He refused to give you all the discounts Surety Guarantee has to offer, and it could have cost you hundreds of dollars a year in extra premiums. The next time you see him, ask him why he didn't give you the best price we had. Better yet, give me another chance at your business, and I'll make sure it never happens again.*
>
> *Sincerely, Larry Johanson*

Looking back, it was probably foolish to send those letters. It felt good at the time, but the feeling quickly ebbed. My motivation was revenge, and when Ted got the letter from the people I sent it to, it would show him that I wasn't about to back down. I wanted him to know who turned him in. I was the guy who said I'd do it, and I'd be a coward if I didn't. Ted had revenge on his mind, but he let pride get in the way. He should have been sneakier about it. He should have waited a year.

He got hit with a lawsuit a week later, and so did the agency he worked for.

Wild ducks have a natural curiosity of foxes. It seems strange, after all, foxes are one of the predators that ducks best avoid. Generations ago, Native Americans lured wild ducks into their snares and traps with tame foxes. Today, the Nova Scotia duck-tolling retriever has a remarkable likeness to a wild fox, even though the American Kennel Club recognizes it as a breed of dog. "Tolling" dogs are bred to cast into fields when passing ducks are overhead. When the ducks circle closer to the dog, the dog is trained to lure the birds to the blind where the hunters are hiding. It seems odd but it works.

Somehow, I thought that Ted was leading us into a trap. He disregarded everything—my warning, the company's, the image of a long, expensive lawsuit. It seemed odd for him to abandon good sense and invite trouble the way he was. The company would never believe that Ted was capable of setting a trap. The company would never believe that he was crazy like a fox.

Seven

THANK GOODNESS IT was almost duck season. At last, an escape from the rat race. Duck hunting is one of those activities steeped in ritual and ceremony. You wake up early. You make coffee and a huge breakfast, then pack a lunch and some snacks. If you're lucky enough to sleep where you hunt, all that's left is to load your gear into the boat, which is usually done under the beam of a flashlight. You taste the air, and see if the weatherman on the weather-band radio was correct about the strength and direction of the wind. Over and over, you cross off items on your mental checklist. It's a long ride back to the dock to pick up a forgotten license or a box of shells. Even worse, it's a long cold ride back to the dock for a pair of gloves.

Phone calls to Gerry Buchanan up in the Sault were more frequent during the fall. I enjoyed hearing Gerry's plans for opening day because of the excitement in his voice. He always had a new place for his blind, or an unusual sighting in the marsh. There's a trick to avoiding the crowds on opening day, and Gerry had a knack for doing just that. As a safety net, we each bought a Canadian license in addition to our

Michigan small game licenses. If the masses on opening day on the Michigan side got too crazy, we could always slide across the border and hunt the Queen's marshes.

The night before duck season, I drove to Gerry's cabin, downstream from Clyde's drive-in. The whole way north I imagined the cabin, with the long drive and the beautiful view of the water. It was very rustic, built many years ago on a shoestring budget. Only about 600 square feet, it had four rooms—two tiny bedrooms, an even smaller bathroom, and a kitchen/living room. Its walls were dreary, dark stained wood, but Gerry had cool stuff on the walls. He had a picture of two old men, taken at the turn of the last century, with a mound of brook trout in their midst. I've seen the photo before in fly shops and restaurants in trout fishing country. He had duck hunting prints too, of mallards dive-bombing decoys, or canvasbacks swooping over vacated duck blinds. In the frames, he stuffed the curly tail feathers from the drake mallards he's killed over the years.

It was almost dusk as I pulled into the driveway. A skunk waddled across the drive, destined for the beach. It was probably prime loitering time for skunks—the salmon run had recently ended and there must have been lots of carcasses in the shallow water. Mess came out to meet me, wagging his tail like mad and unafraid of my truck. Mess wasn't afraid of much, and if I had arrived a minute later, he would have been nose to nose with the skunk. I opened the truck's door, patted Mess on his graying muzzle, and grabbed my jacket. The air in the Upper Peninsula always seems cooler, more vigorous than below the Mackinac Bridge. It felt good to have three days of hunting ahead of me, and life as a Surety Guarantee agent far away. Three doors down, I noticed the only other light in the row of cabins. A man in a camouflage jacket and hat stood on the cabin's stoop, smoking a cigarette, and keeping an eye on his retriever as it hosed down the shrubbery. There'd be at least one other party in the marsh tomorrow.

Gerry opened the cabin door and extended his right hand. Our hands met, our faces smiled. It was good to see him again, especially under such excellent circumstances as the eve of opening day.

We exchanged pleasantries. He took my overnight bag and gun case, and walked indoors. I grabbed my sack of provisions from the grocer and the martini case I had stuffed with the two main ingredients for Manhattans. As he put away the supplies, Gerry told me that he wasn't that much ahead of me in arriving at the cabin. He had problems at his agency. His assistant spent the day at home with a sick child, and like most Fridays, his office was busy. Most of the problems at his office were the same as at mine. I really didn't want to hear about it now; I had food and spirits on my mind.

So with a little nudge, Gerry quit complaining and agreed to go to dinner. He reached into the cupboard and pulled out a milk bone the size of a hot dog. Mess's tail thumped the cracked linoleum floor. He knew the sound of the bones in the box, and the routine when Gerry left the cabin.

We left Mess to his milk bone bliss and headed out to Gerry's Explorer. Three steps from the cabin door, I noticed a hole in the screened porch, and the unmistakable hum of a huge diesel engine near the water. A down-bound freighter churned by us—its bank of lights passing like a train on tracks. In a way, I envied the lonesome life of a seaman. The only stress they had was the specter of dying on the Great Lakes, and that hadn't occurred since the *Edmund Fitzgerald* sank in the 1970s. Gerry clicked the Explorer's car doors open and we jumped inside. It smelled like the marsh, wet dog, and gun oil—the scents that all great duck hunts are made of.

"What's the story with the screen door?"

"The hole in it, you mean?"

"Yes."

"We've got a problem with skunks in the neighborhood. I made the mistake of leaving a few beer cans in there one night earlier this fall, and the sonofabitch scratched his way inside to slurp out the leftovers. It was horrible. That damn skunk drank the remains of the beer cans and became real belligerent. He wasn't a very good drunk. I heard him slamming into the other stuff on the porch, so I got up and tried to shoo him off the porch. Of course Mess heard it first, and started barking like an idiot. So there I am, in the middle of the night, in my underwear, trying to rid the cabin of this skunk, while shit-for-brains is barking like he needs an exorcist."

"How were you trying to get it off the porch?"

"I had a landing net, but the damn thing kept getting stuck in the splinters on the floor. Finally it worked though, and the skunk wandered off. But the next night, it came back again. What a mess. I had to shoot it in the butt with a BB gun. I'm surprised it didn't spray us. The BB gun sure put an extra jump in its step."

I laughed at another one of Gerry's stories. As usual, it was based on his failure to plan ahead or take care of things. His grounds-keeping skills were just as bad as my own, but he was proud of his—I wasn't proud of mine. One of these times his malfeasance would cost him more than just an embarrassing situation, but until then it was fun to laugh at him and pretend that I didn't have my own set of grounds-keeping ailments.

We drove by Clyde's on the way to an old-fashioned Upper Peninsula watering hole where they served fresh fried whitefish on sourdough Kaisers. The parking lot was full of old pickups and SUVs adorned with Ducks Unlimited bumper stickers and license plates. It was one of those few days a year when the yoopers (residents of the Upper Peninsula) tolerated bands of strangers in their towns. Restaurant owners, motel owners and lodges liked duck season; it meant lots of easy money from the folks downstate who came up to visit.

When we walked in the bar, a few of the locals were playing pool under the watchful eyes of mounted smallmouth bass painted to look like perch. There were many mounts on the walls—deer, fish, turkey, and of course, the mandatory antlered jack rabbit. Most of the men were wearing camouflage clothing, drinking, and laughing. It was a joyful time.

Gerry and I found a seat near the window and under an enormous muskellunge. The waitress looked like she had been put through the wringers. Her hair, once tucked into a neat little bun on the back of her head, now drooped over her eyes. She puffed air from the corner of her lips, sending the tufts of hair slightly higher on her forehead.

"I'll have a Manhattan."

"Rum and Coke, please. And if you will, a twist of lime." Gerry was always so polite. He had Eddie Haskell's manners in public, but could be a bit edgy when he was in the company of friends.

"Nice crowd tonight," I mentioned.

"Not bad. We haven't been this busy since last deer season. I'm sure the resort owners are smiling. Looks like there will be more than a few guys in the marsh tomorrow. Hope we don't run into any jerks."

"I hope you have a plan for avoiding the crowds."

"Don't worry, I've got a plan. We'll get our birds..."

The waitress returned with our drinks, took our order, and

Gerry and I raised a toast to the morrow. We took a sip and looked around the bar. Guys were swilling their beers, shooting pool, drawing maps of the marsh on bar napkins, and making trips to the men's room. I spotted duck hunting guide Joe Latourneau at the end of the bar; he was pointing to someone I didn't recognize with his index finger and middle finger. He had a cigarette between his fingers and a smile on his face. Every time I see Joe it reminds me of a story he told me about three duck hunters who almost died one windy fall afternoon. It was a hell of a story, one that I'd never forget.

"The two of us set out after breakfast for Long Point Island, here on Munuscong." Joe told me the story in an ice shanty, several years ago, while the perch fishing was slow. He crouched over a five-gallon bucket, peering into the plate-sized hole cut through the 12 inches of ice. His pack of smokes made a small bulge the breast pocket of his wool, quilted shirt. His smokes didn't last long; they were constantly in either his hands or mouth. "By the time we got set up, the wind was howling, and the ducks were flying. Boy, were they flying! We had diving ducks and puddle ducks too. But then, we started losing the decoys. The wind was blowing so strong that the anchors wouldn't hold. My guys in the boat wanted to leave so we picked up as many decoys as we could, then headed for shore in my big 18-footer. Halfway back to the lodge, we spotted a bag of decoys bobbing in the surf. One of the guys hauls the bag aboard and looks at the name on the bottom of the decoys. 'Holy cow' he says, 'it's the guy's in the other boat!' So we motor upwind, and the waves are like this," he gestured, cigarette in hand, as if he was tracing the back of a picket fence.

"Finally we see these guys huddled together on a tiny muskrat house, up to their armpits in water." Joe just sat there, jigging his little ice rod in one hand while smoking with the other. "They were too weak to move when we got there; it was too rough to haul them in, so one of us had to jump out of the boat and push them aboard. Next thing you know, we've got three guys in the bottom of the boat—and they're all about dead. Even my boat couldn't take that much extra weight, so we threw our decoys, shells, everything overboard to help make it lighter. Two of the guys were in the stern, bailing as fast as they could, but we'd take on just as much as they were tossing out."

"What happened?" I asked.

"I got on the ship-to-shore radio, so the ambulances met us at the dock. I found out that they had severe hypothermia—their body temperature was only 90 something. The hospital had them soaking in saline solution for some reason, and they kept them there for a week. Boy, it was bad. We all could have died."

"How big was their boat?"

"They had a 16-footer, but it was a flat bottom, not a deep-vee like mine. I guess they took on a huge wave that knocked them right out of the boat: dogs, guns, you name it. The boat was swamped. So they swam for the muskrat hut and stayed there till we picked them up. The dogs swam in circles until they were tired and tried to crawl up the backs of the hunters. They had to drown the dogs. Yeah, drowned their own dogs. One of the guys said he couldn't hold on any longer, and almost gave up. I guess we got there just in time."

Every time I see Joe, I think of that ghastly story, and his words "They had to drown their dogs."

I'm not sure what Gerry was thinking about, but suddenly he asked me, "If I got something going with an outside company, would you be interested in getting involved?"

"What do you mean?"

"What do you think I mean?"

"You've got something going on the side?"

"Well, not exactly, but it could happen soon."

"What d'ya mean? That's a violation of your contract. You could lose your job."

"I've already lost my job, thanks to the company. It's the same old thing, if you back a Surety Guarantee agent into a corner, he'll find a trapdoor and use it."

"I haven't found that door, but it may be what I'm looking for." The waitress brought our whitefish. Gerry wiped his beard with a napkin and took off his watch. It was almost a ritual with Gerry to take off his watch and wipe his beard at mealtimes.

I weighed the gravity of Gerry's inquiry. As Surety Guarantee agents, we were considered captive, which meant that we couldn't represent any other company. He did have a point though; the company had priced us out of the market...Was he thinking of leaving Surety Guarantee too, or was he thinking of taking on some additional companies?

Periodically, the company ran checks on our insurance licenses through the insurance commissioner's office to make sure that we weren't representing any other companies. If they found another company, they could fire us immediately. "What's this trapdoor you have?"

"Please, keep this quiet. You know my wife has her insurance license, right?"

"Sure."

"Well, we've been talking to several companies about getting licensed with them, with her as the agent of record. Her office would be next door to mine, so we could get around the part in our contract about 'soliciting' for another carrier.

If her name is on everything, there's no way they can pinch us. Are you with me so far?"

"Yup." I couldn't believe what I was hearing. Gerry was as straightlaced as they come, not too awfully adventuresome, and not likely to put together a devious plan like this one. He took two big bites of his whitefish sandwich and the tartar sauce oozed out one side. He nodded approvingly, then wiped his beard again.

"There are two problems that I can see now. One, there are some start-up costs involved. Most companies tie into a computer server that is quite expensive to initiate, about $20,000 off the bat."

"And what's the other problem?"

"Insurance companies require a certain amount of premium in order to keep your appointment. You need at least $500,000 in new business in the first year."

"That's a lot, but it's not really high, especially if you have a few producers working under you."

"That's where you'd come in."

"Anybody else?"

"I was thinking of asking everybody—Jack, you, me, Dan and Allison in Oscoda. I figure the more agents we have on board, the harder it will be to get rid of us all. Plus, if they don't find out about it, we could really line our pockets with some serious dough. I mean adult money. Imagine what we could do when someone calls to complain about his or her rates going through the roof? We'd tell them that 'we're working on it' and lo and behold, my wife calls them up and gives them a great quote."

"Why do you want Dan in on this?" I asked.

"Why not?"

"You know...the guy writes some suspect business. Remember that time he got caught for writing a mobile home as a modular?"

Gerry winced, nodding his head.

"Or how about the time he insured the plumber who was doing underwater welding on a nuclear power plant two states away from here?"

Gerry laughed at that one, but confessed that we would really need to get lots of premium on the books if we were to keep our appointment with another company. "I'll keep an eye on Dan. If he gets out of line, I'll be the one who'll punch his ticket. Let me handle him."

I let Gerry have his way, because I really had no choice. It was Gerry's deal, not mine. "If Scott ever found out about any of this stuff, he'd have our asses."

"I know, I know. There's no talking to him. He's hopeless. He's never done anything for us. That last meeting with the rate revision was pathetic. He called me the other day and wants to come up duck hunting later in the season. I kinda agreed, but you may want to come up again so I don't have to listen to his baloney all by myself."

"I'll take all the shot out of his shells so he doesn't get anything all day."

We ate the rest of our sandwiches and finished our drinks quietly. The bar was beginning to thin out. I laid a business card on the table, because you never know when the next sale will come from.

We paid the tab and headed back to the little cabin on the big river. Mess barked once, maybe twice when we opened the door. He was balled up on the couch beneath the print of the noble canvasbacks swooping over an abandoned blind. Tomorrow would be a big outing for Mess, and for all of us.

We would shoot six ducks on the state side of the St. Mary's River, and then 11 more on the Canadian side.

An hour after shooting hours ended, I got served with a lawsuit while sitting at Clyde's drive-in.

Eight

THINGS PROGRESSIVELY GOT worse for the agents, the folks who worked for the agents, and the people who bought policies from the agents. The agents saw a spike in their monthly commission checks because the company was billing at such exorbitant rates. The typical home insurance premium was being renewed at a 50, 60 or 90 percent increase over last year's rates, which had been increased the year before in the same intervals. In other words, two years ago, a policyholder's home insurance rates may have been $360 for a $100,000 home, but last year the $360 turned into $570, which this year turned into $1,000. If the client had a claim along the way, their rate got an additional jab in the shorts—a 50% additional increase. So, over the two years, a client with a claim could go from $360 to $1,500.

No wonder people were mad when they got their renewals. They felt like they were getting ripped off, and the agents bore the brunt of their frustration. They called and voiced their complaints. They called to leave the agency, to have the agents start the paperwork to initiate their refund checks.

The company justified those increases by opening their books. Almost. They showed the losses. They showed the salaries, write-offs and expenses. But what they never showed were the gains they made on their investment income. They wanted us to think that they take the money in paid premiums and put it in a sock somewhere, bearing no interest. When someone has a claim, they pull a little out of the sock and hand it over. When someone has a bigger claim, they take it out of the sock and put it in a drawer, known as a "reserve" that bears no interest as well. If a claim takes more than a year to settle, the money stays in the drawer for that entire time, gathering dust. Those reserves go against the loss ratio picture for the agent and the company for as long as the claim isn't settled. If the claim is litigated, the reserve could stay on the books for a number of years. When the claim is settled, and the money is paid from the reserve, the company doesn't credit the agent's loss history, or modify their returns with the insurance departments. It's just one of the ways the company works the system to paint a horrible loss ratio to justify the increases.

Gradually, the company became more and more brazen. They were almost like a drug dealer. Drug dealers don't start out driving stretch Jaguars with gold rims. They start out by selling drugs to their friends, then their friends' friends. Gradually, they expand their circle of clients. Gradually, the money rolls in to where they spend it foolishly. Those purchases draw attention to themselves, which is when the cops come in and take them out. Drug dealers are like squirrels at the bird feeder—the police take one out, and another one takes its place.

The company became more and more flagrant with their lies and deception. They made foolish statements and wild predictions. They were ripe for the taking, and I was the one who would be the ringleader. I was a squirrel hunter too.

Nine

When I opened the envelope, I forgot all about our excellent day in the marsh. I forgot about the juicy cheeseburger, chocolate shake and fries I had on my plate. I had no idea what it could be. All I could see was the Isabella County Courthouse emblem on the brown manila envelope. I spun around, only to see the two men in cheap suits dash away in their Chrysler Sebring. They had undoubtedly driven several hours to serve me with it, but why?

I opened the envelope, peeked through the top, and the mystery was solved. In the upper left corner was the name "Ted Buxton" and below that, under "vs." was "Surety Guarantee" and my name. Somehow, I was getting sued, along with Surety Guarantee.

I flipped through the pages, and several things struck me—breach of contract, defamation of character, and $1,500,000. Both Surety Guarantee and I were getting sued—Surety Guarantee for refusing to pay the remaining portions of Ted's book value, and me, for sending out those letters to all his clients. Defamation of character? Heck, I was only telling the truth. Ted was grabbing at straws. There was no way that he'd collect anything; there was no way that he'd get away with it. But the bigger question hit me after Gerry took a look at it—who was going to defend me?

Ted got served with his lawsuit, all right. Surety Guarantee was suing him for three times the $30,000 they paid him. Under Michigan law, Surety Guarantee was entitled to triple the damages, because, they alleged, Ted took the list of clients and converted it to his own benefit.

Ted alleged that Surety Guarantee violated the contract, for not paying the rest of his book value. He thought that he was entitled to the other $60,000. My letters, which he thought were defamatory, were sent at the direction of the company executives. How could they deny me a defense in all of this?

Monday morning came, and I was on the phone with Scott. He couldn't believe that Surety Guarantee was getting sued, either. He couldn't believe that I was named. "What a moron that Ted has turned out to be. What is he thinking? He steals our policies, and then we're the bad guys in all of this."

"You read the letters I sent out. Were they that bad?"

"Which letters?"

"You remember the ones I showed you and Don at my office a few months ago?"

"Oh, those letters. I'm trying to remember what they said."

"You know, about 'the old agent didn't give you all the discounts'?"

"Can you fax me a copy?"

"Sure, but what's Surety Guarantee going to do about this lawsuit against me? And when do I get to talk to the company lawyer?"

"Fax me a copy of the lawsuit too, and I'll get the ball rolling."

I faxed everything to him and waited. A day or two went by without any response. I left a message at his office but he didn't call me back, imagine that.

I phoned Don Tadrick, but he was just as evasive. "Scott told me you might be calling. We were served Monday morning, and we turned it in to our attorneys. They'll prepare our answer to his suit, and…"

"*Our* answer?"

"Yes, Surety Guarantee…"

"What about my response? I was named in it too, you know."

"Sure, right. We'll have to see about that. But let's not forget you were one that sent out those letters."

"Listen, those letters were sent out with your approval. You read them at my office that afternoon with Scott. Then I faxed them to your home machine, remember? I need you to make up your mind and let me know if you'll defend me or not."

"I know, I know. Let me get right on it."

"I don't understand how you could deny me legal representation. Those letters were done without malice, and in the scope of my employment with Surety Guarantee."

"You're not an employee of Surety Guarantee. You're an independent contractor, remember."

"Just call me back with your decision by Friday afternoon."

I slammed the phone down and cursed. Caroline heard my tirade and wanted to know what happened. I was livid. "You know what? They set a new standard of incompetence every day."

"What happened?" she pressed.

"This blasted lawsuit...that's what happened. I'm going to get even with them."

"What do you mean?" Caroline whispered, "Who?"

"Them...all of them. I am sick and tired of getting screwed by those cheats and liars. You'll see."

Ten

IN ITS PUREST form, selling insurance is fun. The folks I meet, the friends I make, the bonds I solder. It's fun when you have a product to sell, and you figure out a way to sell it. It seems simple enough on paper to sell insurance; after all, everyone needs insurance. They have to buy insurance from someone; it might as well be from you, right? It's no fun shopping for insurance, and if clients feel that their agent isn't charging too much, they typically stay with that agent.

Selling insurance means that you'll meet some interesting characters. I made an appointment with a couple in their 70s for life insurance. The appointment was made for noon the next day, so they wouldn't have a chance to forget about it. When I arrived the next day at noon, the wife was in her bathrobe, and the husband was nowhere in sight. She yelled at the old man and he came out of a back room, also wearing a bathrobe. He had a martini in his hand and a stagger in his step. I sent them a letter a few days before our appointment, explaining everything about the policy for which they qualified. So I figured they read the material, liked what they saw, and in their minds had already committed to the contract. They didn't ask any questions or object to my suggestion to write up the application.

They answered the medical questions without hesitation, although most of them merely required a simple "no." When I got to the part where they needed to sign the application, the old man could hardly hold the pen, or see the paper. He sat there, starring at the paper like he was seeing several. I asked him to sign on the top line of the application again. He sat there, head bobbing, fingers gripping the pen like a tissue. "Aw shoot, I'm just snookered right to the gills. I'll just sign shorthand."

Sure enough, he signed it, like he did when he was in first grade. The underwriters weren't impressed. They rejected his application due to "alcohol use." I didn't have the heart to tell the old man that I was the one who notified the underwriters.

Another time I wrote a policy for a guy that called our office on the eve of his birthday. It's common for the dregs of society to buy insurance just before their birthday because insurance is a requirement for renewing their license plates. Surety Guarantee was competitive in that market, so it was no surprise that he bought a policy from us. His policy was in effect for a month before it lapsed for non-pay. Along the way, he hit a parked car, whose owner came into my office with a set of estimates and a beleaguered look on his face. His own agent offered no help whatsoever, so he was impressed with the way we got going on his claim.

When the smoke cleared a week or so later, the guy with the damaged parked car came in with his policies from another agency. Despite the fact that we were substantially higher in price than his existing policy, he liked the way we handled his claim and he bought our policy anyway. Years later he still had some policies with us.

And last, I had an appointment with a woman who needed auto, home, and possibly life insurance. I had no idea that she didn't live alone, or what her marital status was, but knew she lived in one of the more affluent neighborhoods in town. It was a warm summer evening. Sipping a glass of wine, she invited me out to the deck where we talked about safe topics like the weather, her perennial garden, and her occupation. People like to talk about themselves. They like to feel important and interesting. By watching them, and patiently listening, I make them feel like I really care. But really, what they tell me will later be used to help close the deal. If a client tells me about his gun collection and all the valuable pieces in it, I'll be sure to tell him about the limits on their policy. As an agent, you want to be informative, but compassionate. You want to make clients feel like you're their friend, so it'll be harder to leave you when another agent bangs on their door.

Anyway, this woman's hot button was her antiques. She wanted to make sure that they would be covered after a fire. How do they get replaced? Would she get the same kind of antiques for her older ones? I soothed her worries, but she wanted to reemphasize the value of her collection. She asked me if I wanted a glass of wine, and I accepted. A minute or so later she returned, white wine swirling in my very own egg-shaped glass. Our appointment was going well, and it was a nice summer evening. I didn't want to make her feel uncomfortable by drinking alone.

She asked me about my hobbies. I told her about my outdoor column and my love of photography. She read my columns, but admitted to not seeing any photos. For a while, I thought I was being interviewed; maybe I was. She brought the bottle of wine to the deck and poured more into our glasses. By then I had most of the applications filled out, and had her money in hand. I could have left, but we were having a nice time. Her stories became more and more funny, or so she thought. I laughed along with her.

When the topic came back to antiques, she told me again how important and valuable they were. Now she was tipsy. I should have been on my way, but she wanted to show me her most valuable piece. I followed her down the hallway to her bedroom, where a medium-sized oak cabinet stood. Hell, I didn't know anything about antiques, but she went on and on about who made it and how old it was. To validate her claims that it was an antique, she pulled out a drawer and flipped it upside-down on the bed. "Oh shoot! This is the wrong drawer. Here, give me a hand," she said, tossing panties of every size and color back into the drawer.

"What are you looking for?" I queried, not feeling especially comfortable handling her underwear on our first date. She spun around, yanking another drawer, and flipped that one on the bed next to the first. The second drawer was filled with bras—big ones, little ones, red ones, and black ones. There were lacy bras and flowered bras, smooth ones and pointed ones. Her antique dresser was the Noah's Ark of women's underwear.

"It's the seal that the woodworker emblazoned on the bottom of the drawer to *vaallidite* his work. This one isn't it either. Oh shoot!" The next thing I know, there's a mountain of undergarments on the bed, and I'm hearing footsteps and car keys jingling down the hallway. Oh great, I thought. Here comes her husband, who's going to see his wife slurring her speech and me ogling over her skivvies. This guy's going to tear my limbs off and beat me with the stumps. I held my breath and watched the door to the bedroom.

To my surprise, a woman darkened the doorway, and she was just as attractive as the first. She introduced herself politely, then waltzed over to my hostess and planted a kiss on her cheek. I breathed a sigh of relief, and so did my hostess, when she found the emblem on the bottom of the drawer.

Eleven

JACK CALLED NOT long after I hung up the phone with Don and Scott. Somehow he had heard the news of the suit against me. He wasn't surprised that Ted had filed it. He wasn't told that Surety Guarantee was going to sue Ted, but he probably could have figured it was going to happen.

"Hi, Hanson—what a twisted web we weave, when we make an effort to deceive."

"Shut up, will you?"

"Ha-ha-ha. I'll tell you, I'll tell you what a horrible chain of events. Four months ago we were the best of friends, and now we'll be on the Jerry Springer Show. Ha-ha-ha."

"Very funny." Jack had a way of infusing humor into dreadful situations.

"Ha-ha-ha. What the hell are we doing, suing each other for a few lousy policies, and a few bucks? My gosh, has it come to this?"

"I know. The big losers in this are Ted and me, but if we had a decent company standing behind us, neither one of us would be in this predicament."

"True enough, but what are you going to do now? How much does Ted want for his suit?"

"$1.5 million and I don't have that kind of dough to fend it off. Heck, I couldn't hire a lawyer for very long. Don and Scott say that they're going to let me know if Surety Guarantee is going to hire a lawyer for me. They're denying having any knowledge of reading the letters I sent out to all Ted's clients. They're denying telling me to send out whatever letters I wanted. It shouldn't come as a surprise, I guess."

"No, you should've known better. They'll deny anything that will hurt the mother ship until the cows come home to roost." Jack was filled with *non sequiturs*.

My phone was ringing nonstop. Jamie had her hands full that morning. It was a typical Monday—car crashes over the weekend, vehicle changes, the latest round of renewals that shocked my clients, and of course, more cancellations. What was worse, I got my latest commission check and to no surprise, Mt. Pleasant's revenue had slipped again. Instead of being $7,000 like I anticipated, it shrank to $3,500 a month. October only netted $3,000.

Jack tried to console me, "I would have sent out letters too. I don't know how you worded your letters, but the only way to survive in your shoes is to slam your predecessor. You've got to get in there and save those people money. You've got to motivate them to come in and see you."

"I know, and that's what I had in mind—anything to stop the hemorrhaging of policy runoff. At least now Surety Guarantee has stemmed the tide. They told me that a cease and desist order was filed at the same time as the suit against Ted."

"What are you going to do about a lawyer?"

"I don't know—you know that I've only got a few weeks to answer this thing."

"I wouldn't count on Surety Guarantee."

"I know. Isn't that ironic, how close your statement was to the Surety Guarantee's motto: 'Surety Guarantee: your assurance is guaranteed.'"

"You know, you might be onto something there."

"What?"

"Don't you have a policy with Surety Guarantee?" he asked.

"Yes, I've got a lot of policies."

"Don't they have an obligation to defend you in cases like this?"

"Sure, I guess, but intentional acts are excluded. You know that!"

"You weren't intending to defame him were you?"

"No," I said. "I never thought of that. What a great idea—I owe you one. I've got to run and call the claims office."

"Don't forget, though," he paused.

"What?"

"You'd better not let on that you *intended* to defame him. That stuff is excluded."

"Right."

"I'm serious. You won't have coverage if you do."

"Thanks, Jack. I owe you one. They'll cover me."

Twelve

GERRY CALLED THE following day with an update from the Upper Peninsula. The weekend's cold and blustery weather changed to an old-fashioned helping of Indian summer. By Tuesday the temperature was back into the low 60s, and all the pageantry of fall's splendor was in full bloom. The first two weeks of October draw the "leaf fudgies" to the Upper Peninsula for a color tour. In summer months, tourists are nicknamed "fudgies" because of their penchant for the homemade fudge that is produced by the ton in most northern Michigan towns. Several folks stopped by Gerry's office to pay their premiums, even though their agent was from "downstate."

"I think my office is part of the allure for those people," he said. "They must think that the ducks on the wall are cool. Every year, I get more and more people in my office just to see the ducks and pay their premiums. Even the blue-haired women complain about their rates."

"Never mind, what's the duck report from up there?"

"Everything has simmered down. We did about the best of the other guys I talked to. My brother-in-law..."

"The cop?"

"Yup. He launched the boat at 2:30 a.m. and had to wait in line at the ramp! There were guys all over the place. Finally he found a place to hunt near the refuge, but it took two hours of driving around by flashlight. They ended up with three ringnecks, two buffleheads, and a teal."

"Not bad, but not as good as us."

"Right, but at least they made it through their Clyde burger without getting served by a couple of jokers in cheap suits."

"Not you, too. Jack called me yesterday to rib me about it. I tell you, you've got to have thick skin in the insurance business—especially in this district."

"What did Jack want?"

"He actually helped me out. You know how I was worried about paying for a lawyer? Well, he told me that I may have coverage under my business owner's policy, at the very least they'd owe me a defense."

"Who handles that?"

"Surety Guarantee, of course." Jamie was eavesdropping. She glanced across the room and our eyes met. Her wonderful green eyes. I told her about the lawsuit on Monday morning, and she had an interest in its outcome. She didn't agree with it. Jamie was starting to become invaluable around the office, although at first she mispronounced clients' names. She called Bob Caston, "Rob Hasson" and Ryan Orvis, "Brian Gorbins." All I could do was smile until she recognized the names and voices of our regular callers. Almost everybody liked her. Good help is hard to find, and I was lucky to have Caroline and Jamie on my side. "Did you ask anyone else about that *alter ego* agency?"

"I talked to Jack today, and he's in."

"Anybody else?"

"That's it for now. I'll call the other guys tomorrow."

"Let me know if there's anything else."

"Well, there is one other thing. Scott called me today about some lady from our office that filed a complaint with the state office. Seems that I was rude to one of my clients last week when my secretary was off. Heck, I wasn't rude—she didn't buy my excuse for why her premium doubled. She bought Scott's story, and the problem went away. Anyway, he wants to go duck hunting with us the week after next. Said that he's interviewing a prospective agent up here, and he wants to give it a shot."

"Lovely."

"What am I gonna do, turn him down?"

"That's a good place to start."

Thirteen

MARK HENDRICKSON, THE Surety Guarantee adjuster, called my office the following day. He was a young guy, not far removed from college, with his whole career ahead of him. I enjoyed his sense of humor and the way he could make my clients feel like they were special. He handled many claims out of my office, so I had a chance to watch him in action. Often the claimants left with a smile on their face and the check in their hands.

"So, it seems the cows have come home to roost," he said, sarcastically.

"You've been talking to Jack haven't you?" I asked.

"Sure, we're always talking. He likes that whole 'cow to roost' thing. That guy has more claims than any other agent I know."

"Yeah, but he's got a ton of policies, too."

"What's this mess you've gotten yourself into?"

"It's a mess all right. Can you believe my former friend has stooped to this level?"

"Former friend?"

"Yeah, we were friends, but how else can you explain this? I told him that I was going to turn him in if he rolled his policies. Now he's turned the tables on me. I can't believe it."

"So what about these letters you allegedly sent?"

"I sent them, sure I did. Anybody would have. Heck, Scott and Don knew about them. They read them and gave me the go-ahead to send out whatever I wanted. I had to write those letters if I wanted to save any of the policies. I do have coverage for libel, right?"

"Well, kind of."

"Come on, Mark. I have 'broad form liability' on my office policy. You and I both know that it covers libel."

"Right, but when did you send out those letters?"

"A few months ago, clearly when my policy was in force."

"But did the alleged incident occur while your policy was in force?"

"What do you mean? Did Ted quit while my policy was in force, or did he start rolling policies while my policy was intact?"

"Something like that."

"Oh Mark, this thing is covered. Why don't we get down to business? I need to respond to this suit in a week or so. Why else would I have a policy that covers libel?"

"You remember the routine. I'll respond to it, send out a reservation of rights, and then get down to brass tacks. It's the best I can do right now, but at least we'll get an answer to the lawsuit."

"You've got a duty to defend, but I know it's what you've got to do. Send me the reservation of rights if you have to. But you'll see, Scott and Don won't deny knowing about the letters. They read them before I sent them out."

"That's good; it won't hurt your case if they knew about it."

"Oh, they knew about the letters; you'd better ask them about it."

"We will."

I hung up the phone feeling a little better about things. At least my policy would kick in and answer the lawsuit. If nothing else, I'd have a lawyer on my side, even if they later deemed my letters, and the resulting damages, outside of the policy coverage. I'd cross that bridge later. For now I had what I was after, and that was a lawyer to defend me.

Fourteen

DUCK HUNTER DAN called me from Oscoda on Monday morning. Usually Mondays are busy for an agent, so I thought it was odd that he called with the weekend's hunting report. He and his son paddled a mile or two out into the marsh of Saginaw Bay and shot a handful of teal and wood ducks under balmy skies and sun-soaked days. It was slow gunning, by anyone's standards.

"We need another blow like we had on the opener," I lamented.

"We sure do. All the birds around here are educated."

"They avoid blinds like the plague."

"A little weather would bring down the dumber birds from up north."

"Gerry is up north—have you talked to him lately?" I set the bait and he took it.

"Yes, and he had an interesting proposition for me."

"What do you think?"

"Sounds interesting. I mean, what a great idea. He said that he's got a company now that's ready to go. We'll all be sub-producers, but they don't need our licensing information, so we could get it by Surety Guarantee. Did he tell you that?"

"He wasn't that far along when we last spoke."

"I might as well tell you. The company he came up with is Michigan Miners. Not a bad company, but not one of the big boys either. Their production requirements aren't that bad, and their software is Internet-based. Their rating software comes to the agents via CDs. All we do is rate a prospect online, print out the application, have the client sign it, and send it to the Sault for Gerry's wife to sign. A week or so later, the policy arrives and we collect the commission. Gerry's talking to a lawyer about setting up the corporate papers. He should have the new company set up by the end of the week."

"And what happens when Scott finds out about it?"

"Why would he? It's Gerry's wife that's the licensed agent. And none of us are on the corporate papers. They don't have squat on us."

"We gotta do something. I lost five more policies yesterday. My checks keep getting smaller. I can't blame the people for leaving—heck, one guy saved $400 a year by switching."

"It's just as bad here—I've lost 350 policies since New Year's. But no more. I'm in, and I'm going to make some money at it. Down the street at Allison's office they lost 300 policies."

"Is she in on this too?"

"Roger," he said, derived from the aviator's vernacular. "She's sick and tired of it. She's losing money and hates the company's guts. This is our way out."

Dan had a way of exaggerating. I figured that he hadn't lost that many policies. I also suspected that Gerry's scheme had some holes in it, too. But why not look into it? If we could skirt Surety Guarantee and still help out our customers, it would be worth a shot. If nothing else, it would be an opportunity to offset the losses we were experiencing in our agencies. For many of us, our careers were in the balance. For most, it was do or die.

Fifteen

THE SUIT WAS answered by the end of the next week. Mark Hendrickson got what he wanted—a signed reservation of rights letter. I still thought it was wrong that my policy had to answer the suit instead of Surety Guarantee. I tried to block it out of my head as I drove up north again—to Gerry's cabin and to take Scott out for his inaugural duck hunt. If I could talk to him alone, I was sure I could convince him that they owed me a defense; that they would pay for any resulting damages and/or judgments.

I stopped for gas and a sandwich in Gaylord—a popular place for tourists traveling up and down I-75. It was dark when I climbed back in the truck, pointed it north, and opened the paper wrapper of my burger. A new Suburban in the passing lane drifted by me doing 10 over the 70-mile-an-hour limit. I barely caught the orange hues of hunter's caps in the cab of the truck and dog crates in the back. Bird hunters.

In my head, I was with them for fifteen miles down the road. It was a good year for grouse numbers, and I was sure they would have good gunning if their dogs were worth a lick. They must have had a pair of patch-eyed setters in the back; English setter owners drive fancy SUVs. Perhaps they had a secret covert of thorn apple, hazel bush, and aspen, where the ferns grow tall as belt loops and the grouse rocket into fragrant stands of balsam. I could smell the pungent aroma of wet aspen leaves and hear the silver-sounding twang of the bells on the dogs' collars as they scoured the uplands for game.

When my imaginary hunt, and supper, were finished, I turned on the radio. It's amazing how well AM radio's reception improves after the sun sets. I heard the weather for Cleveland, Toronto, and Chicago, and finally the Upper Peninsula of Michigan. *"Tonight's forecast is for strong southeast winds and clear skies, but watch out for tomorrow. A low-pressure system located over the arrowhead of Minnesota is pumping warm air into it. But by noon, that system should be right on top of us. The winds will clock around to the north and northwest and gain strength. By three we expect sustained winds in the mid-20s, with gusts topping 30 miles per hour. Highs tomorrow will be in the 50s, but falling through the afternoon..."*

It brought a smile to my face, the same way Jack smiled when he cut his sailboat's motor and felt his boat's silent lunge. This was the weather that all duck hunters crave. This was the weather system that would bring down great numbers of birds. It would be a shame to ruin such splendid weather by sharing it with a dope like Scott. He was a complete idiot, but I wasn't about to let him hose me on Ted's countersuit. I needed him in my corner, if it was possible. He couldn't deny reading the letters. He lied about a lot of things, but he couldn't deny that. Once he agreed to it, the company couldn't deny me a defense. They had to provide me with a lawyer; they had to pay for any damages. I was determined to get that out of him, and forgive him for all the other lies he told us at the same time.

The cabin's light was on when I pulled in the driveway. A familiar Chrysler 300m was parked next to Gerry's Explorer. It looked out of place; after all, this was the rugged Upper Peninsula, on the precipice of its most fabled marsh. Most folks who live there drive four-wheel drive vehicles so they can get around in the winter. Three-hundred inches of seasonal snow has away of making four-wheel drive a necessity. This is a place for function rather than style.

Mess greeted me at the door with a bark and a profusely wagging tail. It thumped at the couch that partially blocked the entryway. Gerry had a dishrag in one hand and a stained Williams Sonoma apron around his neck. The cabin's usual musty aroma was overpowered by the smells from dinner—garlic toast, venison spaghetti sauce and whole-wheat noodles. Gerry and I shook hands.

"Howdy, man." I knew that cheesy greeting anywhere. Scott poked his head around the corner of the kitchen.

"Yessir. Sounds like a duck hunter to me!" His oxford's sleeves were folded up to the elbows, and a dollop of soapsuds fell off his hands and into Mess's water bowl. Mess watched the suds with interest, but was disappointed with their flavor. Secretly, I think Mess hoped the suds were potato chips or bits of spaghetti. He had an eye and a nose for table scraps.

"Kind of warm out there today. And breezy!" Weather is always a good topic for icebreaking an awkward setting, but Gerry always had a way of diffusing those settings too.

"You hungry? We just finished dinner but there are some leftovers in the fridge. The grill is still on for some garlic bread. What else do we have, Scott?"

"No thanks, really. I would like a drink though. Is that Manhattan mix still up in the cupboard? Any cherries left?"

"All kinds left. Scott, are you ready for a duck hunting tradition?"

"Sure, I'll have one. These dishes are almost finished."

"I'll get my gear. Gerry, you pour the drinks." I went back outdoors without a jacket. The hole in the porch screen was still there, and the grill's flame silhouetted a brace of grouse on the rickety table outside. Gerry had some luck today. I pulled my sleeping bag out of the truck, a heavy wool shirt hanging behind the driver's seat, and my overnight bag stuffed with all the necessities for a weekend with the boys. Gerry had the drinks poured when I returned to the cabin. I threw my bag onto the upper bunk in the second bedroom; Scott had the lower.

"Shot some grouse today, Gerry?"

"Yes, Mess and I went for a walk," he said, gesturing south, toward the marsh. Sometimes a grouse or two picks clover out of the trail, making easy targets for bird hunters. Even dyed-in-the-wool duck hunters can shoot grouse when they fly straight away down a logging road. "The first one flew down the trail, and Mess put up the second one when he jumped into the alders. I let that one have it too, and Mess had two to retrieve. I'd better clean those birds before long. It's warm out there!"

"Did you bring warm clothes, Scott?"

"I'll be all right. My new waders are neoprene, and the jacket I brought was my uncle's—he wore in the marsh for years. We'll see, though. I'm in your hands. I can't wait to try duck hunting. Sounds like we'll have some good weather for it." Scott jiggled the ice in his glass, then stuffed an index finger inside, swirling the cubes. He sat on the couch, under the canvasback print with the little mallard tail feathers tucked under the frame. He didn't know it, but Mess's short brown hair was melding into the fabric of his blue oxford. Scott would learn things the hard way at duck camp.

Gerry and I sat in the lounge chairs that flanked the fireplace. I had a table light next to me, and my drink sat on a coaster with a Royal Coachman trout fly printed across its face. Gerry crossed his feet and Mess curled up between us, only raising his head when a gust of wind shook the storm windows.

"So, what time should we get up?" I asked Gerry.

"Well, maybe we should decide where to hunt."

"True. What are our options?"

"We could try it right out here, but with three guys plus Mess, the canoe isn't an option. And the south wind has probably blown a lot of the water out of the big bay, so the big boat isn't an option there, either. We could set up on the edge of the shipping channel, near the first row of cattails, but I have a feeling that the ducks are going to want to get into the inner marsh and out of the wind...." He raised his drink to his lips, tilted his glass, and swallowed. He set the glass on the threadbare arm of the recliner and wiped his beard with a hanky. Scott and I followed Gerry's lead, and took a pull of our own. The little cabin was filled with the sounds of jingling ice cubes and the crackling fireplace. "We could try something way out of the ordinary. Remember that one time we hunted the upper river?"

"A few years ago, off the lock piers?"

"Yes. It was a day like tomorrow, wasn't it? There was lots of south wind, and those ducks couldn't wait to get into the decoys. They bucked that south wind all the way from the prairies."

I could see the wheels turning. The locks at the Sault see hundreds of freighters a year—some upriver-bound for Superior or Duluth, others headed down to Chicago, Erie or Cleveland. He was already thinking about a blind for his big boat. He was thinking about a decoy set, and if the bumpers for the boat were still out on the porch. The lock piers require a unique blind, made to look like part of the seawall. Gerry had a collection of oil canvas tarps—the relics of a garage tent and a power company's salvage yard. They were in chunks eight-feet long and four-feet wide, and varied in color from deep gray to marl brown. Grommets in the corners made it easy to tie them to the boat. We laid them over the outer edge of the boat, and from a distance, the kaleidoscope of canvas looked a lot like the rust and rock pierhead. It worked several years ago, but we hadn't been back there since.

"I think we should go there. It just might work. I'll get the tarps and bumpers out of the shed and make sure the boat is ready to tow. Scott, you pull three bags of decoys out of the Explorer and strip those short decoy lines off. Hanson, there's a big spool of decoy cord on the porch. We want at least 25 feet of line for each decoy."

Our restful evening suddenly took on a more urgent pace. Gerry and Mess disappeared outside. Scott jumped to attention and dashed into the bedroom. I could hear him shaking the dog hair from his oxford and the jingling of his belt as he changed clothes. We scrambled into action. Scott brought in the decoy bags, and I was pulling the thick, green cord off the spool in arm-span lengths. He asked for the scissors. I handed him my pocketknife, and he pulled out the longest blade.

"Good dinner we had tonight," he said, slashing at the cord's knot.

"Oh yes, Gerry does it right." A pregnant pause gripped us. I had my chance to bring up the topic of the lawsuit. "I don't understand how this all works with Ted's suit, I really need the company to come through and help me out…" Scott kept snipping, so I reminded him that he saw the letters I sent out: "You know those letters I sent out—did you think they were defamatory?"

"Wait a second—I don't know what letters you're talking about."

"The ones you read at my office that day with Tadrick."

"I didn't read those. I forgot my reading glasses that day, so I went along with what Don read." Strange, I never knew Scott to wear glasses or contacts.

"Why did you approve it then?"

"I didn't want to undermine Don's interpretation."

"What do you mean by 'interpretation'?"

"Maybe I don't mean that. He said that he didn't read them either, and he said that you're an independent contractor. I think you're on your own. I never told you to send them out. You did that all by yourself."

"Come on, we're on the same team here, aren't we?"

"Hey, I'm sorry. We're in a tough business, in tough times. We can get through this, though."

"Get through what?"

"You know—our suit—and Ted's."

"I still say Surety Guarantee owes me a defense."

"Aw, Hanson, can't we drop this tonight? I just want to get along and have fun duck hunting. Are you ready for me to tie on those long leads?"

"Sure." I handed him a dozen ends of cord, and milled through the decoy weights. "You know, I guess I don't understand how this all works. We put our faith in you, and you let us down over and over again. What happened with the last rate revision? You said that we were going to get back into the auto and home insurance market, but the company pulled the rug out from under us. We'd have had more respect for you if you admitted that they pulled a fast one. You're human, how do you dismiss the hopes of three dozen agents without giving it a second thought? I think it's pathetic. Where's your integrity, man?"

"Hanson. You just don't get it. Surety Guarantee has done so much for you. We are one of the largest insurance companies in the country, and people will buy from us because of who we are, not how much we cost." He never did try to defend his integrity. He couldn't.

Gerry stormed in out of the bluster and asked how things were progressing. He answered his own question when he saw the pile of cords and decoys. The glaring stare and pulsing blood vessels in the side of Scott's head were easily recognizable as a sign that he was getting angry. I didn't try to make him mad, but a little terse criticism was exactly what he needed. One thing is for certain—he could care less about me, Gerry, or any of the other agents. He was looking out for his own career, even if it meant that he had to abandon the rest of us.

Gerry disappeared into his bedroom, and then reappeared in a red union suit. "I think we should hit the hay. We'll need to get up extra early tomorrow morning. Oh shit! I forgot about those grouse." He slipped on his boots, and grabbed a paper plate and a sharp knife. Scott didn't want to go another round so he said goodnight and disappeared into the second bedroom. I sat in the recliner and finished my cocktail—staring at the heap of decoys, the waders turned inside-out to dry, and the fire breathing its last gasp. That son of a bitch. He lied about his lies. He lied about the truth, if that was possible. He embodied all that is wrong with big business. He was an unscrupulous man with no integrity, no morals.

He may have been able to trample on everyone else in the world, but he chose the wrong guy in me.

We were, after all, just a few Midwestern insurance agents, working for a huge conglomerate, looking for a way to avenge our frustration. We had been lied to, cheated on, and used as middle men for the deceptive practices of the insurance company for years. They raised the rates so high that our clients left our agencies in droves. They raised the rates so high that our clients thought that we were crooks—that somehow we were a party to the collusion—that we broke their trust. But we weren't crooks or cohorts; we were honest businessmen, in small towns across northern Michigan, in the wrong place at the wrong time. Our only recourse was to get even by playing the game the same way the insurance company operated. They were masters of deception, lords of the lunacy, and we were merely products of that madness. Who could blame us if we got together and beat them at the same filthy practice?

Some people sit on the sidelines and watch the company they work for do horrible things. Some people scratch their heads and wonder why they're out of a job but the bosses are rolling in dough. They can't believe that the guys at the top would use them as pawns in some sort of scheme to pad their own pocketbooks.

It seemed as though the executives at the top of Surety Guarantee knew nothing other than to raise everyone's rates. In my estimation, it wasn't because *they had to*; it was because they *could*. It was their little way of padding their pockets, lining their nest eggs. They never thought about the consequences—to the agents, the clients, or the agents' nest eggs—they were concerned only with themselves and their well being. We were just pawns, but we had an axe to grind. The company underestimated us, that was certain. We weren't going to let the bosses at Surety Guarantee pad their pockets without getting a piece of the pie.

We chose to be proactive and shut them down before they had a chance to demolish the company, and our careers in the process. This is our story, and how we took them down.

Sixteen

THE SAULT POLICE called the Coast Guard station from Traverse City that afternoon to help with the search. They have a giant helicopter used for search and rescue, but in light of the horrible weather, decided the better of it. The sheriff's department had a boat used for patrols and rescue, but that took over an hour to get into the water. While our boat was resting at the dock, theirs was getting launched—loaded with cops, some of them wearing dive suits. A giant bow-light silhouetted a hound on the prow—tail-wagging, nose tasting each molecule for the missing person. By nightfall, the weather was poor enough that anyone out on the water was taking their lives into their own hands. Mother Nature had a bit of a snarl.

Gerry's brother-in-law Darren Whitefoot met us at the ramp at about 7 p.m. He hugged Gerry on the dock, under a pool of mercury lights. I could hear his gun holster crinkle—that unique sound leather makes. His white lieutenant's shirt was crisp and sharp under his navy blue jacket. Gerry had tears in his eyes, and his voice was hoarse from yelling. The whole ramp and parking area was a blur of blue and red lights. The state police had a showing, the county, and even the city cops were there. They were combing the cockpit of our boat with their flashlights—lifting the lid of each little crevice, and depositing the empty shotshell hulls into plastic evidence baggies. They were looking for clues that weren't there. I never thought that an accident like Scott's would garner so much attention. I mean, the guy fell overboard and drowned. What's the big deal? It happens every day, right?

Darren asked us what happened, and was quickly joined by one of the state police detectives. Gerry went first: "Oh, shoot, Darren. We were on our way in and he must have fallen over. Hanson was standing next to me at the helm, and had a duck still in his pocket. He turned to put the duck in the live-well and returned a second later. Next thing I know, we make the turn into Mosquito and Scott is gone. Gone! I'm like holy crap! Where the hell could he be?"

"Sure, sure...Did he fall out or jump out? Did he drop something overboard and then try to reach it?"

"Jesus, Darren, I dunno. We had a helluva hunt today; I mean there were birds all over the place. I was trying to keep the boat in one piece. The surf was way up. Next thing I know he's gone. Gone!"

"Was he wearing a life jacket?" the state policeman asked, looking in my direction.

"No. You know, we never wear them. In fact, we were joking on the way out that Scott was in 'good hands' just like the insurance commercial. Gerry did everything by the books. You know, he wasn't hot-dogging or anything. He didn't take any chances. It was rough out there. He fell in."

"Who was he?" Darren asked, pulling out a small pad of paper from his breast pocket.

"He was our District Coordinator, Scott Husted."

"Where was he from?" Darren asked, facing Gerry. Darren's

sister and Gerry's wife, Molly, had a tissue to her nose, and her arm inside Gerry's.

"Downstate. It was his first time hunting. We should have had life jackets on. God this is horrible—I can't believe it."

"I know, Gerry. Sounds like this could have happened to anybody."

"Hanson and I are experienced. This guy was a new-bee. We should have held his hand. Jesus—you guys gotta find him."

Gerry's wife pulled on his elbow—nudging him toward her van. She said goodbye to Darren, and the detective shook his head. I called him back: "What about the boat?"

"Oh crap." He pulled his hat from his head, running his fingers through his hair. His wife kept walking—mad that I pulled her husband away from her again. "Lemme pull the Explorer around and let's get this thing loaded up." He stumbled to the Explorer, and backed down the ramp. I held the lines and reeled it up the trailer. Gerry eased it out of the water and parked at the top of the ramp. He jumped out and left the driver's side door open. "Would you mind taking the boat back to the cabin?"

The state police detective piped up and said, "Not so fast. We're treating this like a crime."

"How's that?" I asked.

"We've got a missing person here, and we don't have all the facts. This incident is under investigation. We'll take the boat to the post, and you'll have to come in and give us your statement."

"When?"

"Right now."

"Okay then. Is it okay if I drive there, or do you want to take me?"

"You'd better come with us." Now Gerry's wife was really mad. She asked her brother why it was necessary. I jumped in the back of the squad car, and watched the activity. Darren was getting an earful from the detective after she stormed off. It seems that Darren forgot the rules about handling legal situations involving relatives.

The dispatcher's voice on the radio inside the patrol car was blaring nonstop, describing everything from a domestic dispute to a fender bender outside the Big Boy restaurant. When the detective opened the door I could smell his cologne; it smelled like Brut or something cheap. He called the dispatcher and asked if she reached the power plant manager.

"Ten-four," she said, "he's waiting for you at the post." He then asked if the dragnet at the plant had found anything.

"Standby," she paused, but then advised "negative."

Several minutes later we were at the post, and I was led into a small, square room where I sat for nearly an hour. No sign of Gerry, the detective, or the boat. I had to wonder what they wanted with the plant manager. I wondered if the dive team found anything at the mouth or the dragnet at the other end. I knew the odds were long in finding him—the weather was dangerous, the current was a bulldog, and it was dark. Even if they did find him, they couldn't prove it was anything but an accident, and I wasn't about to admit that I didn't try my best to save him.

Finally, the detective reappeared with a metal clipboard and a stack of carbon paper. He grabbed a pen from his sport coat pocket, pulled the chair toward the table, and sat down. Without looking my way he started: "My name is Detective Gary Plouf of the state police, I am going to be taking your statement. Please state your name and spell it for me."

Detective Plouf went on and on about things that I thought

weren't very relevant. I couldn't understand why he needed to know about my family, my education, my years of duck hunting experience or my marital status. After 15 minutes of questions, I asked him why it was necessary.

"Mr. Johanson, we've got a suspicious disappearance. We've got to investigate it as if it were a homicide. You were the last guy to see him alive—that's makes you a big piece of the puzzle."

"Does it make me a suspect?"

"You become a suspect if we determine that his disappearance was a murder. We're just trying to find out the facts of what happened tonight. You have a problem telling me the facts of what happened?"

"Of course not. The facts are that he fell overboard, wasn't wearing a life jacket and drowned before we could save him. That's it."

"Who was he?"

"Scott Husted, but I'm not sure of his home address."

"Did you two work together?"

"Not really."

"What do you mean?"

"He was our District Coordinator, he was our overseer."

"Was he your boss?"

"No, no. He was only there to try to help us. His..."

"Did he?" For the first time during the interview, the detective looked me in the eye. His were gray, under hooded, furry eyebrows.

"Well...not really. He only had bad news for us, but I don't think it was entirely his fault. The company really put him in a bad spot. But what does this have to do with the accident? With tonight?"

"I'll ask the questions."

"Do I need a lawyer?"

"Why would you ask that question unless you have something to hide?"

I hate the way I alienate people sometimes. The detective was just doing his job. "You're right, I have nothing to hide, but I don't want to give up any of my rights. So let me start again. I still had a duck in my pocket, and I wanted to throw it in the box under Scott's seat. When he got up, a wave hit us, and he fell overboard. That's it, case closed. It was an accident plain and simple."

"Did you have any other business relationship with Scott?"

"The only thing close to that was that I rented office space from him."

"Where?"

"In Mt. Pleasant—on the west side. He bought the building and I rented from him."

"Now that he's gone, who gets the building?"

"Detective, this interview has turned into an interrogation. I get the feeling you're trying to lead me into some sort of confession, and you're not going to get it. We were out duck hunting and something went horribly wrong. It was an accident. It was an accident. It makes no difference who was my landlord, or what our business relationship was. I guess you'll have to wait till his will is read to find out who will own the building. But I'm leaving now. You charge me with murder, or I'm outta here."

The detective had heard enough. "Let me give you some advice."

"Shoot."

"You watch your step. This thing is far from over."

"Very well. I need the keys to Gerry's vehicle…Where is it parked?"

Seventeen

THE FOLLOWING MORNING I awoke to the sounds of freighter blasts along the St. Mary's. Perhaps one of them was the *Reserve* now through the locks and ready to negotiate the lower reaches. The cabin was quiet. No Mess or Gerry. No skunks outside, getting into mischief. I put on a pot of coffee, brushed my teeth, then got dressed. The boat was still attached to the Explorer until I wheeled it around the yard and unhooked it next to a stately white cedar. It was cold, perhaps close to 20. The ball on the Explorer stuck to the trailer, so I took my hands out of my gloves and warmed the aluminum sheath. Without hesitation, I reached into the livewell and admired our haul from the day before. The birds weren't frozen, but chilled. They made a fine pile.

I pulled out that beautiful drake canvasback and the pair of redheads. I laid them on the picnic table, pulled the garbage can from the porch, and set it near the edge of the table. It would be easy to throw handfuls of feathers into the can—there was no wind. I took my time—sipping coffee and plucking birds until they were done to perfection. No sense in rushing a time-honored tradition as plucking ducks. When you take your time and handle each bird, you replay the hunt in your head. You pay reverence again to the bird, the places it lived, and the grand passage of migration. But the task of cleaning and drawing the birds was interrupted by the constant gnawing of my conscience. All I could think about was Scott, flailing in the frozen surf, clawing for help and getting none. I tried to help him, but I didn't try very hard. If my best friend fell overboard, I would have done more. As much as I despised Scott, I never wished him any harm.

An hour later, I had the birds stowed in the freezer and my gear loaded into my truck. I left Gerry's keys in the door for the gas tank. We've always left them there, come what may. My car phone didn't have service when I fired up the engine. By the time I reached the Mackinac Bridge, I would have service, and oh, the calls I'd make.

My first was to Gerry, to assure him that everything was all right with the boat and the cabin. He still was in an emotional coma. Scott's wife called Gerry and forgave him for what had happened. It was rumored that they were having trouble, and now that he was out of the picture, she could collect all that life insurance and fade away. But there wasn't much life insurance, we discovered. He cancelled his half million policy when he quit the agency force, and when things headed south with Surety Guarantee, he let his other policy go; it was worth $150,000. Rumor had it that the only policy he had was a decreasing term policy that was worth $33,000. It was one of the first policies Scott ever bought, and over the years it dwindled to a paltry sum. That pompous hypocrite—he preached the benefits of life insurance, but had next to none.

Jack was next on the list, but he had heard the news already. He couldn't believe it. His whole office was in shock.

"Oh Hanson, I'm so sorry. What happened?" I proceeded to tell him my story, and his voice grew silent. The chain of events shook him, perhaps because he was also a man of the sea. He knew the torture Scott must have gone through when hypothermia kicked in, how it sapped his strength.

Duck Hunter Dan wasn't in his office when I called, but he called me back a short time later. "How the hell did that happen? Oh my God. Man, I can't believe it."

Allison's reaction wasn't much different than the others. She couldn't believe it. They all couldn't believe it at first. None of them had a bad word to say about Scott. None of them brought up the secret agency, and how with Scott out of the picture it would clear the way. None of them brought up the securities licensing exam and how he hung it over our heads, which was now a moot point. Then again, none of them ever said that he was a good District Coordinator, a good man, or that they would miss him.

Eighteen

IF WE WERE going to build our secret agency, we needed to have a proper foundation. There's no sense in haphazardly throwing up a structure without the basics taken care of. Our plan was put into action. Duck Hunter Dan had a relative who was a lawyer. He formed the corporation, listing Dan's wife, Gerry's wife and Allison's husband as officers. The papers stipulated how the commissions were to be cut (paid to landlords, utility companies, phone companies, and bank accounts to avoid the agent getting paid directly), how the quotes were entered into the system, and how the policies were issued. Furthermore, if and when the corporation was sued, the papers maintained how the defense was to be paid for. Additionally, if any of the officers abandoned the corporation, any policies that were in their control would be forfeited to the corporation, and the company's defense would be paid from that agent's commission. "Abandonment" was defined as any act, admission, or cooperation with any outside group, organization, or company that could be considered a threat to the board of directors or its shareholders. So, in a nutshell, we were all in it together. If someone bailed out, they had a lot to lose. If someone became a traitor, they would lose even more. We all figured there would be a suit against us eventually, so we needed to start our defense before the whole thing ever began. Surety Guarantee executives routinely lied about everything, and nobody ever tried to prove them wrong. Surety Guarantee executives made proclamations based on falsehoods and nobody ever called them onto the carpet. Surety Guarantee had a string of victories under their belt in cases just like Ted's, and with each passing day of the agents sitting on their hands, they gained more and more confidence. They were downright arrogant, and ripe for the picking.

Our plan started with a paper trail. We agreed that we needed to make the company perfectly aware of what was going on in the field. That way they couldn't deny knowing about the problem when the chips were down.

Jack drafted a letter to the state executive stating that he had lost 250 auto policies and 95 home policies since the beginning of the year. He went on to ask if the state executive had any plans to rectify the situation, and if he was aware of what the pricing structure was doing to Jack's agency and other agencies just like it.

Allison wrote Newark—the home office—where the Vice President of personal lines saw policies and premiums as only numbers. She said that she was losing policies faster than she could write them, and that if the current pricing structure continued, she would be out of business by the first quarter the following year. She also asked what the executive was going to do about the situation.

Duck Hunter Dan whipped a letter off to Don Tadrick that stated his Surety Guarantee rates were sometimes twice as much as the competition. If the client had a good credit score, the disparity was less, but still, his average rates were more than 50 percent higher than the competition. "How can I sell any new policies with rates like these? How can I maintain my current book of business?"

And me? I wrote the big enchilada—Mr. Phidler himself in the ivory towers in Newark. My angle wasn't that of an agent, but as a customer. I expressed my disappointment over the pricing of my renewal. I told him that my auto renewal went from $350 to $540 for no apparent reason. My driving record was clean; I had no claims or at-fault accidents, but they still raised my rates through the roof. When I called around and got quotes from other companies, they came back with rates that ranged between $310 and $435. Surety Guarantee was higher by a country mile. "Why was it necessary to raise my rates so high?"

But we didn't stop there.

We looked back at the memorandums that the company sent out to the agency force. One of them, from the state executive, was a cry to turn around our homeowner's rates. In doing that, he outlined criteria for homes that were susceptible to future claims.

Most of the homes described were built more than 30 years ago, and according to the memo "needed immediate reinspection by the agency force." Attached to the memo was a list of homes to be inspected, photographs taken, and a form that needed to be filled out. I had 337 on my list. What was really disturbing was the company stated: "This is not an optional program. You must reinspect the homes in your agencies within the next 60 days, or your binding authority will be revoked. Turn in your inspection reports to your District Coordinator at the end of each week."

How the hell was I going to inspect that many homes in that little time? How the hell could the state executive tell us how to spend our time when we were supposed to be independent contractors? And so I wrote him a letter of my own.

Dear Mr. State Executive,

I have been a Surety Guarantee agent for 10 years, and as a rule, enjoyed my relationship with the company. However, after reading your latest memorandum regarding the re-inspections of 337 homes in my agency, I can tell you now that there's no possible way to complete this task. My loss results over the years don't warrant this action, and my contract with the company states that I am an independent contractor—responsible for spending my time as I see fit. Furthermore, our attrition rate is so high that a comprehensive reinspection plan for home policies makes no sense.

Please explain how you can call us independent contractors, yet tell us that we are on your time schedule. If you're suggesting that our contract can be broken, I would be willing to entertain possible articles for modification. Please respond to my concerns at your earliest convenience.

The state executive was just arrogant enough to abandon his good sense in favor of his own agenda, which was the demands of the home office. For Michigan's state executive, the end justified the means. The contract between the company and the agent, called the "agent's licensing agreement" was supposed to be the end-all for the relationship between the parties. The executives conveniently forgot about its terms when they wanted to, and enforced it when it helped their cause.

If the executive responded, it would slit his throat when we went to court.

Nineteen

JAMIE TOOK THE news of Scott's death unusually hard, I thought. She really didn't know Scott very well, but offered, "He was always so perky on the phone." She cried, and I gave her a tissue. I sat on the edge of her little side table, and she was seated at her desk. We were quiet for a moment or two, until she stood up and gave me a hug. It was the first time we touched other than when she came to the office for an interview and shook my hand. It was a great hug—satisfying in every way. I could smell her perfume and the slightest hint of hairspray. Her body next to mine felt right. We fit. I didn't have to stoop, and she didn't have to stand on her tiptoes.

I could see the day when we would hug for some other reason. I felt that she was growing closer to me, and I knew that I was to her. Our conversations became more and more personal. She had issues with her kids' grade school teachers and her mother. All I could do was listen and watch her open up to me. I admired her tenacity in raising her sons by herself on the modest wages I could afford to pay her.

She was my sounding board for our strategy against Surety Guarantee. I phrased my "moral dilemmas" the same way callers do when they call Dr. Laura's talk show. We laughed together a lot, but this business with Scott was the first time I ever saw her cry. She seemed like a strong individual on the outside, but she had a tender spot too—beneath that wonderful figure.

It was odd to see her vulnerable like that. I was responsible for it, and I didn't want to see her hurt that way again. I am a bit protective of the people that take care of me at the office. When clients or claimants become verbally abusive to my staff, I stand up to them and make sure that it doesn't happen again.

It was especially easy to feel protective of Jamie. She had those enticing eyes and a demure personality. She trusted people, but she wasn't naïve. She'd look you in the eye, but would stab you in the back if you took advantage of her.

But despite my burgeoning attraction to her, I tried to keep our relationship strictly professional. You have to be that way if you want to survive in the business world. Some guys conjure fantasies of sweeping a coworker off her feet, tossing everything off her desk, and having sex right there. That's asking for trouble, but many men harbor those fantasies. Jamie would be fine candidate for such an encounter—she had a beautiful body and a pretty face. I knew better, but not every man would. As long as she was a good and loyal employee, I'd protect her, pay her as much as I could afford, give her time off, and harbor images of someday the two of us going out on a date. Maybe three or four dates, if I could work up enough courage to ask her out. For now I bit my tongue and watched her saunter gracefully around the office like a doe grazing in a springtime meadow.

Don Tadrick was one of those men that would have a hard

time with temptation. I could see him slobbering all over Jamie if given the chance. He would cross the line of good taste and make suggestive comments to Jamie or any of the other women he works with. There were rumors from the women in his old office that he had crossed the line, but nothing could be proven. It apparently boiled down to a case of "he said, she said." That's how Don ended up as our marketing committee chairman (a.k.a. The Gestapo); the woman threatened a lawsuit if he wasn't reassigned. Surety Guarantee was good at settling claims, and that seemed like a favorable settlement for all parties concerned.

Still, Jamie and I had a plan to take down Tadrick.

Twenty

Mark Hendrickson called later that day with good news. Surety Guarantee was going to answer the complaint against me, supply a defense, and pay for any damages.

"Shocking though, about Scott. I saw it on the news over the weekend and thought about you guys right away. The news broadcast never mentioned the name of the guy who was missing, so I wasn't sure who it was. I never knew that Scott was a duck hunter."

"He wasn't."

"What happened, then?"

"He fell overboard."

"Just like that? Come on, what happened?"

"There's really not much to it. We were duck hunting in rough seas, and he must have fallen overboard."

"Have they found him yet?"

"Can't say for sure, but they're having a service for him tomorrow at a church around the corner from the District Office."

"Are you going?"

"Well, sure I'll be there. How 'bout the claims office?"

"Don't know. I imagine some of us." The conversation lingered for a minute. I tried to think of some claim that needed attention, but couldn't come up with anything. Mark had also run out of things to say. I had all I wanted—the good news about the lawsuit.

"Oh, hey, about this business with Buxton—will he be at the service?"

"I doubt it. He hated Scott. Hated him. Why?"

"I need to talk to him about his claim."

"What claim? He's getting sued by Surety Guarantee, isn't he?"

"I dunno about that…Buxton has been sued for sexual harassment."

"What? Are you serious?" I was damn near yelling, and Jamie looked at me across the room. She knew the tone; she knew that there was big news in the making.

"For Christ's sake, please don't say anything. Forget it. I shouldn't have said anything."

"Not so fast. Come on, Mark, you can't leave me dangling here like this. Besides, it could help my defense somehow."

"Nah."

"Mark, Mark. We go back a long way. You can share this with me."

"Ted is getting sued for sexual harassment, and I wanted to take his statement about it, but since he's no longer a Surety Guarantee agent, he's been hard to reach."

"If he's at the service, I'll pass on your message, but I won't say anything. What's the story anyway?"

"Did you know his secretary?"

"Sure, sure, almost hired her."

"What kind of person was she?"

"Are you taking my statement now, or is this off the record?"

"Off the record."

"She was nice…pleasant. We always joked around on the phone when Ted wasn't there. Like I said, I wanted to hire her when Ted quit, but he told me that she really wasn't interested. Said she'd been acting really weird by the end."

"What do you mean *weird?"*

"I dunno, 'weird,'" he said. "Why?"

"She's alleging, and again, please keep this quiet…that he swatted her on the ass."

"Oh bull! Ted wouldn't do that in a hundred years."

"There are witnesses. Lots of them."

"Bull!"

"Really."

"Where?"

"He did it at the country club."

"Ha! You're lying!"

"Nope! What they're alleging is that she was in her Wednesday evening golf league, and they had some sort of awards ceremony on the first tee in front of the bay windows. The emcee is handing out prizes for the "prettiest swing," "lowest score," "most improved"—stuff like that. Out of the crowd steps Buxton. He runs up behind his secretary, lifts her skirt, and swats her on the caboose. The two dozen women there gasp and try to grab him, but he escaped in a golf cart."

"Seriously?"

"Serious as cancer."

"That was dumb. Why would he do that?"

"That's what I need to talk to him about."

"But why are you involved?"

"He had his office policy with us."

"Yeah, but sexual harassment is excluded."

"Not if you paid extra for the endorsement. And he paid extra for years."

"Is he covered?"

"If all this is true, he should be."

"And if all this is true, what kind of dough are you looking at to settle this thing?"

"Who knows? There are a lot of influential people at that club. Even though she wasn't a member at the club, her dad is a pretty powerful member there. He's a Dean at the Business School at Central Michigan University. I'm sending Buxton a reservation of rights letter, but I'm also sending in a reserve request to the regional office for $250,000."

"The home office ought to like that."

"They don't have a choice."

Twenty-One

I WAS EARLY FOR the service the next day. I sat in the middle of the church, left of the aisle. It was the first time in five months that I wore my dark flannel suit. I always liked that suit and felt confident in it. As I sat there, the altar boys were lighting the candles and doing the ritualistic errands associated with a Catholic service. An easel at the foot of the pulpit had a large felt board resting on it. It displayed several dozen photos—all the good times in Scott's life. The funeral program was on my lap. I looked at the front cover of scribed roses and the words "Scott Husted, 1954-2004." Inside was the usual mumbo about what a great guy Scott was and how much the family appreciated everyone coming to the service.

Gradually, the church began to stir. The rear of the church first filled with strangers—must have been neighbors wanting to pay their last respects. They shook off the cold, removing their topcoats. There were far fewer people than I would have thought. Scott always seemed to project a jet-setting image to the agents.

Gerry Buchanan was early; he made good time from the Sault. I nodded to him as he made his way up the aisle, and he turned into the pew just ahead of me.

"Morning."

"Any redheads at the bridge?"

"Couldn't tell—it was still dark when I came through. They gotta be there, though."

"Have you been hunting at all?"

"Not really, Mess and I shot another pair of grouse at the cabin yesterday when I went down to winterize everything. Thanks for cleaning the birds and taking care of the boat."

"Sure. Heck, what else was I supposed to do?"

"I know, this has been hell. God, this has been horrible."

"Gerry, you can't blame yourself for what happened. Christ, it was an accident."

"That's what everyone keeps telling me, but it doesn't feel right."

"What do you mean, 'everyone'?"

"Everyone—my brother-in-law, my wife, neighbors, everyone."

"What does your brother-in-law say?"

"Nothing, really. They still don't have a body." He turned his head and watched the same thing I did—the strangers filing indoors and the altar boys lighting the incense in a small, gold pail. The smoke wafted toward the cathedral ceiling. I picked out several familiar faces—District Coordinators from other areas of the state, our state executive, and several of his minions from the state office. Jack was walking up the aisle toward us when Gerry turned back to me. "I think we should have a meeting after the service. You know, the five of us, about the new enterprise."

"Good idea."

The service began simply enough. The priest thanked everyone for coming, and then proceeded to rejoice in Scott's passing into the loving hands of Jesus. That was always a comforting feeling for me.

One of Scott's nephews read from the New Testament, and then the priest read the sacrament. The organ piped in with the first few bars of "On Eagle's Wings," and the attendees muttered along with their heads buried in the hymnals.

The priest then introduced the state executive as "wanting to say a few words about Scott." At the pulpit, the executive began:

"Thank you, Father. Ladies, gentlemen, friends, relatives, co-workers, and acquaintances, we will all miss Scott Husted. We will all miss Scott Husted." His voice echoed through the cavernous church; it bounced against the massive organ pipes and dainty stained glass. "He died in a way that he lived his life—trying new things, experimenting with a fresh activity, in a setting that was far from comfortable. And, he did it in the company of his co-workers. He loved the agents in his district as much as he loved his children. He would do anything for them. He'd go the extra mile. I can't think of a more loyal supervisor, a more honest person.

"Scott believed that we were all family members in the business world. He had the integrity, the morals, and the ambition that most of us could only dream of..." I looked at Gerry, and he scowled, surprisingly.

"When I first met Scott, he was an agent, just starting out. He became an accomplished insurance agent by selling the coverage that his customers needed. His clients knew the value of having him as an agent. He didn't cut their coverage, or sell them anything less than what they needed. They bought from Scott because he promised to take care of them when they had a claim. That's one of the highest honors you can bestow on an agent—they're a symbol of trust, and have a very important job."

The executive went on and on. It was almost as if he liked to hear himself talk, and it didn't matter to him whether what he was saying was anywhere close to the truth. In the most humble of times, in the most candid moment, the executive still hadn't a clue what Scott's life was all about. Duck Hunter Dan, seated next to me, looked at his watch. Jack, next to Gerry a row ahead of us, turned his head sideways and whispered "Blow me." We all snickered.

Our little outburst didn't get by Tadrick, who sat a couple rows ahead of us and on the opposite side of the aisle. He glared our way, like a nun would do in catechism if the students were acting up. It worked. We were perfect gentlemen for the remainder of the service, but the lies kept coming.

When the service ended, Don pulled me aside and asked if I was going back to my office. I admitted yes, but I had to reinspect a few houses along the way. He acknowledged my commitment, but said that he'd "meet me there in an hour or so."

An hour would be just perfect. I phoned Jamie on the way to the bar to tell her the news.

Twenty-Two

FROM THE CHURCH, the five of us (Gerry, Jack, Duck Hunter Dan, Allison, and I) met at our usual watering hole. It was barely noon when the waitress brought us three Bloody Marys and two coffees. Gerry took off his watch and stirred in a couple sugar packs, wondering rhetorically if it would be the last time we met at this bar. After all, without a District Coordinator in Saginaw, we might meet somewhere else in the future.

"Ah, baloney. They'll get someone else in here by the New Year, and forget all about Scott by Valentine's." Jack always had a way with words, blunt beyond compare.

"Some legacy for Scott, huh?"

"You gotta hand it to him, he did work hard."

"But who was he working for—himself or the agents?"

"You forget, he worked for the company, and we were just peons."

"All right you guys, we've got to cover some material." Gerry started in, "Michigan Miners has given me five disks to load into your computers. These are simulated disks for their authentic software. They want us to look over their way of doing business. In a month or so we'll get together with them and go over this again. We should be aware of the underwriting criteria, the application process, and their billing procedures. Molly had some cards printed up. She has a different phone number than mine, so don't call my office and expect her to answer. She's no longer an employee of my agency. She's on her own now with Michigan Miners."

Duck Hunter Dan didn't comprehend what was said, "How do we print off the applications?"

"Dan, they print out automatically when you upload the information. Take the disk, plug it in, and wade through it. Everybody understand that? Molly started quoting this week and it's really easy. The best part is we're really competitive too. Everyone, we stand to make a ton of dough."

"Any idea how long it takes to get a policy issued?"

"They say about five days, if everything was entered properly. In 30 days we get paid. Does everybody understand?"

Allison crossed her arms. "We've really got to watch ourselves here. I don't think we should be blatantly marketing to our Surety Guarantee clients, but give our spouses and assistants every opportunity to help them out."

"What are you trying to say?"

"You know. Pigs get fat, but hogs get slaughtered. Let's not get stupid. We've got to distance ourselves from the process of writing the business. If someone calls you and asks if there's anything you can do, toe the party line and tell them that you can only represent one company." She reached into her breast pocket and pulled out a folded piece of paper. "Then," she said, "give or send this to your client. It's a list of several other companies in our area. Molly's name is on the list. There's an affidavit at the bottom stating that you had no involvement with the client canceling their Surety Guarantee policy. In other words, make sure that you insulate yourself from the process." Allison handed out copies of the paper, stirred her Bloody Mary, and took a quick sip. She was a smart businesswoman, and was accustomed to getting exactly what she wanted. Well, almost everything.

Jack and I looked up from reading to notice the waitress and her low-cut T-shirt. It was right up Jack's alley. She leaned between Jack and me, and after glancing down at the woman's chest Jack raised his eyebrows, Marx Brothers' style. It was like we were adolescents in eighth grade all over again. Perhaps we should have been more serious. Allison picked up on Jack's little stunt and rolled her eyes at me. I think she was mildly amused with the barbaric simplicity of some men.

Anyway, our idea was to have the licensed agents in our offices give the quotes, write the policies, and handle their billing. If the client chose to call Molly in Sault Ste. Marie, and Molly in turn called Jamie or Caroline in my office, then what harm was there in that? I wanted to see my assistants get ahead, and if they could earn extra money by selling policies at a more reasonable rate, why should I stop them?

Now there was no turning back. We took that first step toward oblivion, and the next would be much easier. We were on our way, but there really was no choice. We could continue being devoted Surety Guarantee agents and watch our book of business slip through our fingers, or we could take charge of our destiny and put our relationship with Surety Guarantee in jeopardy. It was a tough decision, but there seemed to be no other choice. Doing nothing was not an option.

We could have quit Surety Guarantee all together, but the

non-compete clause saw an end to that. The book value payment would have been nice, but it wasn't enough to secure our life style for an extended period of time. We could have honored our contract with Surety Guarantee, but we felt cheated by the company that was supposed to be fair. Honorable individuals would have stood by and watched everything disappear for the sake of their honor, yet we were honorable people not willing to pay the price. Our motivation for revenge was fermented in their deception.

Twenty-Three

AN HOUR LATER I arrived at the office. Don Tadrick's dumpy little Mercury Sable was parked next Jamie's Jeep Wrangler. When I walked into the office, Don was standing on Jamie's side of the office, hands in his pockets, jiggling the change inside. He seemed unusually glad to see me, like there was something he was trying to hide. I had a hunch what it was, and judging by Jamie's body language, I just missed something important. But, she wasn't visibly shaken, so I let it go.

I acted as if nothing appeared amiss, "Hi Don."

"Hi, Larry. Sorry about the accident."

"Oh, thanks. I tell you—it was really scary." Our hands met, even though I really didn't want to shake his.

"Really." He looked like he didn't believe me.

"Oh, shoot, Don, the wind was howling, and the surf was nasty..."

"Wow...It's amazing that you and Gerry made it."

"What do you mean?"

"Well, it seems lucky that you two survived the storm, but Scott didn't make it...Get those re-inspections done?"

"What? Oh sure. Yep."

"How many do you have to go?"

"Plenty. Probably a couple hundred or more."

"Jamie tells me that you're still losing a lot of policies?"

"Not a day goes by and we don't lose 10 or 15, and these are good people, Don. I wish there was something someone could do. Anything. It's been the worst I've had with Surety Guarantee. Our pricing structure is abhorrent—you know that. Maybe we shouldn't dance today. Besides, I'm sure you know what you're doing."

"Okay…Just as well." I shuffled through the few envelopes on my desk, and then looked across to Jamie. I could only see the back of her head, but there was a tissue to her nose. Poor thing. There was more to this picture than I first suspected. "What I wanted to talk to you about is the suit with Buxton."

"What about it?"

"So far the courts have ruled in favor of our injunction, so now he or his agency can't write any of our business. The attrition you're seeing isn't from his office, I suspect. That's the good news."

"Why do I get the feeling that there's another shoe about to fall here?"

"There is some bad news. It's about the countersuit against us."

"Us?"

"Surety Guarantee and you."

"What problem is that?"

"Ted seems to hang his hat on whether or not we knew about the letters you sent out to your new clients."

"Is that all? I thought it would be a lot more serious than that."

"What do you mean? It is serious."

"Why's that? I showed you and Scott the letters before I sent them out. You knew about it, no doubt."

"The letter I read wasn't very incriminating."

"The letter you read was the letter I sent out with your approval."

"That's not true."

"Oh really. Now you're going to deny this?"

"For the record, I am."

"You're pathetic. You know, at the funeral today, when they talked about Scott and what a great man he was? What are they going to say about you? It's no wonder morale is so low within the agency force. Management lies and denies everything. Absolutely pathetic."

"You watch yourself, mister, or there'll be hell to pay."

"What the hell is that supposed to mean? Screw you, Don, off the record," I whispered. "And you're the one who's going to pay."

"We'll see about that. Your deposition is coming soon."

"See you in court, then...*Adios!*" Don tugged on his belt, buttoned his sage-colored sport coat, and stormed off. We never raised our voices, or led on that we were arguing. It was just a simple disagreement between colleagues. Tomorrow, it seemed, we'd shake hands and have a working relationship all over again. That seems to be the way Surety Guarantee deals with its customers and its employees—stomp on them and expect them to bounce back.

I thumbed through the stack of messages from Jamie and Caroline and found nothing urgent. The mail was also unremarkable—more bills, a few more cancellation notices from disgruntled clients. The middle part of the week is always calm. It seems that most of the insurance action happens on Mondays and Fridays, when folks purchase new vehicles or the toys that need policies. I was trying to act busy, hoping that Jamie would tell me what had happened with Tadrick before I arrived. She was on the phone, across the office, scribbling notes in earnest, and somehow managing to type at the same time. One leg crossed the other, and her heel flicked in and out of her shoe. With each twitch, her calf changed shape. Even the smallest parts of her body were fun to watch.

At last she hung up the phone, finished her note, and uncrossed her legs. I pretended not to notice any of that, for fear that she might think I was weird. Still, I wanted to show that I cared, that I wanted to know what happened. I thought quickly, and asked for some clarification about one of her messages. She answered my question, and sat there, like she couldn't believe what had just happened.

"I get the feeling I missed something important."

"Larry, you're not going to believe this."

"What happened?"

"About a half hour ago, when I got back from lunch, Don was parked in the parking lot. He was *right* behind me when I unlocked the door, fumbling with the change in his pocket. It was horrible."

"Jamie, I hope he didn't do anything."

She nodded, and gestured to wait. "So I opened the door and came inside. I threw my coat on the rack and checked the answering machine. I finished up, turned around, and there he is—sitting at my desk. I asked him if he would be more comfortable waiting at your desk, and he said that he liked the feel of my chair. He said he liked the shape of my seat."

"What an ass," I said, regretting the pun.

"I know." She missed my joke, took out another tissue, and dabbed her nose. "So the phone rings and I walk over to your desk to answer it. While I'm on the phone, he's over there rummaging through my desk. I finish on the phone, and tell him that I want my desk back. He spins around in my chair and throws his legs up on the desk, so I'm trapped between him and the desk."

"Oh Jamie, I'm so sorry."

"I should have smacked him. Ohhh, I was so mad. So I tell him, 'Mr. Tadrick, I suggest you get away from me or I'll scream bloody murder.' He stands up and says that I'm acting tense, I need to 'loosen up a bit.'

"That would have been bad enough, but then he puts his hands on my shoulders and gives me this phony massage. His hands were there for a second and I said, 'Stop it.'

"He lifts his hands straight up—like the cops are pointing a gun at him. 'Sorry, sorry' he says, 'but I think you're too uptight about things.' And then here's what really got me. He said that he could do big things for me, and what an important man he was in the company. Somehow he must have thought I'd be interested if it would help my career.

"That was about the worst of it. He tried to make small talk afterward, like it was no big deal."

"How long were you alone with him before I came in?"

"Not really long. I don't know, 15 minutes, but then Jody Robertson came in and dropped off a premium. You know how short she is with us, but today I really piled on the charm. I wanted her to stay longer, but she left after five minutes. The whole time that jerk was sifting through my desk, like he was looking for something."

"Like what?"

"I dunno, but sometimes I catch my little boy looking through my underwear drawer, and he had the same little smirk. I don't even want to think about it."

"I know. Did you remember our plan?"

"Sure did."

"Well done. Now you know what kind of people we're dealing with. We'll have our day, Jamie. You know that don't you? "

"That's why I keep going. Now I know what kind of an jerk he really is. I hope you guys hang him up by his ears."

Twenty-Four

SURETY GUARANTEE HAD a lot on their plate besides the subterfuge that we had come up with. They had multiple lawyers on staff, and they were going to make sure that they were busy around the clock. Strange, most companies try to avoid paying lawyers. It seems that most companies know that the only parties that win when lawyers are involved are the lawyers themselves. Not Surety Guarantee. They had an agenda, and steamrolled anything in their way. When Surety Guarantee was sued for their practices, they merely denied it and put up a fight. Their strategy was to outspend their opponents, because they had more money than their opponents. Firms from all over the country competed for Surety Guarantee's law work; they were a fat cow with the smarts of a plump steer. In anyone's book, they were a formidable opponent because they had deep pockets to spend on lawyers.

But when you're right, you're right, and when you're wrong, you're wrong. Surety Guarantee tried to press their agenda, but it lacked the conviction of righteousness. When your cause has its roots in deception and half-truths, it's destined for failure from the start. Little by little their world came tumbling down upon them.

A group of Surety Guarantee employees in Pennsylvania sued their employer for unfair business practices. The suit alleged that company managers required employees to return to work after their shifts were over. The employees got together and filed their suit class action style. They won, to the tune of $80 million.

When the employees in Michigan heard about it, they realized that the company was pulling the same kind of lunacy here. They filed suit too, and everyone who wasn't a manager was rooting for them. They won $33 million.

Soon there were other suits. Some agents in New Jersey sued the company for their accounting practices. At issue was how they "charged back" commissions when a client cancelled their policy before the renewal date. Here's how Surety Guarantee got in trouble: If an agent received a 10 percent commission on a $1,000 policy, it meant the agent earned $100. If the client cancelled, or was cancelled, a day before the policy was up for renewal, the agent was "charged back" the whole $100 even though the agent technically earned almost the whole premium. They should have "charged back" the commission on the premium that was returned to the customer. The company got burned in New Jersey by the agents and District Coordinators, and they changed their practices throughout the operating territory.

The state of Florida sued Surety Guarantee for "price gouging and deceptive practices" because of the way Surety Guarantee priced and marketed their home insurance policies. The company doubled or tripled the home policies of clients whose credit scores were less than modest. What's worse, they didn't tell the clients about the rate change, or how the rates were determined. The Attorney General thought this was unfair, while the Surety Guarantee executives, naturally, thought it was warranted. In a memo to the agents, the executive in charge of legal affairs said that the action by the state of Florida was "unfair and unwarranted. Surety Guarantee has paid nearly $650 million dollars in claims the last few years—an average of $350 for every home policy in force. In fact, we have lost $500 million dollars in Florida the last few years alone." The letter went on and on, but what I couldn't understand was how any company could lose all that money, but still stay in business. Their logic was backward. You stay in business to make money, not lose it. Surety Guarantee was excluded from this equation. They seemed to have a knack for losing money year after year, but still stayed afloat. They did it because they had creative ways of "cooking the books" to make it look like they were losing money. We all knew there were lying, cheating idiots at the top of the company, and we roared with delight when Florida lawyers stepped in and spoiled the Surety Guarantee facade. Surety Guarantee denied the charges and pulled out of insuring Florida homes. The same executive stated in another memo "We don't believe that pulling out of the home insurance market will affect our auto policies."

The dumb ass. Not affect auto policies? Why would someone feel confident with Surety Guarantee for their autos while their home policy was cancelled? When their autos lost the auto home discount, why would they pay the extra premium? It was a prime example of how little the executives knew about the insurance business, how their bombastic decisions rolled downhill.

Closer to home, Surety Guarantee was sued by the Michigan Chiropractor Association for the way they paid bills.

Apparently the company didn't believe in chiropractic treatment as it related to the recovery of the insured. Imagine that, finances played a part in the decision of whether or not their client should receive treatment? The courts agreed with the chiropractors, and won case after case, until it went all the way to the Michigan Supreme Court. Surety Guarantee lost the appeal, and now they pay reasonable chiropractic bills, just like the rest of the insurance carriers in the state of Michigan. The only difference is the notoriety Surety Guarantee realized by "paving the way" for the other carriers in Michigan. Bad publicity never scared Surety Guarantee. They took pride in challenging the chiropractors when they should have been paying what was reasonable and customary. They would have been money ahead.

Then there were the cases in Michigan like the one against Ted Buxton. There were plenty of agents that left Surety Guarantee and couldn't resist the temptation of rolling their books to another carrier. Some of the agents were stupid and invited trouble. Other agents were lazy and made no effort to conceal their intentions. Regardless, Surety Guarantee made hay. They bowled right over those agents and sued them for three times what the damages were, which I later discovered was the law. Surety Guarantee quashed them one after another, because the agents didn't have enough money to combat them in the legal arena. With each victory, Surety Guarantee became more and more confident, less and less prepared. Surety Guarantee hired the same firm for each case, and their successes made them negligent. Surety Guarantee was becoming careless, over-confidant, and ripe for the taking.

Twenty-Five

"HELLO, LARRY. THIS is Kyle Holbine. I've been hired by Surety Guarantee to handle the case against Ted Buxton."

"Oh hello, Kyle, hang on a minute." His phone call caught me off-guard, and I scrambled to find my notes. "Sorry about that. What was your name again?"

"Kyle Holbine, from Detroit, the law firm of Gosczling, Miller and Stroh."

"Gosczling, Miller and Stroh? Sounds like a brewery, not a law firm," I thought.

"Surety Guarantee has hired me to handle the case against Ted Buxton."

"Okay, Kyle. What can I do for you?"

"Larry, I need to ask you a few questions regarding this case, and I'll be perfectly honest with you. There's a long row to hoe with this case, and it's still very early in the ballgame."

"Sure. Sure. There's a lot that needs to be discovered, I'm sure. You're not the same lawyer that the company hired to defend me against Buxton's countersuit are you?"

"No. But I need to get some information from you."

"I'll do anything I can to help your case, but at the same time I don't want to compromise my own defense. You understand, don't you?"

"Well, sure I do. Really, when the facts of this case are decided, and the truth is told, justice will be served. I have absolutely no doubt about it, so whether the truth comes out now or later, I'd just as soon find out what it is. Does that sound fair?"

I hemmed and hawed for a minute, then conceded, "Sure. Go ahead."

"Chronologically, I'm trying to establish the timeline between the time Buxton left Surety Guarantee till now. He turned in his resignation in June, right?"

"Yes, something like that."

"Then what happened?"

"I approached the District Coordinator about taking over the accounts, which was approved."

"What do you mean?"

"I put together a business plan for the second agency. It included staffing, marketing, solicitation, advertising, networking, stuff like that."

"When did you take over?"

"I think it was July."

"When did you notice that he was rolling his policies to his new agency?"

"Almost immediately. Clients came in and said they were canceling their policies. I'd ask them who they were switching to, and they came right out and told me. Tadrick said the company wanted proof that the clients were leaving. So from then on, I asked the people who were leaving to sign a statement that they were going to take their business to Buxton."

"When did Tadrick tell you he needed proof?"

"He and Scott stopped by the office early on. It was the same day that he read the first of several letters I sent out to the customers."

"Tadrick read the letters you sent out to the clients?"

"He and Scott both did, and they agreed the letters were okay. He'll probably deny it though, knowing him."

"What do you mean by that?"

"We've since had a conversation about the letters and he said he was going to deny knowing about any letters. What's worse, I think, is that he not only read one letter, but he basically gave me full approval for sending out whatever I wanted."

"When was that?"

"That same day that Scott was there. Have you talked to Don about the letter?"

"Yes, but he's my client and whatever we discuss is confidential, you know."

"But since I'm not your client, you can share our discussion with him, right?"

"Something like that."

"Well, then is there anything else we have to discuss?"

"What are your thoughts about Surety Guarantee?"

"Why is that relevant?"

"I'd like to know if you're going to be a hostile witness or a favorable one, that's all."

"Oh, I get it. You don't want to have a loose cannon on the stand if it comes down to it."

"Right."

"You know, Kyle, I'm not sure where or when Surety Guarantee went bad, but I can say that they're doing a lot wrong. They just don't get it. They continually make decisions that are counterproductive..."

"Like what?"

"Like what? How about claims? They pay independent adjusters $800 to look at a $300 boat claim. They fight paying what's reasonable and customary if you want to see a chiropractor. They put junk parts on new cars after a claim."

"Anything else?"

"How about marketing? They have taken such huge increases on our auto policies that they've chased most of them away. Now we're left with the junky policies. And homeowner's insurance? Absolutely pathetic. We're twice or three times what most carriers' premiums are. For what? Our losses aren't as bad as half the other carriers, but still we've got to be the most expensive. It seems that management is daring their policyholders to leave the company or get gouged."

"How do you know that Surety Guarantee losses aren't as bad as the other companies in Michigan?"

"Because I get copies of the year-end reports from the insurance commissioner's office."

"Why do you do that?"

"Because I want to stay on top of the situation in Michigan. This is my business, and the more information I have on my competitors, the more prepared I am. It didn't take long to realize that what the Surety executives were telling me was far different than what they were reporting to the state."

"It sounds like you don't have much trust in the management."

"I've got good reason to doubt their integrity, don't I?"

"Larry, why would someone in Ted's position bail out of Surety Guarantee and start over like that? I mean, the guy is in his late 50s and has 10 years to go before retiring. Were things that bad?"

"Kyle, they were worse than bad. I don't know how to

explain it to you so you'd understand. When your day consists of nothing but answering complaint calls from people whose rates have gone through the roof, you kind of become jaded. When you look yourself in the mirror every morning and realize that you're a party to the extortion coming from Newark, you start to feel a little bad about yourself. When you try your best to do a good job but when your check comes it's smaller this month than last, you think that you've made a horrible career move. Every man has his breaking point, and Ted found his before the rest of us. Is it bad, Kyle? It's absolute lunacy."

"I never knew. I mean, I had an idea that Surety Guarantee was in trouble, but I never thought that much trouble."

"You've seen cases like this one before, right?"

"Sure. We've won them all. You don't want to mess with Surety Guarantee and their contract."

"What do the other agents say about the rates, about management, about the working conditions?"

"It really doesn't matter what they say or think about Surety Guarantee, we still win the cases. Surety Guarantee is mismanaged, but they hired me to handle their cases."

"Then why do you think Surety Guarantee is in trouble?"

"Hey, I'm a consumer too, and I've seen their rates. They're horrible. Heck, I tried to give them some of my business but I couldn't afford it. And Tadrick, off the record, doesn't seem like the sharpest spade in the shed. He knows the rates are bad. He knows that Surety Guarantee is gouging the public."

"You don't say."

"He knows it. And I know it too."

When our conversation ended, I hung up the phone and smiled. The tape recorder in my hand captured our entire conversation. I opened the hood on the recorder, took out the little tape, and labeled it with the date and time. Then I opened the desk drawer and threw it on the stack with the others.

Twenty-Six

IT WAS THE week before Christmas and schools were on vacation. The insurance business usually falls flat during that time of year because people are preoccupied with holiday festivities.

It was, however, a great time of year to have a meeting for our new agency group. Gerry made arrangements with Michigan Miners to meet us at the Holiday Inn in Gaylord, Michigan for a training and marketing session. Gaylord was a convenient location for all the agents to meet, because we all had a 90-minute drive. Everyone would be there, and since we technically didn't have anything to do with the new agency, we had to invite our staff. Caroline and Jamie were excited to close the office and go up north for the day. Allison and her crew had the notion to spend the night there and take their kids. Next thing I know, Gerry and his family planned to spend the night too, and Jack, his family, and the three staff members that worked at his office followed suit. Who was I to be the party pooper? Not only did we close the office, but I rented a twelve-passenger van from the local rental franchise and a room and a suite at the Holiday Inn.

It was fun planning our getaway. Caroline and Jamie were excited about the prospect and weren't put out by sharing a suite. After all, this was a business trip with kids, and they knew that you don't kick a gift horse in the mouth. Their boys were all about the same age, and I knew that they had a lot in common by the discussions we had about them. And what school-aged boy wouldn't have fun at a Holiday Inn, with a pool and loads of pinball machines to play with? For two weeks before our getaway I heard less complaining from Caroline and Jamie, and that alone was worth the expense involved with the meeting.

Early the Friday before Christmas, we met at the office and piled into the van. The boys took the back seat, and it wasn't long before I heard the telltale beeps and electronic gibberish from their handheld games. Caroline sat next to me in a bucket seat while Jamie sat behind us in the middle. I only had an overnight bag, but the girls seemingly packed enough for the whole weekend. Neither Jamie nor Caroline had much experience traveling for business, but they didn't need much. They were both excellent employees and I was proud to have them with me. It was a privilege to have them on the team.

About 45 minutes into our trip we stopped for coffee and a restroom break. Caroline put a six-pack of mini bottles of wine on the counter behind my coffee. Jamie followed her lead, and put a two-liter bottle of Diet Coke on the counter. It seemed that cocktail hour was shaping up.

"Got any hard stuff to mix with that, Jaim?"

"I packed a little bottle of rum for later. After all, what would a Christmas party be without a little something to spice things up?"

"Not a very festive drink, is it? Eggnog maybe?"

"Bah humbug! You can drink whatever you want and I'll have this."

"All right then, I will, but you've got to try one of my Manhattans."

"Sorry. I tried one of those and nearly got sick. That was years ago."

"Boys, put those munchies up here on the counter. The bus is leaving in two minutes. Last call, Caroline." She signaled no, and I gave the chap behind the counter the nod to ring everything up.

Before I knew it, we had $30 in munchies, booze, and coffee in paper sacks. Nothing like a little junk food to get the body jumping.

When I got to the van, Caroline handed me the phone. Before I answered, I started the van, buckled my seatbelt, and pulled out of the parking space. Caroline and Jamie had strange looks on their faces—like I was walking into a trap.

"Hello?"

"Hi, Larry, this is Paula Richardson, and I got your number off the answering machine at your office. I hope it's okay to call you, but I really need your help."

"Sure, Paula. Sorry we had to close the office, but we're on our way to a meeting. And with it being a holiday weekend and all..."

"Listen, Larry. I'm going to look at a new vehicle later today and I'd like to get a quote on how much you would charge me for insurance."

"Sure. What do you have now?"

"I've got a 10-year-old Chrysler, remember? I'm thinking about a new Sebring. How much will it cost?"

"Oh shoot, Paula, don't let insurance stand in the way of what you want. If you can afford the car payments you can afford the insurance. We'll be back in the office on Monday, and I'll take care of it then. Okay?" Caroline was on the verge of snickering, because she somehow enjoyed watching me squirm. Plus, she was the one who put my cell number on the answering machine, which was probably a good idea, but nonetheless, bothersome. Paula agreed to my suggestion.

When I hung up, both girls were laughing. It's fun to laugh at the boss. It's fun to laugh at yourself. It's even more fun to laugh at your clients that are a pain in the neck. Caroline had an impersonation of Paula, and even added an extra layer of whininess. Instead of one car for a quote, Caroline's Paula wanted eight or ten cars quoted, with and without the discounts... We laughed all the way to the motel, while my phone rang two or three more times.

As we pulled into the hotel's parking lot, Jack's gang was there, unloading their overnight bags. I honked the horn and asked how to get to the Michigan Miners meeting.

Jack said that he didn't know Michigan Miners "if Don Tadrick was in the vehicle with us." We shook hands, and introduced each other's staff. We all laughed when we realized what the voices on the phone actually looked like. The folks at the Holiday Inn must have known we were coming because they had our check-in papers halfway finished when we got to the counter. Our rooms surrounded the pool on the first level, and my room was next door to Caroline and Jamie's suite. The boys led the charge to the suite and tossed in their bags before trotting down the hallway to the gaming room, their mothers yelling something intelligible after them.

The meeting was about to be started, so I unzipped my overnight bag and pulled on a pair of camel-colored trousers. I could hear the women talking next door, but I couldn't understand what they were saying. Probably just as well. There are certain things you don't discuss as an employer and employee.

As much as I was drawn to Jamie, I knew I had to maintain my distance. Still, I couldn't get her out of my head. I thought about her almost every minute of the day. I recounted our conversations, and replayed the cute parts of each one. I liked the way she looked, dressed, worked, and smiled. I liked the way she laughed at my jokes, and flicked her heel in and out of her shoe when her legs were crossed. But, oh, that blasted conscience! Why is it that the things that you want the most are the things you shouldn't have? Why couldn't I have met her at a bar, or a PTA meeting? Why did I hire her? If she weren't an employee, I could pursue her with both barrels, so to speak. The last thing I wanted was a sexual harassment suit like the one Buxton's assistant hit him with. "Keep your cool," I reminded myself, "and if something happens, keep your cool."

Scott would have been proud of that redundant statement.

After changing my trousers, I walked down to the lobby where Gerry, Allison, Dan, and Jack were standing around the coffee machine. The meeting with Michigan Miners was scheduled to start in less than 10 minutes, and most of us wanted a few more gulps of coffee to keep us alert.

Jack couldn't help but jab me about Jamie's looks. He talked to her on the phone several times a month, and often inquired about her looks and asked if she was proficient at giving "oral binders," which is an insurance man's way of saying "you're covered." Now that he saw her, it really piqued his interest. I tried to play down her looks, preferring to emphasize her contributions to the agency. But there'd be no fooling Jack; he enjoyed looking at her just as much as I did.

We got off to a great start with Michigan Miners. The

meeting began with four little words so unusual to our way of being treated: "Welcome to Michigan Miners." After introducing ourselves, we jumped right into their underwriting philosophy. Within five minutes of that discussion, we knew that their philosophy was much different than Surety Guarantee. Michigan Miners viewed their agents as their lifeblood, rather than an encumbrance. Michigan Miners liked their agents, and were counting on them to help put policies in force. It was refreshing to have a company come to the agents collectively with the reasons why we should place business with them. What a change of pace. All we ever heard from Surety Guarantee were excuses why our rates were twice as much as everybody else's. But since Surety Guarantee was the only company we could represent, they rammed it down our throats.

The marketing representative gave us disks to install in our laptops. Within 10 minutes we had the software installed and were hooked up to their website. The representative led us around the homepage, which eventually lead to the auto rating pages and the uploading of applications. It was painfully simple. It was adorably easy. Michigan Miners was hugely competitive compared to the abysmal rates that Surety Guarantee had given us. We all shook our heads in disbelief. It was like the future just whacked us in the face, and it looked absolutely splendid. We could make some serious money with Michigan Miners. We could rejuvenate our careers and our image. No longer would we be the red-haired stepchildren of the insurance world. We could offer our clients a competitive insurance product at a reasonable price, and it set really well with the whole gang. There were smiles all around. There was backslapping and handshaking. We couldn't wait to get back to the office and begin selling insurance all over again.

After lunch, the home insurance scenario was just as encouraging. And then they unveiled the cherry on top: commercial, which had never been possible with Surety Guarantee. Michigan Miners wanted body shops, dry cleaners, excavators, and dentists. It felt like we grew another appendage. Before, we only had two arms—auto and home insurance. Now we had a third; we could sell the stuff that developed some premium and the almighty commission.

When the meeting ended close to 4 p.m., we were all in great spirits. Jack and I took orders for the liquor store and drove the van down the street. Gerry and I wanted whiskey Manhattans. Jack had to have his vodka tonics. Their wives wanted rum with Jamie, and those that didn't were interested in Allison's wine. Duck Hunter Dan wanted beer— "and plenty of it." It was great. We were all together, having fun.

Jack rolled down the window at an intersection and asked a woman walking her dog if he could give her a quote on her insurance. The woman said no, but he said that he had the best rates and the most dedicated staff in the entire state of Michigan. I didn't let her rebuff his advances, because I punched the accelerator and sped away.

Ten minutes later, we were back at the motel. The gang had four or five poolside tables pushed together and buckets of ice on each. Almost everyone was wearing a swimsuit, along with a T-shirt or cover-up. Jamie had her bottle of rum on the table next to the Diet Coke, and Caroline was already three-quarters through her first baby bottle of wine. Their sons were tossing a foam football from one end of the pool to the other, and hollering the rebel yells of kids having a good time. Jack tossed the bags of booze on the tables and we both disappeared into our rooms to change clothes.

The agents sat together and discussed the situation with

Michigan Miners. We all agreed that this could be our big break and we had to make it work. There was plenty of laughing, and plenty of drinking. After an hour, Gerry suggested that we order pizza. That was just about the time that Caroline was hit in the back of the head with the soggy foam football. She pushed back her chair, unzipped her cover-up, and dove into the deep end of the pool, screaming, "You're dead, son!"

We all laughed at her, but a dip in the pool did seem like a great idea. I joined Caroline. Gerry jumped in with his wife, Molly, then Jack and Jamie. Caroline had her son in a headlock, and was giving him fake punches to the top of his head. I grabbed the football and tossed it Gerry's way, who in turn fired it at his wife. Round and round we went, until that became boring. Jamie's son splashed her, and then furiously swam away. He was no match for her, though. She caught him within a few strokes. Gradually she drifted my way, and splashed me the same way her son did to her.

"Hey, quit it! Where'd you learn to swim like that, anyway?"

"Like what?"

"You forgot how observant I am. I saw your freestyle there, after your son. You looked like a killer whale chasing a harp seal."

"He-haw. Now I'm a whale?"

"Okay, okay, just keep splashing me, but I don't think you'll catch me as fast as you did your son."

"Sounds like a challenge?"

"You up for a little race?" I pried.

"Three laps, freestyle, no jump start."

"What are the stakes?"

"I win and you buy breakfast, if you win I'll buy dessert."

"Let's go." We were at the end of the pool where the gang

was seated, and I couldn't help but announce our little race to the spectators. The boys cleared the center of the pool while the women yelled their encouragement to Jamie. I bobbed my way down to the far end of the pool, and must confess, looked at Jamie and the way she filled out her purple one-piece suit. Chlorinated water is no fun on the eyes, but the view was worth the sting.

We shook hands, and her son gave the command "ready, set, go!" I pushed off the wall, taking a long, underwater track. Jamie was stoking away in a flurry of splashes. When I resurfaced and began flailing, we were neck-and-neck. She knew how to flip-turn, but my longer legs gained a small lead. I could hear all kinds of shouting from the crowd while we were at that end. By the time we made the second turn and headed for home we were still tied. I turned on the afterburners, but she stayed right with me. At the end of the race, I stretched and won by a hair—a lot of hair. Jamie's supporters said that she won, but there was no way. I won fair and square. "Great race, Jaim, but you owe me." She was out of breath, and waved off my victory.

I sat next to her when the pizza arrived. Her sons didn't need any supervising—they were eating their pizza, drinking pop, and having fun. She did a good job with her boys. She never did lead on where she learned to swim so well, but then again, neither did I. When the pizza was gone, I told everyone that Jamie was buying dessert.

She slugged me in the arm, and mentioned that dessert was for me, not everyone.

"Okay. Does that mean that you're conceding defeat?"

"I never said that!"

"Then what are you saying?"

"Never mind. Besides, they don't serve dessert here."

That kind of bantering went on throughout the night. We all had a lot to drink, but it was great, friendly fun. After midnight the conversations became more sedated. There still was giggling—at Jack's imitation of Tadrick, and Caroline's story about me on the cell phone. Duck Hunter Dan and his wife turned in, and Jamie looked in on the boys. Allison and her husband rounded up their children and turned in too. Jamie came back and told Caroline that the boys had crashed. Caroline pushed the chair back, and mumbled that she had better move them onto the cots in their room. I put the cans away in their cardboard cases, and threw away the pizza boxes. I poured the leftover drinks into one cup, and tidied up a bit. It was late, after all, and I had been up for a long time. I gave Jamie a hug and said goodnight.

Several minutes later in my room, I drank several glasses of water, ate a couple aspirin, and brushed my teeth. I flipped on the television and the bedside light. Nothing was on, but the surfing was good. Highlights of hockey and basketball games dominated the sports channels. Jerry Springer had a couple of losers on his program—something about love gone awry, I imagine. The next thing I knew, my eyelids were getting heavy.

I barely heard the tiny click of the door between our rooms, but I did notice the bed sway ever-so-gently when she pulled back the covers and crawled in. I was on my side and she was facing me. By the glow of the television I didn't see any clothes under her chlorine smelling blonde hair. She touched my hair above my ears and I stirred. When her hand moved to my earlobe I opened my eyes.

"Hello, Jaim…you must be the mermaid I beat in race a few hours ago."

"Mr. Johanson."

"Not enough space in room 116?"

"No, I couldn't resist the thought of you all alone over here, in your very own big bed."

"Really…sounds like a moral dilemma. I have a moral dilemma too, Dr. Laura."

"Welcome to the program, how can I help you?" By now her index finger was seductively tracing my lips.

"Well, you see, Dr. Laura, I made a bet with this person."

"I see, sir. Do you have a gambling problem?" Her finger now eased down my chin, below my Adam's apple, over my bicep to the hair on my chest. My voice quivered, but her touch felt absolutely incredible.

"If I deny it, I'm showing the first signs of addiction, right?"

"Sir, if you want me to help you, you better ask the doctor your question," she purred.

"Sorry. Sorry. Please don't yell at me. I am a very sensitive man. I had a bet with this person and won, but she didn't pay off the wager."

"What does this person owe you?"

"Dessert of my choosing."

"What do you have in mind?"

"What would you suggest?"

"Sir, I don't have a crystal ball. You'd better think of something."

"Would horizontal refreshments be too much to ask?"

"Go for it."

I pulled her head toward mine, and we kissed. At last, our lips met. At last, I could taste her mouth—hinting of rum, and feel her tongue exploring mine. Her breath rained heavily on my cheek. My hand moved down her back to her round, firm ass—cut like cloven halves of honeydew. She wasn't wearing a thing. Heavenly.

"Keep your cool," I thought, but it was really hard. Everything was. She gasped in the throes of passion so loud that I thought she'd wake up Caroline next door.

Twenty-Seven

AT SEVEN THE next morning, I woke up and took an inventory of my faculties. Slight headache, but my stomach felt fine, which wasn't bad considering the number of Manhattans I had the night before. The television was still on, glowing softly in the corner of the room. The sheets next to me were still tucked under the pillow, and the bedspread hardly had a wrinkle in it. I buried my face in the pillow next to me with hopes of detecting any remnant of her, but there was none. Jamie never did visit me last night; we never did make love like I so vividly imagined. So much for that, I lamented. She was an excellent lover too—responsive, uninhibited, and was blessed with a body that Venus would envy.

I could hear life starting to stir next door—the boys were anxious to get their suits back on and go swimming again. If Jamie had been with me last night she would have left during the middle of the night. She was smart and thoughtful. She must have figured that there was no sense in stirring up controversy with Caroline. No sense in making her children insecure about sharing her with somebody else. I was beginning to imagine her catlike departure, even if she never came to me in the first place.

We should have been lovers, even though it was less complicated this way. If I was more up-front, perhaps it would have paid off. I was gentlemanly, humorous, flirtatious, and understanding—four lethal ingredients for a man chasing a woman. But, oh, the chase is always more fun than the kill. It's always more fun luring ducks to the decoys, and the anticipation of that final act of killing, than the actual act of squeezing the trigger. The same argument could be said for seducing a woman—especially one with whom you've never had relations. The final act of making love isn't as much fun as the acts that lead up to that event. The steps that precede sex are the best. For Jamie and me, I thought the best part of our evening was the playful splashing we did in the pool. I also liked the way she socked me at the dinner table when I told everyone that she was buying dessert. Who knows what she saw in me. I certainly earned some brownie points when Don Tadrick made sexual advances at her and I showed such compassion. I think I made her laugh at me when I had to answer all those calls on the cell phone.

I wondered where I went wrong. Why didn't she give me a kiss when I gave her a hug? Maybe I should have paid her more compliments throughout the night—about the way she picked up on the Michigan Miners program, about her purple swimsuit, about her long, shapely legs. Seducing a woman is a lot like blackjack, I think. Play one card too many and you're busted. If you don't play enough cards, you end up well short of 21 and out of the ballpark.

I crawled out of bed, brushed my teeth, ate three more aspirin, and turned on the shower. What a shame—it would have been fun to shower with her. I pictured her blond hair, flattened, with the warm water spattering against her emerald green eyes. It would have been fun to pour a giant dollop of shampoo on her head and work it into a thick lather. Maybe she'd throw her arms around me and get busy with the soap. I imagined how soft and firm her breasts were, and how they swayed as she raised an arm to wash away rivulets of suds.

I wondered if Jamie was having those same thoughts. I wondered if she would be open to the notion if the opportunity ever happened again. With less than a week to go before Christmas, I put a plan together to woo her, or at least play more cards at blackjack.

Now there would be no turning back—for Jamie, me, and the other agents. Today we had no policies in force with Michigan Miners. No commission, either. By the end of the next week we'd have 100 policies on the books and $20,000 in premiums. In a week we would convert 50 Surety Guarantee clients to Michigan Miners, and save them several hundred dollars apiece in the process. There would be many weeks like that to come, with many policies to be converted, at a huge savings to our customers. At last it felt good to be in the business again. At last we could look ourselves in the mirror when we shaved in the morning and feel good about the career we chose. We weren't going to let the crooks at the top of Surety Guarantee rape our clients and gouge our income.

When I opened the office on Monday, I received my underwriting results through the third quarter. In typical Surety Guarantee fashion, the results for the third quarter were released when the fourth quarter was nearly over. If I were in charge, I'd have the results much sooner than that. After all, why should I have to wait three months to see the effectiveness (or in Surety Guarantee's case, ineffectiveness) of a rate revision?

My numbers on the report were good. Through the third quarter, I had about $150,000 in homeowner's premiums and $50,000 in losses. According to the Surety Guarantee way of computation, that netted a loss ratio of 85 percent, but in reality, according to industry standards, it should have been 30 percent: 150 divided by 50 equals 30. The auto was just as confusing: $650,000 in premiums, divided by $210,000 in losses equaled a loss ratio of 75 percent? It should have been close to 30 percent as well. Surety Guarantee always maintained that the "breakeven" loss ratio was 60 percent; so, they were losing money in my little agency. By industry standards they would have been making money hand over fist.

Making money for Surety Guarantee's executives was a twisted paradox. They had the loss ratios to show that they were making money, but in order to really make a killing, they needed to show that they were losing their shirts. They couldn't just make an honest dollar; they had to make a killing. Somewhere along the line, someone came up with a demented accounting philosophy that rewarded losses and punished profits. Somebody in the company hierarchy embraced those practices. Somehow those people were promoted to the top of Surety Guarantee management. But where was the board of directors? I'm not sure if they bought into management's shortsighted style, or if they were so naive not to know the difference.

On a single line of the report, I noticed a summary from a subsidiary of Surety Guarantee based in Florida. "Country Mutual" was a small insurance company for Florida residents who had lost their preferred status either because of underwriting reasons or multiple car crashes. I had a County Mutual client move from Florida to Michigan, and his one little policy showed up on the report. His policy generated $1,000 in premiums, and he had no claims, but the Surety Guarantee report said that his policy had a loss ratio of 85. It should have been zero, but it was just the way Surety Guarantee cooked the books for their benefit. If we asked for an explanation of their methods we'd get the same old rhetoric: They had so many write-offs and expenses built into their equations that they were destined to lose money. They filed those inaccurate loss ratios with the insurance commissioners all over the country. No wonder they claimed they were losing money. No wonder they had to justify raising the rates so high. No wonder we all thought they were crooks. No wonder so many agents and clients were leaving their ranks. Their accounting methods bordered on criminal.

Surety Guarantee seemed to be in a death spiral. They unveiled a new auto rate (based on the second quarter results) that was supposed to be introduced the first of February. They assured us that they were taking a five percent decrease. None of us were excited by the news, because we knew five percent was still 40 percent short of where it should have been to make us competitive. When I got back to the office, I pulled up my rate for my truck's insurance: $550 for six months. For kicks, I changed the effective date on the quote to February 2. My new rate, with the five percent reduction: $603. That's just how it worked with Surety Guarantee. A five percent reduction actually raised the rates. They were crooks, plain and simple.

But all was not lost: Michigan Miners' rate for my truck: $375.

Twenty-Eight

ON MY WAY into work on Monday, I stopped at the flower shop and ordered a dozen red roses for Jamie. I asked the woman behind the counter to help me with my secret plan. We removed the name of her shop from the card I selected, and then she inscribed my message: "*To Jamie, Deck the halls with boughs of holly? Roses smell better and are much more jolly! From Santa.*" I gave the lady an extra $5 to deliver them after 4:30 Monday, so they wouldn't be frozen when she got home from work. I knew the day would be especially busy at our office for Jamie because we were closed on Friday.

From there, I stopped at the ritziest hairdresser's in town and paid $90 cash for a gift certificate that could have been used for a hairdo, manicure, makeover, or whatever they do in women's salons. When I explained to the woman behind the counter that it was a secret Christmas present, she agreed to help me and addressed the card and envelope herself. On the card, she wrote: "*To Jamie, Don't let Jack Frost nip at your nose. Let these people work on your fro. From St. Nick.*" I dropped by the Post Office and sent the card and certificate to her home. The handwriting on the card wasn't mine, so Jamie wouldn't recognize it.

Jack called me on the cell phone when I returned to my truck. He had received his third quarter results too, which were similar to mine. The dirty bastards. They were taking advantage of the agents, their policyholders, and the trust that so many of us had cultivated over the years.

He called to say that he bumped into Don Tadrick at a Bob Evans restaurant in Petoskey. Apparently, Tadrick was in the neighborhood training Scott's replacement, who was yet to be introduced.

Jack pulled up his auto renewal on the computer and discovered his premiums were going up as well. It probably wasn't a good idea that he ran into Tadrick, because the wounds of another rate hike didn't sit well with either Jack or his wife, who ran the office. She was the one who bore the wrath of clients who called the office to complain. She was the one who had to deal with customers whose monthly billing plans were messed up beyond recognition. She was the one who had to manually go into the company's antiquated computer system and add discounts that were mysteriously removed.

Both Jack and his wife used Tadrick as a whipping post. They wanted answers to questions about the future of Surety Guarantee, about their billing plans, about the mysterious five percent discount on car policies. Tadrick didn't know. He was just the last stop for the crap that ran downhill from Newark, and the complaints that ran uphill from the agents. He was a good foot soldier that toed the line in a horrible situation. Still, he didn't have much integrity. I thought he was a snake, and so did everybody else.

When Jack and his wife asked Tadrick about the five percent discount, he didn't have much of an explanation. The company did give a five percent discount, but the "base rates" went up 10 percent; when combined with the removal of the member discount, it resulted in another 10 percent increase. He denied knowing about the base rate or the member's discount business. It was another example of their smoke and mirror marketing.

Jack's wife was beside herself.

"Then why do you lie, and tell us that our rates are going down?"

She had a good point. There was no reason for lying. Tadrick couldn't give an explanation. Pathetic. The hell with Surety Guarantee. They weren't going to ruin my Christmas spirit. I liked taking care of the only woman in my life at Christmas time. It was fun shopping for Jamie, and I wasn't finished yet. The bath and beauty shop was next. A $50 coupon goes a long way there, and the clerk behind the counter seemed impressed with my plan. She even giggled when I had her write the card: *"To Jamie, 'Twas the night before Christmas and all through your house, it smelled of perfume, bubble bath lotion, and such. Merry Christmas, from Kris Cringle."*

I put the card in the console of the truck, and made plans to mail it on Tuesday so she'd get it Wednesday, Christmas Eve.

Twenty-Nine

TUESDAY, JAMIE STOPPED me outside the front door of the office, under the big balsam tree. She was wearing her black leather coat, the one with the fur lapel. She looked like a little Christmas angel—with the snow landing on her black earmuffs and her straight, blonde bangs. The Christmas lights had blown off their hooks and she braved the bluster to repair them. Someone less conscientious wouldn't have noticed. No wonder the office ran like a well-oiled machine since she came onboard.

"Is that you, Santa?" she asked.

"Ho, ho, ho! Blitzen ate my beard just south of Nome." Jamie laughed.

"Thanks for the roses."

"What roses?"

"Right. You can't deny it."

"Deny what?"

"Didn't you send me those roses?"

"No."

"Come on. You did to!"

"No, really I didn't. How many were there?"

"A dozen, red ones. They're beautiful."

"Aw, that's nice. Why did you think I sent them?"

"The card said that they were from 'Santa.'"

"Oh, I see," scratching my chin, "when I said 'Ho-ho-ho,' you thought I was Santa."

"I thought you were Santa before I got to work today. I thought for sure it was you."

"Can't you think of anybody else that would have done this?"

"No."

"Your sister? Anybody at the boys' school? Church?"

"Nope, nobody."

"Are you seeing anyone?"

"When? I haven't had a date in forever. This is weird. I thought for sure it was you." She followed me inside to the rack where I helped her out of her coat and hung it next to mine.

"Sorry, Jaim. It wasn't me, but it sounds like you have a secret admirer. Someone really wants to get to know you."

"I hope he's not a stalker. I hope it's not Don Tadrick—sick."

"Don't be silly. He may have the scruples of an alley cat but that isn't his style."

"That's true."

"Just think, if it's from Santa, Christmas is almost here and all the fun will be over soon."

"True enough."

"Anybody call?" she shuffled through her desk and came up with a pair of pink papers.

"Mark Hendrickson, and somebody from the Yellow Pages."

"What did the Yellow Pages guy want?"

"Your ads in the phone book are up for renewal soon, and he wants an answer on what you want to do."

"Thanks, Jaim...Hey, how about dinner tonight? I've got something surprisingly special picked out, and I'd like to share it with you...Not that I couldn't tell you about it, but it would be better as a surprise." I was rambling, but that always happens when I get nervous. I was even more nervous when I lied, and I didn't have anything other than a couple of plump ducks from the freezer. "You'll probably like it, I mean, what I have in mind. You know, for dinner. I like it. I think it's delicious."

"Sure."

"I'd like to tell you about it but I think it would be better off as a surprise." I was stammering and her response didn't register.

"What time?" she smiled.

"I can give you directions too. It's really easy to find."

"Larry, I'll be there. Sounds like fun. What should I bring?"

"Sure, okay. Great." Finally, it registered. She accepted! I felt happier than a kid with a new balloon. "I'll see you about six, and I promise to have you home by eleven. Don't want you to be sleepy for work tomorrow."

"I've been sleepy before," she giggled.

"Of course, we all have...at our old jobs." I glanced her way and she was still smiling. For some reason my cheeks felt warm. For a simple conversation, a pleasant dialogue, it meant so much more.

"So what should I bring?"

"Dessert...remember?"

"Oh yes, the bet from our race up north. I knew you'd never forget about that."

"The Lord didn't bless me with many gifts, but a good memory is one of them."

"I'll surprise you too. See you about six." She turned, gracefully answered the telephone, and then mouthed the words "I need directions," her free hand scribbling an imaginary note. Her talents seemed endless; her work ethic enchantingly productive.

I gave her the "okay" gesture back, then looked through my stack of messages. Mark Hendrickson called from the claims center and told me more about my claim. My attorney's name was Nikki; *her* name was Nikki Mammel. Hopefully she'd be good enough to fend off Ted Buxton and his band of goons. She already filed an answer to the lawsuit, even though she had yet to contact me. Apparently, they file an answer to the lawsuit, then figure out the best way to defend it. Mark said I should be expecting a phone call from her soon. I asked Mark what kind of reserve he put on my claim, but he either lied and said that it was too early for that, or he didn't want to tip his hand and disclose that information. After all, it could hurt my case if it got into the hands of the counter-plaintiffs.

Then I asked him if Buxton ever called him about the sexual harassment case. Buxton did call him back, and Hendrickson took his recorded statement. Buxton didn't deny swatting Sarah on the bottom, but contends that he only did it because he thought it would be funny. There was no malicious intent on his part, and because he worded it that way, the claim would be covered. Ted knew that "intentional acts" are excluded from coverage; we all knew it except the company. They were too ignorant to suggest that Ted's stunt may have been intentional. They were too busy gutting the company to realize that maybe a few agents were trying to get their share of the pie.

"Still have a reserve of $250 on that one, Mark?"

"How'd you know that?"

"You told me, remember?"

"Oh, I guess I did...Yep."

"How far are you from settling?"

"I dunno. Her lawyer wants $750,000 and is rounding up witnesses, trying to pad the case. He's asking everybody about it, and what their opinion of Sarah is now that it happened. Seems like her dad is the one driving the case. He's not going to see his little girl dragged through the mud like that."

"So what did you offer?"

"$175,000."

"Jeez, that's a lot of money for getting spanked in front of a bunch of golfers. Sexual harassment is pretty hot topic now, I guess."

"I know."

"I'd hate to think what my case is worth to Ted's team!"

"We'll see what it's worth when the facts come out. Your lawyer should be calling soon, and we'll get to the bottom of it."

Thirty

AT FOUR I said goodbye to Jamie, swung by the post office, and mailed her coupon. From there I made it to one of those grocers that has almost everything that the big chain stores don't. I picked out a fresh looking bundle of Romaine lettuce, feta and Parmesan cheese, croutons, and a small tube of anchovy paste. The man behind the counter suggested a box of wild rice and bottle of dry white wine from somewhere in California. I'm never sure what wine goes with what; it all tastes the same to me. I paid for everything quickly, tossed the bags on the passenger seat, jumped in the driver's side, and started the engine. A second later, I turned off the engine, jumped out of the vehicle and ran back inside. Forgot the candles, a loaf of French bread, and something flowery for a centerpiece.

A half hour later I was home in Big Rapids. Before changing clothes, I turned on the oven and set the barely thawed ducks in a pan of warm water. They were fine birds—plucked neatly and drawn with a surgeon's skill. Not a pinfeather was on them—not a BB hole marred their appearance. I put the bottle of wine in the freezer on a bed of ice, and set the heads of Romaine to soak in cold water. I only had 20 minutes before she was to arrive.

What to wear? She had seen me wear nice clothes day after day. I needed something different, something unpredictable, like I had a huge wardrobe. In honor of our first date, I thought about wearing a tie, but that would be too stuffy. If I dressed too casual, she might think less of me. It seemed like I stood there for five minutes, pulling a shirt off the rack, noticing the wrinkles or a cracked button, then putting it back. Finally, I decided on a sharp denim shirt, khaki trousers, a woven leather belt, and a pair of heeled moccasins.

Without a minute to spare, I donned a white apron, put on some soft music, and had the candles erected in a diminutive pair of holders on the round, oak table. I rummaged through the refrigerator, found some tart apples, and cut them into wedges. They made a nice bed in the bottom of a baking pan. I filled the pan half full of water, sprinkled on a handful of pickling seasoning, and then stuffed the ducks' cavities with white raisins. Before loading them into the oven, I put a couple pieces of bacon over the birds so they wouldn't dry out. I set the timer for sixty-five minutes, and moved on to the next task at hand.

I didn't get far. The doorbell rang. It was Jamie, waiting patiently, hands clenched behind her, breath steaming from the cold. The front door was seemingly stuck, or I lost my bearings.

"Come on in."

"Thank you."

"Right on time, as usual. Any trouble finding it?"

"Nope, but the roads are a little slippery."

I took her coat and hung it inside the closet. "Nice place." Her head was on a swivel, admiring all the tasteless features of a bachelor pad. "Oh this is cute, 'golf with your friends,' huh?" She pointed to the framed poster I had near the hallway, the one with Larry, Moe, and Curly dressed in golfing attire.

"Would you like the nickel tour?"

"Sure, but let me put this in the freezer first." She followed me to the kitchen, where we found the wine.

"Are you ready for a glass?"

"That would be great, where are the glasses?" I pointed to the china cabinet, next to the table. I heard the glasses clink as she brought them over. I was busy, plunging the shiny, spiraled corkscrew between the lips of the tall wine bottle. I could smell her standing next to me, fragrantly. "I never thought of you as a big wine drinker."

"You're right. Sometimes it tastes good, though," I confessed.

"What are we having, anyway? Smells good." She reached for the handle of the oven door, but I stopped her.

"It's a surprise, remember?"

"Ooops...I can wait."

"Would you like to help me wash the lettuce?"

"Sure." She pulled up the sleeves of her black cashmere sweater, took off her watch, and jumped right in. I laid a towel on the counter and set her glass of wine on the bar above the sink. She picked it up, puckered her lips and tipped the glass.

"Here's to Michigan Miners." She smiled, raised her glass to mine, and took another sip. Her lips left a perforated smudge of pink on the edge of the glass.

"Do you think about work a lot when you're not at the office? I mean you seem like you have a lot on your mind," she suggested.

"I think about work all the time, unless I'm duck hunting or something."

"Why is that?"

"I dunno. I guess it's because it's my own. I mean…I own the business. I'm responsible to nobody but myself. There's a lot to worry about. You, Caroline, your kids—everyone is relying on me, in a way, to take care of them."

"I never thought of it that way."

I measured the ingredients for the wild rice, checked the timer, and turned on the burner.

"What happens to people?"

"What do you mean?" I asked.

"You know. What happened to the people that work for Surety Guarantee? Somewhere they went wrong. Somehow they lost their ethics. They don't care about their agents, or about the lives they wreck, not to mention the policyholders who pay too much. What happens to them?"

"Greed, plain and simple."

"I think they're crooks. You're right."

"They *are* crooks," I nodded, but the conversation lulled for a second.

It was nice having her in my house, working side-by-side again. When she finished washing the lettuce, I grabbed another towel, patted it dry, and opened the tube of anchovy paste. Jamie held it to her nose and furled her eyebrows. I didn't miss a beat, pouring enough olive oil in the bottom of a wooden bowl to make a saucer-sized puddle. I took her hand, still on the tube, and gently squeezed. A small stream of brown paste oozed from the end, until it broke free, into the bowl and its slippery coating. She screwed the top back on, while I found a clove of garlic and the press. We were working in harmony now, just like at the office. I took the large wooden spoon and pushed the mix around the edges—coating the sides in a translucent sheen of pungent flavors. The rice boiled, and I cut the flame. She tore the lettuce, leaf by leaf, with her long, shapely fingers.

"I usually squeeze half a lemon on it now, before the lettuce is all gone."

"Coming right up," she obliged. "In the fridge?"

"On the bottom, in the drawer. There should be one or two in there."

"Here we go. I got it." I looked her way and smiled, pleased with the way things were going. "I'm famished. This all looks so good, and smells wonderful…is this salad some sort of secret too?"

"Not really, it's just that I'd rather have a hearty Caesars than a spineless tossed salad any day. This stuff is strong and bold."

"Just like you, Larry."

"Aw, come on. I'm really a pushover, deep down."

"I'm just kidding. I'm sure you are." She laughed again.

I poured more wine, set the table, lit the candles and checked on the main course. Just dandy. She put the finishing touches on the salad—just the right amount of Parmesan, feta cheese and croutons. I asked her to sit down, and then pulled two plates out of the cupboard. This wasn't going to be a family-style dinner but a sit-down type. It was fun to wait on Jamie; I was trying my hardest to impress her.

I scooped a bed of rice on each plate, added some steamed green beans, and carved a few slices of duck from each breast. When I did, the juices oozed into the bed of shrunken apples. Done to perfection. I laid the duck slices on our plates, and covered them with a boiling mixture of currant jelly, Worcestershire sauce and butter.

"Wow, this looks wonderful. I never knew you had these talents."

"Thank you, but you'd better try it before you say anything else."

"Now can you tell me what it is?"

"You really want to know?"

"Yes."

"Why don't you see if you like it first?"

"Okay then." She picked up her fork and knife, made a few cuts, and then raised a bite to her mouth. I could only watch as she chewed, smiled, then swallowed. "It's good. What is it?"

"Duck."

"Boy, it's different. It tastes a little like beef...but sweeter. That sauce is excellent, what do you call it?"

"Shotgun sauce." She took another bite, and seemed to relish the flavor. She was hooked. "Glad you like it. Sometimes if you overcook it, it'll dry out, and then it's ruined. Didn't you eat a lot of duck when you were growing up?"

"Not really. My dad hunted deer when I was a kid, and we ate it a lot as hamburger. We didn't have Caesars salad either. It is strong!"

"I told you."

We laughed together over dinner, the dishes, coffee, and her dessert. She conceded defeat up north in our little race, and told me all about her swimming lessons as a kid. Before we knew it, the evening had come and gone. She never did get the nickel tour of my house, but that was okay.

She never asked about the ducks we ate, or where they came from. I didn't have the heart to tell her that the ducks were shot on Scott's last day alive.

Thirty-One

I MET MY Yellow Pages representative in Big Rapids on Wednesday morning. Instead of renewing my Surety Guarantee ad in the phone book, I decided to make a change. No more Surety Guarantee ads. No more Surety Guarantee phone numbers. It was obvious that my future was with Michigan Miners. They were the ones that had the most competitive auto, home, and commercial insurance programs. They were everything that Surety Guarantee wasn't. But I really couldn't put my name or picture in the ad. Caroline and Jamie would have to agree to have their photos displayed. Our second or third phone lines would be Michigan Miners' first line. Caroline and Jamie would also have to change the way they answered the phone. Instead of "Surety Guarantee," we'd have to change it to "Insurance office" or "Risk management center." It would have to be something generic—something nonthreatening that wouldn't throw off Michigan Miners personnel or Surety Guarantee if they called.

I agreed to the ad, and gave the salesman our new phone numbers. I'd worry about Caroline and Jamie's picture later.

Caroline was surprised to see me. Most of my visits were announced.

"Merry Christmas to you, too."

"I'm sorry; I didn't mean it like that. Merry Christmas," she said.

"What's up?"

"Not much. I'm about ready to drop-kick this computer into next year."

"Why?"

"Oh, I don't know, it's the same old thing. Discounts removed, change of coverage lost, I swear it gets slower and slower everyday."

"Sorry…Hey, I have something for you." I reached into my breast pocket and pulled out an envelope. "Here you go. Merry Christmas. I really want to thank you for another great year. Despite all the trouble, I want to thank you." I handed her a Christmas card with a short stack of $100 bills inside.

Caroline said thanks, several times, and said that she'd have something for me the next day.

"Heck, I don't need anything. Well, I guess I do need something, but it has nothing to do with Christmas."

"What's that?"

"I made an appointment for you and Jamie to have your pictures taken at a studio in town. It's for the new Yellow Pages ad."

"Together?"

"No, but that's not a bad idea."

"Sure…no problem. When's my appointment?"

"Next week. I'll let you know. Sell anything? How many policies did we lose here this month?"

"Not too many. Johnson's told me to tell you thanks, but they found it cheaper down the street."

"They had a bunch of cars, too. Didn't they?"

"Five cars, a house and their two personal watercraft. They said they saved $500 every six months."

"Ouch."

"The Wilcoxes and the Georges left too. They had a Cadillac, a Lincoln, their home, and snowmobiles. Wilcox said our rates were twice as much as their new agent's."

"Okay, I get the picture. That's horrible. They've been with us a long time, and what…now they're saving half? We need to start incorporating Michigan Miners into our routine."

"How do you want it done?"

"Let's do this. If someone calls to complain about their rates, or if they have more than three vehicles, switch them to Michigan Miners. At least give them the option. You'll have to watch the computer to see who's coming up for renewal."

"Got it."

"Oh, and one other thing. All new business now goes to Michigan Miners. There's no sense in wasting time and quoting them with Surety Guarantee. We might actually start selling insurance again."

"Okay."

It was ridiculous. We kept losing our asses, but all the company could do was raise the rates. I had a copy of my third quarter results with me in Big Rapids. Through September, I lost 350 auto policies. Man, I worked hard to get those. I poured my blood, sweat, and tears into my agency, and now the company methodically gutted it. It had been six weeks since Jack wrote the state executive about the policies he lost in his agency. It had been about the same amount of time since I wrote him about the re-inspections of our current homeowner's policies. The state executive didn't respond to my letter, and Jack's had also gone unanswered. I suppose no response was a response on his part, but that wasn't going to help our case if our little secret agency was going to get into legal trouble. We needed to goad him into responding. So I sat down and wrote him another letter.

Dear Mr. Executive,

I regret to inform you that I have only been able to reinspect four homes since my last correspondence. All four homes are in fine shape and I would consider them excellent prospects for our homeowner's policies. Please be advised that of the 337 homes I had to inspect, 111 have cancelled their policy for reasons most likely attributable to Surety Guarantee's pricing strategy. It is with deep reservations that I bring this observation to your attention: Surety Guarantee's pricing is abhorrently skewed.
When can we expect some relief?"

I sealed the envelope, put a stamp on it, and dropped in the mail on my way to see Jamie in Mt. Pleasant. Things were dead there so we had a chance to chat.

"Made it home all right?"

"No trouble. Not even a close call. I had a great time last night, except I went through three pieces of gum. That garlic had more lives than a cat."

"I know, I know, that's part of the joy in eating a Caesars salad." Just then the phone rang—Nikki Mammel.

She seemed pleasant enough, and in between the shuffling of papers, seemed to think that the crux of the case was whether or not Surety Guarantee knew about the letters I sent. I told her unequivocally that Tadrick and Scott knew about the letters. She, of course, said that Tadrick denied knowing anything about it.

"Listen, Ms. Mammel, Tadrick knows about them. He was at my office, and stood next to my desk and read one letter, then gave me the go-ahead to write whatever I wanted as long it helped save our business. Does he deny saying that, too?"

"He denies knowing anything about those letters."

"Just like that? No knowledge?"

"Basically. In a nutshell."

"What does that do to my case?"

"Well, it certainly doesn't help it. It makes you look like a loose cannon or something. You're out there writing these letters without any regard for whether or not the information contained in them is true..."

"And if Surety Guarantee did know about the letters?"

"It would shift some of the blame from you to Surety Guarantee. The allegations in those letters can be considered defamatory, but I would think that if they came with a big insurance company's blessing, it definitely adds more weight to the damages."

"How do I prove that they knew about it?"

"I don't know. The only witness that would have known about it was Scott, and he can't help you now."

"Wait a second, my assistant Jamie was here in the office. She remembers Tadrick coming in here. I bet she'd remember. I'll ask her after we're finished talking. Maybe she'll agree to testify."

"Okay, good—that would help."

"The lawsuit said that they wanted $1.5 million. Have they given you any indication of how much they'd settle for?"

"No, no. It's way too early for that. We need more information. We need to get copies of the people you sent those letters to. We need records, depositions, all that."

"When do we get started?"

"I'll send you a subpoena and ask for everything. Then we'll take your deposition. In the meantime, why don't you talk to your assistant and see what she remembers. We may also take her deposition."

"What are the chances this will go over my policy's limit of $1 million?"

"Hard to say. I wouldn't worry about it. Don't let it ruin your Christmas."

"Lovely."

I hung up the phone, ran my fingers through my hair, and gulped the last of my coffee. This was a fine kettle of fish. I knew that Tadrick would deny it. Jamie seemed to be somewhat concerned, but it was Christmas Eve. She was standing at the counter, taking someone's premium payment. I waited until the client finished and said goodbye before asking, "Hey, Jaim, do you remember that time Tadrick and Scott came to the office?"

"When? Weren't they here quite few times?"

"Yes, but I'm after the time they were here at the beginning, when we were sending out those letters?"

"Yes, I remember."

"Do you remember if Tadrick read those letters we sent out?"

"No, I don't remember anything about that. Seems like he was leaving when I came in."

"Okay, that's fine."

"Why?"

"Well, it's about this lawsuit business with Buxton. My lawyer wants to know if anybody from the company read the letters that caused all this nonsense. If we can prove that they knew about it, it will shift liability from me to them."

"I wish I could help you, but I really can't say for sure."

"That's okay. It seems like he did leave shortly after you got to the office. What a mess."

"Don't let it ruin your Christmas. Come on, let's turn on some nice Christmas music and forget about those losers. What d'ya say?"

"You know what, you're right. You're the second person in the last 10 minutes that told me not to let it ruin my Christmas. I'm not going to let those clowns drag me down! On Dancer and Prancer and Vixen…." Jamie turned up the music next to her desk, and soon our office was filled with yuletide joy. "Are you all set for Christmas?"

"I think so. I'll probably wrap some of the boys' presents tonight after they go to bed."

"What did you get them?"

"I got clothes, books and stuff. They wanted a Gameboy and a hockey net. I probably spent way too much, but what the heck, they're at such a cute age." She was sitting across the desk from me, donned in a red and green sweater. I could have looked at her all afternoon.

"When do they go to their father's?"

"Christmas Day, about dinnertime. I get to have them longer on Christmas Day because he wants to take them up north with him on New Year's Eve. They're going up there snowmobiling or something."

"Well that's nice. I mean—that they get to spend time with their dad and mom gets to have them all to herself on Christmas."

"Should be fun."

"Hey, I brought you something." I gave her an envelope with a little sum of cash inside, along with her watch from the night before. "Merry Christmas."

"Oh shoot, I guess I did forget my watch, thanks. You

shouldn't have done that! I've only been working for you for a few months." She clenched her hands around the money, raised it to her lips, and told me thank you over and over again. I could tell that she really appreciated it. I thought for sure she'd bring up the roses again, but she didn't. She didn't bring up the coupon from the salon, and I wasn't about to mention it. It would spoil the fun. Besides, when she checked her mail tonight, she'd have another surprise.

"I should have given you more. Next year will be different. We're going places with Michigan Miners. You've done such a nice job. Why don't you go home and buy something else for your boys on the way—maybe a hockey puck and stick, or another game for their new doohickey."

"Aw, are you sure?"

"Sure. Go on; get out of here, before I change my mind."

She grabbed her coat, cleaned up a few things on her desk, and waltzed out. I stood at the window and waved, through the snow, as she buckled her seatbelt and sped away. I stood there for quite a while, watching the snow fall between the spears of icicles, listening to the likes of Burl Ives and Bing Crosby swoon festive scores. The phone was dead, so was the fax. I wished things were different in my life. I was alone, and lonely—facing the fact that I'd never make the kind of living as long I wanted as I represented Surety Guarantee. How depressing. I thought that being a family man might bring me happiness. If I had my own family, it might help me snap out of this vindictive curse, might help me forget about Scott's accident, and how I didn't help him. What I wouldn't do to be in Jamie's house on Christmas morning with the boys! It sounded like fun. I had to make a few more strides before anything close to that would happen.

On a snowy Christmas Eve afternoon, I put the next phase of my plan together.

> *"Rudolph had a shiny nose, Frosty a big fat belly*
> *bring your swim suit and they'll pamper you, Jamie.*
> *All I ever wanted was to see you smile*
> *Kick back your heels and relax a while."*

I sent the note anonymously to her home with two more coupons: one for a 3 p.m. massage and another for a 4 p.m. makeover at a salon at the local Microtel Inn on New Year's Eve. They had all sorts of cool stuff at the Microtel Inn—whirlpool, spa, weight-lifting machines, aerobics classes, restaurants, and tons of rooms. It was a dopey poem, but so were the other poems I sent her. At least I was consistent. It was a wild idea for New Year's, but since she didn't have any plans, I figured it would be worth a chance. If nothing else, she could go to her appointments, and then go out on the town if she wanted.

Thirty-Two

THE FEW DAYS after Christmas were restless ones for me. I could hardly look at Jamie. She must have figured out that it was me who sent her the goodies, but she never lead on that she knew. Two days before New Year's Eve, she asked if she could leave early on Wednesday. She said something about taking her kids to their dad's, then a doctor's appointment for her mother. How could I argue with that? She had an extra jump in her step, and I figured that she had written me off.

But now I was in too deep. There'd be no retreating. I'd set the stage, done my homework, and had a good plan. I would see the plan through, come what may. It just might work, or I'd fall flat on my face.

"Sure, you can leave early. Happy New Year." At almost one o'clock she left the office. She had on a pair of velvet, low cut navy pants and a red silk blouse. She never smirked or winked, like she knew it was me. She must have thought it was someone else. Whatever the case, I finished working, closed the office early, and headed off to the Microtel Inn.

I discreetly approached the "makeover" counter at ten to

five and handed a note to the woman at the counter. "Please give this to the cute blonde getting the makeover."

Your knees are weak, your face is neat
See Santa where the bubbles warm feet.
Wear your suit, chap your seat,
Don't be shy because today we meet.

I rushed through the men's locker room, changed my clothes, and packed a bag with small bottles of champagne, extra towels, and red grapes. Thank goodness it wasn't busy. There were a few kids in the pool and a few parents gathered around the edge. In the corner of the poolroom was the whirlpool, which was the size of a two-car garage. It was vacant. I took off my shirt, turned the bubbled timer on 30 minutes, and poured a paper cup of champagne. I had to be sneaky with the champagne and glasses; there were signs all over the place warning "no glass containers." It tasted good, so I poured another. My back was to the locker room, my face to the clock. Self-doubt seeped into my thoughts. This was stupid. I shouldn't have done this. I should have been more direct in my note to her. I should have told her who I was. Bah!

The whirlpool stopped churning. It was 25 after five and she should have been done with her makeover by then. She should have been next to me in the whirlpool. Footsteps stopped next to me and I glanced over. The feet were heavy, knuckled, and hairy. How could I have missed that in Gaylord? Jamie, with hairy, knuckled feet? No, they belonged to a middle-aged balding man who turned the bubbler back on and hopped in the other end. I nodded to him, and slammed another cup of bubbly. This was awkward. With only one small bottle of champagne left and too much time elapsed, I decided to leave.

I pulled a towel out of the bag, sat on the edge, and reached for my shirt. Someone caught my wrist in her hand and said, "Is that you, Santa?"

"Well hello, Jaim, what are you doing here?" I noticed the purple suit, the long legs, dimpled smile, and her sweet voice.

"Ha-ha. I'm supposed to meet someone at the whirlpool."

"Mind if I wait with you?" She looked absolutely wonderful. She glowed.

"Please, stay. When my date gets here you can leave."

"You look fantastic," I said.

"Thank you."

"So who are you meeting here?"

"My secret admirer."

"Do tell—want something to drink while you wait?"

"Sure. What d'ya have?"

"*Shampoo, pour vous.*"

"Oh *Ouis, ouis.*" I handed her a paper cup, and the hairy man across the whirlpool got up and left.

"Was that your secret admirer?"

"I hope not; I'm not into fat, balding men. I like the young, studly kinds like you."

"So where is he?"

"I don't know. Strange, I received this mysterious note that I should meet him where the 'bubbles warm feet and chap my seat,' something like that. This man is very creative, but I almost didn't understand where that might be." She reached into the bag, poured another cup, and pulled out the grapes. With each little sip, she licked her lips. She plucked the grapes from the stems with strong, two-tone nails, and dropped them into her painted, full lips. I wanted to kiss her right there, but I didn't want it to spoil the blackjack game. Seduction is so much fun.

"How long do you want to stay here?"

"I don't know; I'd hate to disappoint him. By the way, what are you doing here?"

"Me?"

"Hello? Who else would it be?" She moved closer to me, and her foot stroked the inside of my ankle.

"I was supposed to meet someone too."

"Who's that?"

"This cute blonde I work with. She has the prettiest deep green eyes and a kind and tender heart. On New Year's Eve she skated out of work early to take her poor mother to the doctor."

"Really? Sounds intriguing!"

"Oh yes. I'd like to meet her mother. I want to see if she's as cute as her daughter."

"So where is she?"

"I don't know. Maybe she had a better offer."

"She's foolish."

"He's foolhardy."

"More champagne, please."

"That's it. Cocktail hour is over." Both bottles were empty. She sipped a few more times and poured what was left in the cup into the whirlpool. "Want to blow off our dates and have some dinner?"

"Sure. My knees are knocking, anyway."

"From what?"

"The massage, silly."

"How was it?"

"Oh, it was awesome. They really know how to make you feel good. Just amazing. I could feel the tension just ooze out of me. You should try it sometime."

"Sounds like fun. Lord knows I have plenty of tension." I

handed her a towel and took her hand. She stepped out of the hot tub, dripping wet. I picked up my bag, slipped on a pair of sandals, and walked her to the locker room.

"Meet you in the hallway."

Twenty minutes later she strolled out of the locker room, dressed to the nines in a short black cocktail dress. She could have stopped traffic. "Wow, you look incredible. Let me see you." I took her hand, lifting it over her head and giving her a quick twirl.

"Thank you. I wanted to impress this mystery man who was sending me all those nice things."

"I'll vouch for him, and say that you look incredible. What are you hungry for?"

"Food. I'm famished."

"Me too. They have a nice restaurant down the hall. Want to try it?"

"Sure."

We walked down the hallway, past the pool, spa and salon. We didn't need directions to the restaurant—we were drawn to it like rats to the Pied Piper. We smelled the food, and heard the band and the clatter of plates and silverware. Couples were laughing, dancing, and having fun.

"Reservation for Johanson."

"Right this way, sir." I let Jamie go first, and put a hand on her waist as she passed. She smelled like a waterfall in the springtime. After I pushed in her chair and handed her the small bundle of flowers that I had delivered, the waiter took our drink orders.

"When did you make reservations?" she pried.

"Why, a long time ago."

"Gutsy move, Mr. Johanson."

"Why's that?"

"I don't know. Seems like you've thought of everything. Seems like you're really trying to impress me."

"Is it working?"

"Yes, yes."

"Tell me something, though. You've also planned ahead—the outfit, the heels. You look wonderful. Why would you expect to wear that after a massage and a makeover? Did you have plans for tonight? You never knew that you were going to meet your secret admirer until that note came to you in the makeover."

"Call it a woman's intuition."

"I see. I've heard of that. That allows you get away with murder, doesn't it?"

"Mass murder. Serial murders."

"Yikes. Would you like to dance?"

"Love to."

I pushed back my chair and took her hand. Several steps later we were on the dance floor arm in arm, dancing to a generic version of Chris Issac's "Wicked Game." It was a wicked game we were living. Wicked, that we were setting up the company for a fall. Wicked, that we were going to ruin some people's careers over it. Wicked, that Scott died in the mess.

I wasn't wicked, having her so close to me. I liked the way she moved, the smell of her perfume. It was slightly awkward at first—so close, so fast. I had never even kissed her, and now our faces were only inches apart. "You dance divine," I tried to break the ice.

"Isn't it divinely? '*You dance divinely*'?" She blushed.

"I suppose you're right, an adverb, not an adjective. Anyway, I like the way you dance."

"No toe-stepping yet, either. A bonus."

"You're a good dancer not to step on these feet. I don't need water skis in the summer, my feet are so big."

"Come on, they're not that big."

"I think so. You've got to be self-conscious about something, don't you?"

"I suppose so."

"What are your insecurities?"

"Mr. Johanson, this is only our second date. I don't have any. Other than the way I dance."

"You dance divine."

"Divinely."

"Superb." I smiled.

"Superbly." She giggled. "And I bet you say that to all the girls."

"What girls? I'm as pure as the wind-driven snow."

"I doubt that."

"What? I have no skeletons in my closet—at least none with flesh on them."

"Gross."

"Maybe I should rephrase that. I haven't had any regrettable circumstances with the female gender within the last 10 years. How's that…better?"

"And what about before that?"

"Miss Pickett, this is only our second date, remember? We're still getting to know each other…Nothing *really* regrettable."

"You mean like sleep with a deer hunter," she asked.

"Ha, right. Those deer hunters are rough characters." The song gradually died, and the drinks were waiting for us at the table. I asked her how her Busch Light tasted, and remarked how strange it was that they didn't bring it still in the can.

"Is that what your last deer hunting lover drank? Busch in a can?"

"By the case. She loved it so much that she made furniture from the empty cases. End tables, coffee tables. Anytime she needed more change for the Laundromat, she'd merely return half of her living room set." Jamie nearly fell off her chair laughing.

Two more rounds of drinks and 90 minutes later, we went through the buffet line, which was set up on the dance floor. We talked of our goals, our families, and our goals for our families. We spoke of our taste in music, movies, and our likeness for revenge novels. Tentatively, we agreed to take in some plays or see a concert. We never discussed the business, our working arrangement, or Surety Guarantee, which was just fine. Time raced along. The next thing I knew we were dancing, drinking more champagne, and had those silly noise-makers in our mouths—the kind that have a paper tongue that unfurls when blown. She poked me in the eye with hers. My aim wasn't as good. I shot horrible, or "horribly," Jamie corrected. "I hope you shoot ducks better than you do that noisemaker."

"I wish I could say that I am a better shot. Must be the alcohol tonight. I'm losing my touch."

At 11:45 the crowd was getting restless. There was more yelling and louder laughter than before. Several women were slapping their knees with laughter, and swayed slightly as they walked to the ladies room. Most of the men had their top shirt buttons undone and their sleeves rolled up. A waiter dropped off more glasses of champagne, but Jamie ran to the ladies room. "Don't be long or you'll miss the big countdown."

"Oh I won't miss it."

I sat there, amidst the mass of humanity, watching that dopey tradition of the ball falling in Times Square on television. Jamie made it back just in time for the traditional lighting of the New Year, and of course, a kiss. I wasn't sure how she'd react to it all, so I thought I'd peck her on the lips. That didn't quite do it for her. She wanted much more, so we kissed and kissed, there in our little booth to the sounds of *Auld Lang Syne*.

"Happy New Year, Jaim."

"Let's hope it's the best one yet."

"If we're together it will be."

"Together we will be." She kissed me again, passionately, heartily. I tried to keep up with her, but she seemed ravenous—like a hungry animal gnawing at sustenance. I kissed her, strong, and squeezed her wrist. Only six months ago we were strangers. Six minutes ago we hadn't even held hands, or kissed. We crossed several hurdles with flying colors. We had spent six hours together but it felt like six minutes. Heck, we had worked together for six months without as much as a disagreement. She made me happy and I made her smile. The first five minutes of the New Year were incredible. I didn't want the evening to end, but then again, I knew eventually it would. To avoid an awkward ending, I left.

"I'll be right back. Don't go away." I pushed away from the booth and walked toward the men's room. Before I ducked inside, I stole one last glance. She sat there, legs crossed, as usual, with those shapely calves bobbing in and out of her heel. My, she looked good—good enough to eat. I grabbed our waiter, handed him $20 with instructions to hand her an envelope in five minutes. "No problem, sir, and thank you."

I found my coat in the coat rack, the little beach bag, and walked out of the restaurant, leaving Jamie all by herself.

Thirty-Three

SOME WOULD SAY that my actions weren't very becoming of a gentleman. Some would say that I was a coward. I suppose that under both analyses, I was wrong for leaving her the way I did. For laughs, though, I pictured the waiter with the envelope still in his little black pouch, driving home, reading my poem and chuckling like mad: "Ooops! Sorry sir, but thanks for the $20." I imagined Jamie there, wondering where I was. If the waiter never delivered the envelope, she'd have to wait till January 2 to see if I was all right, and by then she could probably care less.

I sat there, naked, in a Jacuzzi. A pair of fat candles cast flickering shadows on the remote controls—one for the stereo, the other for the television. A giant glass of carbonated water sat on a cork coaster, sweating. I sweated. It was hot in there, but it was a better departure than trying to give Jamie an awkward goodnight kiss amidst the mass of people. I never was a very good closer. The big insurance cases slipped through my fingers. My forte was the mom and pop style accounts—I had a knack for convincing them they were better off with me than somebody else. Same thing with Jamie; I would look foolish asking her if she wanted to rent a room and screw like rabbits, but I could throw my cards on the table and let her decide for herself what she wanted to do. "Probably better off this way," I lamented.

I turned off the television and turned up the stereo—flipping the compact disk player from "random" to "select." Revel's "*Bolero*" was up. *Rat-ta-ta-tat. Rat-ta-ta-tat went the snares.* It was 1 a.m. now and still no phone call from Jamie. She must have rebuffed my invite. It was too much too soon. At least I could apologize when I saw her again at work. At least I could say my invite was gutsy—like nothing I've ever done, like nothing she'd ever seen before. It was a classic case of "nothing ventured..."

I heard a card glide through the electronic channel on the hallway side of the door. I heard the tumblers disengage, and the handle turn ever so slowly. The light from the hallway illuminated the entry to the room. Her body was a curvy silhouette on heels—flowers dangling upside down from her painted nails. She stepped across the threshold without saying a word—black patent leathers gracefully stepping on the bed of rose petals I placed there hours before. The waiter did his job and delivered my last poem and the extra room key to the "cute blonde at my table." She must have liked my poem, my invite, and the notion of taking our relationship to the next level.

I slunk into the deepest part of the Jacuzzi, so that only my head and feet were exposed. *The piccolos were swooning, the snares rat-ta-ta-tat.* It was slightly embarrassing, yet intoxicatingly exciting. We didn't speak, until she sat down on the edge, tracing figure-eights across the water's surface with her long, slender fingers.

"I thought you'd never make it."

"I thought you got mugged in the men's room."

"I'm sorry. I should have asked you up here the old-fashioned way."

"How's that?"

"You know."

"No, I don't."

"Maybe my note wasn't such a bad idea after all. You're here, aren't you?"

"Maybe the old-fashioned way would have worked, if you had the guts to ask me." She took off her watch and set it on the edge of the Jacuzzi, next to the candles, then plunged her hand wrist-deep into the water. She found my feet, and then walked her index and middle finger up my ankle. *Oboes joined the fracas, and the snares louder, rat-ta-ta-tat.*

"My invite was very original, very romantic. It was gutsy, too."

"Okay, I confess. You've really won some brownie points. Now how are you going to talk me into joining you?"

"I don't want to talk you into anything you don't want to. But I will ask you if you'd like a drink. Sparkling water, Jaim?"

"That sounds good." I turned slightly, found a glass and the bucket of ice, and poured the glass full. She took the glass, raised it to her lips, and had a long, satisfying drink. "Mmm, that hits the spot. I think I'm getting chilled."

"It's warm in here."

"Ha, that's how you're going to talk me into joining you. You're going to talk me right out of these panties aren't you?"

"Pretty clever, huh?"

"It's no wonder you sell so much insurance—you can talk an Eskimo into buying snow. Are you going to watch me get undressed?"

"With pleasure." I grabbed the remote, sat up ever so slightly, and turned up the volume on the stereo. *By now the clarinets joined the oboes, and the snares gathered pace, rat-ta-ta-tat.*

She turned her back to me and reached under her blonde mane to the top of her black dress. Slowly she lowered the zipper, exposing her black, snug bra. She turned, now facing me, and wiggled her round hips, letting the black dress fall in a crumpled heap to the floor. "My, my, Jaim. Aren't you amazing?"

"You like what you see?" She spun again, with her arms over her head, showing off her black bra, tangas, and heels. No stockings, garters or baloney, just a beautiful woman in sexy black underwear.

"Oh yes. You're beautiful. I'll picture you like this at the office."

"Dream on, mister. This will never happen at the office." She turned again, with her back to me, unbuttoned her bra, stepped out of her tangas, and sat on the side of the Jacuzzi. Before sliding into the water, she flipped her heels across the room. "By the way, I have a confession too."

"What's that?"

"Your secret plans for tonight weren't so secret." She was sitting next to me, hands exploring my inner thigh. I had my arm around her shoulder, enjoying the feeling of her nails on my loins. She purred.

"How?"

"You never asked where my sister worked, did you?"

"No, why?"

"If you're going to pull off a romantic evening, with secret notes, massages and makeovers, you need to find out if anyone knows you."

Baritone saxophone, oboe, clarinet and rat-ta-ta-tat.

"Let me guess, your sister works here."

"She's the manager downstairs...She's the one you talked to when you called in the reservations."

"Lovely...an inside job."

"Don't hold it against me."

"I'd like to do more than that..." Our eyes met in a gimlet stare—mesmerized by the moment, fixed by the notion of impending bliss. She sat up, straddled me, and held me against her. My hands found her beautiful breasts, barely poking their noses out of the bubbling swirl. They were like treasure—firm, not too big, with areolas as big as silver dollars. She kissed me deeply, then guided me into her warm, moist channel. I felt her take me, all the way, in one deep thrust. She arched her back, daring me to sample the Jacuzzi nectar dripping off her pert nipples. I obliged, heartily. She moaned, I groaned; we were stroking in unison now, with our eyes shut and mouths agape with pleasure. I wanted that moment to last forever.

Oboes, trumpets, tubas, they all joined in. It was that climactic part of the score when all the instruments bellow and wail in synchronized harmony.

The timing couldn't have been more perfect.

Thirty-Four

THE SUBPOENA HAD two parts to it; one was a notice to appear at the deposition, and the other an order to bring all the documents I had that were relevant to the Buxton matter. Nikki said the deposition was necessary to learn what I knew about the case. She also gave me some advice about how to answer questions. "If you don't know for sure, say so. If you're guessing, say so. It's okay to say 'I don't recall.' Keep your answers simple. If they ask you what time it is, you say, 'day time.' Understand?"

"Yes, I understand."

"Oh, and one other thing, don't bring a bunch of extra paperwork with you."

"What do you mean?"

"Don't show up with a lot of extra documents—you know, policies, notes, cancellations, stuff like that. The plaintiff's lawyer will keep asking you questions until he has those documents in his possession, and they might somehow incriminate you."

"I don't know how, but I understand."

"All right then, I'll see you tomorrow."

"Who's going to be there, anyway?"

"Buxton, the agency he works for, Tadrick, and all their lawyers."

"When is Tadrick's turn in the barrel?"

"Right before yours."

"Okay, I assume that you're going to be there...for their deposition?"

"Sure I will."

"All right, I want you to pound away at him. He knows I sent those letters. He gave me approval. I faxed them to his home office fax machine. He told me to write whatever I wanted, as long as it helped save the business."

"Did you ever talk to your assistant about Tadrick reading those letters?"

"Yes, but she didn't remember."

"Then how can I pin him down?"

"Do your best, at least put his denial on record."

"What's up?"

"Nothing. Why?"

"Nothing. I'll see you tomorrow morning at 11."

I hung up the phone and pulled out all my notes from the Buxton matter. There wasn't a lot to it. Or maybe there was.

I had lists and lists of people that I sent letters to. It all started with the "introductory" letter, and all 2,000 households got those. Then, there was the second letter, where I stated, *"your old agent could have given you all the discounts, but he chose not to. It could have cost you hundreds of dollars a year."* Almost everybody got that one.

From there, I sent out the "surly" letters, which Tadrick gave me the "implied" permission to send. Those worried me, because they had some fairly strong language in them:

"Your old agent didn't give you all the discounts because he was more concerned with collecting more commission...He wasn't doing his job, plain and simple. If you want me to save you money, please give me a call."

More than two-thirds of his clients received that one.

And then there was the letter that I sent to everyone that cancelled their policy. I figured most of them had left me for Buxton, and were waiting for a refund check. *"Your refund check should be arriving soon, but I hope you understand that your old agent owes you many, many more dollars. He cheated you out of a fair price, our best value. Surety Guarantee is glad that he left the agency force, and now is the problem of some other company."* That was really dumb. The lawyers were going to have a field day with that one. I must have sent that letter out to at least a couple hundred households.

I had all the records of the people who received each letter. Some of them got all four. Some of them only got three. Everybody got at least the first one, and most of them got the second. Ted and his band of goons were going to sodomize me.

I told Jamie about the situation and she frowned. She never hesitated to show her emotions, and I loved her for it. I didn't need to guess if she was happy or sad, confused or mad. She was angry when Tadrick harassed her, and disappointed when she couldn't help me with the letters he allegedly forgot to read. Through it all she was strong and independent, yet had a soft and sweet side. Through life's ups and downs she was smooth and feminine, graceful and attractive. I liked being close to her; I liked to be with her now more than ever.

Now that we'd slept together, I had to wonder how it would affect our working relationship. So far so good. It was only the first day back to work and nothing had changed. She still answered incoming calls, talked to the clients about their billing issues, and balanced the books. The only difference was the way we looked at each other. There was more eye contact, more flirtatious eyebrows and even a wink or two throughout the hours. At least for today, we could work together, with the lusty thoughts of our first encounters still fresh on our minds. At the end of the day, she patted me on the ass and wished me luck at the deposition.

The following morning I made my way to Ted's attorney's office, a block away from the Isabella County Courthouse. The receptionist directed me to the waiting room, where stacks of periodicals sat on fine cherry end-tables next to luxurious leather chairs studded with bronze rivets. Nikki told me not to say anything to any of the attorneys involved—in the waiting room or otherwise, because they would have a way of using it against me. No need to worry about that—I was the only one waiting. Apparently Tadrick's deposition took longer than what they anticipated.

Shortly before noon, I heard commotion in the hallway. Men were talking loudly, jingling change in their pockets, and making the warped hardwood floors creak and groan. Tadrick walked past with his lawyer, who I assume was Kyle Holbine. Ted and three other men were next; I guessed they were his attorney and his agency's contingent. Pulling up the rear was my attorney, Nikki, who struck me as far different that what I imagined after our phone conversation. She was much younger than I had thought, rumpled, and didn't exactly instill confidence. After a brief introduction, she told me that my deposition would be after lunch.

"Come on, let's go have a bite to eat. Surety Guarantee is buying. I'll fill you in on the case as we go."

"Let me grab my coat."

I put on my topcoat and goulashes, then followed her outside into the cold, wintry air. Another light snow was falling—it seemed that we were stuck in that rut of winter where it snows every day and the sun doesn't shine for weeks on end. Nikki didn't wear a coat, and sloshed through winter's slop in dumpy little heelless shoes. Dandy. I hoped she'd be more prepared for my case than winter's most obvious by-product.

"Well, Larry, it seems that this case will boil down to a situation of credibility—your word, Tadrick's, and Buxton's. Who will the jury believe?"

"What do you mean?"

"Buxton is convincing, but so is Tadrick."

"What's the issue?"

"There are other issues, but the big one in Buxton's case against you is the letters you sent out—who got them, who knew about it, and why you sent them."

"What did Tadrick say?"

"A lot of his testimony today was about the case Surety Guarantee has against Buxton. I didn't ask him much about it because a lot of it didn't have to do with you. I did ask him about the letters you sent out and he denies everything about them. He said that he never read any of your letters. He said he never gave you the authority to send them, either."

"Just like that, huh?"

"I'm afraid so."

"Now what?"

"Now it's your turn."

We stopped at the doorstep of the restaurant, and I wasn't sure if she meant that it was my turn to open the door, my turn to be deposed, or my turn to tell her what I knew about the case. I grabbed the door and yanked it open. She shuffled in, nearly slipping on the wet tiled floor in the process.

We were eating at the Judge's Chambers, Buxton's brother-in-law's restaurant. Sure enough, Ted was sitting four tables down and an aisle over, in the smoking lounge. He was crouched over his mug of beer, apparently listening to the advice of his attorney. Most of the time Ted was smiling, which made me even more nervous. Although he laughed at everything, I could read him when things were going bad. They must have thought their case was proceeding well. He reveled in his good fortune.

I ordered a bowl of chili, and Nikki had a cheeseburger and french-fries. When I heard the laughter from Ted's table I lost my appetite. All I could see was Ted's brother stirring fresh spit in my chili, while Ted's team of lawyers pulled my limbs from their sockets with a team of draft horses.

When our meals arrived, a smart-looking black man in a dark suit and horn-rimmed glasses introduced himself as Kyle Holbine. Nikki had already met him at Tadrick's deposition.

"Hello, Larry, we spoke on the phone last week."

"Of course…I remember. Hello, Kyle."

"I'm sure Nikki will tell you all about the issues here. All I wanted to do is introduce myself."

"Well, nice to meet you, Kyle. How's the case going so far?"

"It's going. There are a lot of issues here, as Nikki will tell you. The complexion of the case will revolve around your testimony, frankly. Tadrick simply verified the facts as we know them—Buxton sent out the letters to his old clients, then wrote them new policies. We all know that's a direct violation of his contract. Our case against Buxton is virtually watertight, but the case he has against us and you is a completely different matter."

"We were just discussing that, Kyle," Nikki chimed in, wiping ketchup from the corner of her mouth. I pushed the chili away from my placemat and crossed my arms. Kyle understood our body language and sauntered off to Tadrick's table, barely saying goodbye.

"It's still your turn," Nikki looked my way. "What do you know about the letters?"

I told her everything, and she shook her head. "Why did you word the letters that way?" she asked, dipping her Kaiser in ketchup.

"Tadrick gave me a blank check to do whatever I wanted, that's why. He said I should write whatever I wanted, as long as it saved the policies."

"He's already denied that."

"I knew he would. They're all liars, plain and simple."

"Just tell the truth when it's your turn on the hot seat. I'll pay for this one, and put it on my expense account to Surety Guarantee."

She must have been a rookie for thinking that she'd impress me by having the company pay for lunch on her expense account. For all I knew, she was a rookie. It would be the Surety Guarantee way—hire the best lawyers to pursue their cases, but assign the rookies to the claimants that needed counsel. It was just another example of how shortsighted they were—a good lawyer could save their claimants money by providing a competent defense. Kyle was sharp and experienced, my lawyer was young, inexperienced, and struck me as a wet dishrag.

My deposition was my first experience with the legal system, other than a few speeding tickets. All I could do was remember Nikki's advice: "I don't recall. I don't recall." As she had predicted, there were several people in the conference room when I got there. Some were seated at the long, wooden table, while Tadrick and Kyle Holbine whispered in the corner with their hands covering their mouths. Ted and I exchanged "hellos" and small talk about the recent college basketball games on television. The court reporter was there too, feeding a fresh roll of coiled paper through the back of her machine. For fifteen minutes we stood there in purgatory—not getting started, not doing anything. Apparently one of the lawyers was on the phone in another office, and didn't think anything of making the rest of us wait. Finally he waltzed in, without as much as an apology. The court reporter swore me in and we got started. Ted's lawyer was first. He was a twerpy looking fellow with ratlike features. He twitched his nose as if he was smelling bits of gerbil food in his cage.

I had to recite my name and address, my affiliation with Surety, and how long I had been an agent. So far, so good. Then he asked what kind of awards I had earned, and what kind of sales I produced. In a roundabout way, I think he was setting me up for something, so I really didn't brag about my accomplishments. Better to be modest than thump your chest like Scott used to do. Sure enough, I think Ted's lawyer was trying to make me out to be a money-grubbing scoundrel—the kind of guy that would slit his friend's throat for a policy or two. Never mind that it was his client who was stealing the policies. Never mind that the company was the one who forced his client to do those things.

After a half-hour interrogation, he arrived at the business of the letters. He had them all, labeled with little thumbnails in a three-ring binder. The second letter captured his attention—the one that stated Ted didn't give all the discounts. "Who did you send these letters to?"

"Almost everybody," I confessed.

"What do you mean, almost everybody?"

"Almost all of Ted's 2,000 policyholders."

"How do you know that Mr. Buxton didn't give his clients all the discounts?"

"I didn't, but I can tell you that Mr. Tadrick read the letter and gave me the authority to send out whatever I wanted, as long as it helped to save the policies."

"Mr. Johanson, I would like to remind you that you are under oath, and that you are required to tell the truth. Mr. Tadrick has denied that, and he said that you sent the letters out on your own. For the record, did he know about the letters, all of them?"

"Absolutely. He knew about them. He read the first two—that's for sure. Scott was there; the two of them were in my office in Mt. Pleasant."

"Who is Scott?"

"Scott was our District Coordinator."

"*Was* your coordinator?"

"Yes. He died in a boating accident last fall."

"I understand that the alleged accident happened while you were there. Is that correct?"

"Yes I was, but what does that have to do with the case today? And yes, it was an accident." I looked at Nikki, who gestured to the lawyer to move along.

It worked, the lawyer rummaged through his papers. He then queried, "How did you know that Mr. Buxton could have saved his clients several hundred dollars a year?"

"I didn't."

"How did you know that Mr. Buxton wasn't doing his job?"

"I didn't."

"How do you know that Surety is glad that he doesn't represent them anymore?"

"I don..."

"How do you know that he is a problem for the new company he represents?"

"I don't know that either. All I was trying to do was save the policies, and if I had to do it by being less than truthful, then so be it. I had Tadrick's blessing. I had Tadrick's blessing and that's all there is to it. I had to do what I had to do." It was grueling. Nikki just sat there. She could have tossed me a life-ring; she could have interrupted the proceedings.

The lawyer who represented Ted's new agency was next. This was the jerk who made the whole gang wait for his important phone call. Half the time I was answering questions he was at the other end of the table, reading some trade journal. He cut right to the point, "Mr. Johanson, can you tell me the definition of libel?"

He had me dead to rights, and I didn't know how to answer it. I looked at my watch. I heard the clock on the wall *tick, tick, tick.* The court reporter was silent. My stomach churned. "Excuse me." I pushed the chair back and stood. The lawyer who asked me the question raised a fuss, but I came back with "Hey, we waited 15 minutes for you. I'll be back in 10." Nikki stood as well, and followed me down the hall toward the men's restroom.

"What is it?" she whispered, clutching my right arm.

"Nothing, I just had to go to the bathroom."

"You do know what libel is, don't you?"

"Of course I do, that's why we're here, isn't it?"

"Yes, of course," she countered, with a confused look on her face. "You don't want to admit that the libel was intentional, right?"

"If the libel was intentional, this whole thing wouldn't be covered under my business owner's policy. I wouldn't have you here to provide me with a defense, and I wouldn't have the company pay for the damages...right, counselor?"

"Right...right." Nikki was still confused, and the concept of me intentionally harming Ted seemed to be over her head. She let go of my arm, and I opened the door to the men's room.

"I don't recall" how the rest of the deposition went; I staggered out of there hoping that they'd settle for something less than my policy limits.

Thirty-Five

I REALLY HATE winter. It's a constant case of trying to stay busy in order to stave off depression. The days are so short, the nights so long. As much as I hate watching television, I can't help it during the winter.

If nothing else, though, it is a good time to sell insurance. People are home at night, and willing to talk to us about their insurance program. They don't go on vacations during the winter either, unless it's to take out their snowmobiles, and we have excellent rates on those.

At least we did have excellent rates on snowmobiles until Surety had the bright idea to raise the rates on those too. Suddenly our rates were higher than just about everybody else's. The most we could do was keep in contact with our existing policyholders and hope they wouldn't leave us. As much as we tried to write a few new policies, the rates were prohibitively high.

Through the winter months, while the lawyers talked about both cases, we seemed to have a bit of a respite from losing so many people to Buxton's new agency. My checks from the

Mt. Pleasant office held their own, and Jamie kept working with me.

When her sons spent the weekend with their father, I spent the night at her house, or she came to mine. We had great times. We went to concerts, plays and movies. We tried eating at different restaurants within an hour's drive of Mt. Pleasant or Big Rapids. I even took her ice fishing and cross-country skiing—just to stave off the winter blues. We were having so much fun together, I forgot all about how long and boring winter can be.

One afternoon after skiing, we came back to my house. I checked the answering machine, hung up my heavy clothes and brought in an armful of firewood. Jamie was already in the shower by the time the kindling flickered. I strolled to the kitchen, poured a little brandy in a snifter, and then poured a glass of wine for my girl. Outside, the day's last chickadees dive-bombed the bird feeder—sorting through the sunflower shells in the hopes of finding one with meat still on the inside. It was mild stimulation—the drink, the warm fire, the cold outside. I heard the shower stop, and the cupboards in the bathroom close. She knew where to find the towels, and made herself at home.

A moment later she was in the leather swivel-chair next to me—towel wrapped around her head like a turban, and a "housecoat" that looked like something my grandmother used to wear. I didn't say anything.

"So, what do you want to do about dinner?" she asked.

"I don't know. I'm getting kind of hungry though."

"I could whip up some goulash or something." She got out of the chair and glided to the kitchen in one graceful swing. I heard her wineglass bump the counter; she found the glass I poured her. "Have any garlic bread?"

"Is goulash and garlic bread good for a sore back?" I complained. She popped her head back into the den, wineglass in hand. "Yeah, right here." I gestured to the small of my back.

"Too much skiing today?"

"I suppose. Maybe a warm shower would help. Check the freezer door for the garlic bread. There's hamburger in the freezer too, but for Pete's sake, I can cook dinner."

Jamie's cell phone rang. She ran to the front door and pulled it out of her purse. I watched as she curled her lip when she recognized the incoming number on her phone's display. Her mother.

"Hi, Mom." I heard her talk. I watched her listen, tucking the wraps of her towel behind her ears. Jamie is so funny. The only thing she tells her mother is "Uh-huh...Really...Wow... Sure...Uh-huh." Her mother is nice enough but she likes to talk, but not necessarily listen. I decided to take a shower while Jamie lost herself in the conversation.

My bathroom is adjacent to my bedroom and has a walk-in closet on the right and a shower on the left, with mirrors all around. If I peeked out of the shower, I could see what was on the television in the mirror and see the bed by looking through the crack of the shower curtain. It's handy when I'm late for work and I still want to catch the highlights of the game, the stock market recaps, or watch the latest weather report. Men are so simplistic.

Jamie and I were still in that stage of our relationship where we couldn't see any faults in each other. I liked the way she ate, raised her kids, cooked, kept her house, and paid attention to me. I tried my best to be a good listener, thoughtful, and always lending a sympathetic ear to her worries. We had fun together and laughed a lot.

Jamie was raised on a farm in the northern Lower Peninsula where she was the youngest of three kids. Just as her mother warned her, she fell for the first man she met. Her sister was a little more blunt; she said that Jamie "would fall for the first swinging organ that paid attention to her." They both were right; he became her husband while she was a freshman at Central Michigan University in Mt. Pleasant. They were wed shortly after she discovered that she was pregnant. The marketing degree would have to wait.

Her older sister never did go to college but married a man who worked for the power company. He got promoted and they wound up in Mt. Pleasant, and that's how she made it to the Microtel Inn. Jamie's older brother left the farm after high school, and wound up going to college in Detroit. He got married early and had a child who was killed accidentally by the neighbors. His two-year-old rode his scooter down the sidewalk, behind the shrubs, and into the path of the minivan backing down the neighbor's driveway. The resulting insurance settlement, and her life's experiences, left Jamie skeptical of men, hesitant to develop trust, and somehow curious of the insurance business.

Anyway, I left the bathroom door open so the mirrors wouldn't fog up. Warm water spattered against my sore back, and I felt it ease the muscles. When I peered through the crack in the shower curtain, I saw Jamie pass by the open bathroom door—still wearing that dreadful housecoat, tucking the towel around her head, and continuing to mumble nothing but small talk. Very small talk. I rinsed my hair and grabbed the bar of soap, but it fell to the floor. I picked up the soap and began scrubbing, stealing a glance through the crack in the curtain. Jamie was sitting on my bed, facing the mirror on the bedroom bureau. She was bent over, rummaging through her overnight bag on the floor. I put the bar of soap to my face, and ears, then gradually lathered the rest of the necessities.

Jamie was facing the shower now, shaking out a black silk stocking. Slowly, she drew the nose of the stocking over her pointed foot then eased it up her shapely calve. Suddenly I forgot all about my sore back. It was fun to watch her. I felt like a voyeur. When she stood up, she turned to the bureau mirror, and all I could see was the back of her housecoat, and her blonde hair underneath the bath towel. She pivoted one way, then the next, on pointed heels and silk stockings. She was modeling for the mirror, still talking to the phone. I turned off the shower, grabbed my towel and nonchalantly acted like I hadn't seen a thing. Jamie was out of sight now, but I hear her tell her mom goodbye, and "Love you too." I found my towel, swabbed a circle on the steamed mirror, and wrapped it around my waist. Suddenly Jamie was behind me, wearing the housecoat and the towel on her head. Her face was warm on my back, and her hands moved under my arms to my chest. She asked me "How was your shower?"

"Good...good."

"How's your back? Any better?"

"Let me check..." I put my hands on my hips and leaned backwards. "I'm still in severe pain," I said facetiously.

"Aw, you poor thing. Here, let me help you." She was still behind me, rubbing my shoulders with her long fingers. I stood there for a moment or two, watching her working me in the mirror. Great fun. Before I knew it, she opened her housecoat and was pressed against me. She nibbled at my shoulder blades while rubbing my chest and stomach. "Now, doesn't that feel good?"

"Oh yes...Don't stop."

"Not here, look at me."

She spun me around, removed the towel from her head and showed me what she was wearing—stockings, black panties, a sleek push up bra, and a snappy black bowtie. My hands found her hips, just above the silk hem on her panties, and I pulled her toward me. Our lips met like hands clapping, our mouths like a firm handshake. I felt her hot breath on my neck and her silky bra against my chest. I ripped the dreadful housecoat from her and it fell to the carpeted bathroom floor. She was free, and hungry for more than just a little lip mashing in the bathroom. Her lips left my face, and traveled south to my neck, my ear lobes, my chest and navel. She unwrapped my towel then looked up at me; I couldn't help but smile. My hands stroked her hair, my fingers, each ear. She was awesome. I reached down, grabbed her by the arms and scooped her up. I had every intent of throwing her on the bed and returning the favors, but she stopped me fast.

"No, no..." she begged. "I want you right here. Come on, right here, right now."

I sat her on the bathroom countertop, covering her in a fusillade of kisses and nibbles, smelling her perfumed nape, hearing her bosom rise and fall with each excited gasp. I was between her legs, feeling her heels stroke my buttocks, pulling me toward her. I wanted that moment of carnal desire and intimacy to last forever. I wanted to keep her wanting, keep her begging. It wasn't long before I ripped her scant panties from her like peel from an orange, exposing her blond mound and succulent crevice. She looked so perfect, so luscious and inviting. I had to have her. I had to dive into her. I had to wait just a few more seconds.

"Come on. Take me, will you? Don't make me beg."

Maybe winter isn't so bad after all.

Thirty-Six

JAMIE AND I had a lot of sex that winter, and we came up with silly names for different scenarios. Safe sex was with the lights off. Voyeur sex was when we watched other people having it on television. Roadie sex was having it in the car. We never did have sex at the office, but we did flirt a lot. Heck, we did more than flirt. Jamie had a penchant for teasing me when I was on the phone or had clients at my desk. She made seductive gestures toward me when my hands were tied, so to speak. One of her favorite tricks was to lick her lips and wink at me. Every once and a while she'd flash her panties or her bra, but only when I had clients at my desk and couldn't do anything about it. It was every man's dream, or at least *my* dream, in my own demented way.

And there were lots of clients at my desk. The new Yellow Pages ads hit the streets and resulted in plenty of phone calls to our office. We were quoting and writing new policies like mad. In January, we sold 110 policies with Michigan Miners, five with Surety Guarantee. In February, we sold 98 with

Michigan Miners, 10 with Surety Guarantee. March, April, May and June were about the same—we sold 15 policies with Michigan Miners for every one with Surety Guarantee. All told, we put $330,000 of premium on Michigan Miners' books that netted $45,000 in commission. Jack's office was the big hitter—he netted $65,000 in new business commission. Gerry, Duck Hunter Dan, and Allison all had about the same as I did. And the strange thing about Duck Hunter Dan was that he no longer cheated. He didn't have to because Michigan Miners' rates were fair. All the incentive to cheat was gone--imagine that. Michigan Miners loved us. They never thought that we could grow that fast. They thought we were superheroes, and were talking to Jack, Allison and myself about forming three "districts"—east, central and west.

Life was good. My business turned the corner. In the spring, Jamie and I worked on her perennial garden, went to her sons' soccer games and went bike riding for miles. Finally, my life seemed to be falling into place.

Too bad Ted couldn't have been around to reap the fruit of our good fortune. In all reality, we were doing the same thing that he was, only we weren't getting caught. We were just as bad as he was, and if he ever found out about our arrangement, our goose was cooked.

One day in June, Tadrick showed up in Mt. Pleasant. I wasn't there, but Jamie told me all about his visit. He dropped off a flyer for the agent's convention that fall on Mackinac Island, and suggested that I attend the Series 6 and 63 courses scheduled for noon the next day. Insurance products tied to the stock market required the extra licensing. He made some small talk about our lack of production, and then he went too far. He stooped to a level that I knew he eventually would.

How else was I going to react when Jamie told me that he

pushed himself on her? When he told Jamie that he could do all sorts of good things for her career, for our rates in Isabella County? How else was I to react when he put his hands on her shoulders and invited her to his room at the Microtel Inn? Jamie flatly turned him down, and threatened to tell me about it. "You're only ruining his career and your job. If he closes this shop or gets fired, you're done."

I listened to the tape recording that Jamie made and couldn't believe my ears. That dirty son of a bitch. He had the gall to proclaim that he could control the rates. I'm glad Jamie told me about it, but I hated the sound of her voice when she rebuffed his advances.

"What's the matter, Jamie, don't you think I can help you? Huh?"

"Mr. Tadrick, you'd better leave me alone. I don't need your help."

"You're going to beg for my help when premium payments come up missing from the night deposit and Larry gets called onto the carpet."

"You're so scummy. You make me sick. I wouldn't let you touch me if you were the last man on earth."

"Come here, Jamie. You're so cute with that tear in your eye."

"Get away from me. No!"

"I'm not going to hurt you."

"Leave me alone or I'll scream bloody murder."

"Don't be a fool, Jamie. I can help you out or be your worst enemy."

"I'll take my chances."

"I'll see you tonight, room 240 at about 10, if you know what's good for you and your job."

"I'll take my chances." I heard footsteps at the office, the bell on the back door ring, and then the phone. Jamie answered it, but she sounded upset. I was irate.

It was five o'clock when Jamie told me about it. I raced to her house from an appointment and gave her a hug at the door. She was still crying when I got there, and her boys seemed quieter than normal. They sensed her pain and welcomed my arrival. We hugged for thirty, forty seconds at the door in a drizzly rain. I played the tape twice to make sure I didn't miss anything. Jamie finished making dinner while I sat in the living room and listened. Her boys set the table, without as much as a stern warning. My blood pressure rose and I could feel my ears getting red. What a scummy idiot. What a jerk.

I skipped dinner and called Jack on his cell phone. He was halfway from Petoskey to Mt. Pleasant on his way to take the securities licensing course that Tadrick thought I should attend. He agreed to meet at my office.

A few minutes later I opened the office. Stacks of messages were on my desk and I jumped right after them. Most of the people had issues with their claims. They hit deer or were involved in other car accidents. As an agent, you've got to hold your clients' hands sometimes. Some of the people had policies with Surety Guarantee and some of them had Michigan Miners. It really didn't matter to most folks what company they bought a policy from—they bought policies from Jamie and Larry, not from Surety Guarantee or Michigan Miners. I spent 45 minutes calling people back and putting out rhetorical fires. Almost everyone was home and eager to hear from me.

Between calls, my phone rang. Strange, I thought, that someone would be calling me at the office, after hours. It could have been Jack, or Jamie, or one of the people who weren't home. Not even close.

"Mr. Johanson? This is detective Plouf with the Michigan State Police in Sault Ste. Marie."

"Yes...what can I do for you?"

"We are still investigating Scott Husted's disappearance, and we have some additional questions for you."

"This thing isn't finished?" I asked.

"No, no far from it," he said gruffly.

"What can I do for you?"

"Do you plan on visiting Sault Ste. Marie anytime? We want you to come into the post and take a lie detector test."

"For what?"

"So we can rule out that Husted's disappearance wasn't intentional."

"I don't think that's a good idea."

"What do mean—that his disappearance wasn't intentional, or that you don't want to go on the box?"

"Both," I was stammering. "I mean, his disappearance was an accident, and I don't have to take a lie detector test to prove it."

"Does that mean you're not willing to come up here?"

"Oh, I'm willing, but not till duck season the first part of October."

"Answer me this, then." He breathed a sigh. I waited. "Some people have said that you hated him."

"What does that have to do with the fact that it was an accident?"

"Is it true?"

"I'm not going to answer that. And who told you?"

"Don't forget, I'm the one who's asking the questions."

"Detective, I'm very busy this evening. While I have you on the phone, why don't I give you a quote on your auto insurance?"

"Very funny. Have you been hunting with any other people from the insurance company?"

"No. They haven't asked, and I haven't volunteered. Listen, detective, you know it, and I know that you don't have squat on me. So leave me alone, will you?"

"I'll see you up north."

"Don't count on it."

Jack rolled in as I finished up the call. He picked up the flier for the agent's convention and rubbed his eyes. He looked like he had been through the wringer. It must have been a long day for him—selling policies, switching Surety Guarantee clients to Michigan Miners, and settling claims of his own.

"Hi pal," I said. "Thanks for stopping by. That was the state police. They still think there's something more to Scott's disappearance—like I had something to do with it, or I had something to gain by it. They wanted me to take a lie detector test. Can you believe it? I'm sorry—long drive?"

"Sure, I can believe it. The guy's just doing his job, but he doesn't have much to go on...everyone knows that. Watch, they'll call it an accident before long. They just want to see you get a little sweaty under the collar."

"I shouldn't let it bother me."

"I shouldn't let the drive bother me either, but it was bad enough. There were deer in the ditches all over the place. I had to slam on the brakes several times...almost wiped out. "

"No kidding. All this just to sell mutual finds."

"Yep. I'm going to be rich selling Surety Guarantee mutual funds some day." Jack had a sarcastic sense of humor.

"Don't forget to write when you get to the top. I'll be stuck here selling Michigan Miners."

"Christ, we'll all be selling Michigan Miners."

"Not if Tadrick finds out."

"Why do you say that?"

"Jack, I don't mean anything by it, but I've got to tell you that I've reached the end of the line with Tadrick. You've got to listen to this."

I pulled out the tape and played it. It didn't take long to hear, and Jack couldn't believe it either.

"Holy shit, man," he said, pacing from one end of the office to the other. "We could really string this guy up. I mean he could lose his job over this. *He should* lose his job..."

"I know. I know." We both stood there, shaking our heads. What a crummy outfit. I knew that Jack wanted something to eat and drink, so we left for the bar around the corner. A few minutes later Jack had a vodka tonic in one hand and a menu in the other. He peered over his bifocals, folding the menu back and forth, as if looking for something more delectable. He put away his glasses, then remarked about the agents convention on Mackinac Island.

"At least it'll be good time for a color tour."

"Early October, you mean?"

"Sure. Should be a great time to go for a drive—all the hardwoods ablaze. But I think we'll be lucky to be around when that happens."

"You mean we'll be former Surety Guarantee agents?"

"Sure, sure," he said.

"I guess we took that chance last December in Gaylord."

"We can't turn back now."

"I know. I wouldn't want to."

"Me either." Jack ordered a chicken breast sandwich, crossed his arms, and took another pull on his drink. I nursed my beer and really wanted his advice about what to do about Tadrick. We weighed our options. We could take the tape and go to the state executive, but he would do nothing with it. Tadrick was the state executive's hired gun; Tadrick did the dirty work that the executive couldn't. The tape could come back and bite us in the tail if they were going to fire us anyway. That was not an option.

"Why don't we send Jamie to his room and see if it helps our cause?" Jack always had a way of breaking a stressful situation with humor.

"Right," I said, laughing. "Come on, Jamie. Please? Take one for the team. That would go over like a fart in a church pew." We laughed again. Jack's food arrived and the conversation stopped. He pulled leaves of lettuce from the pile under the bun with his fork, and tucked them neatly inside his mouth, smacking his lips in the process. I watched him eat, hungrily, while I ordered another round of drinks. He seemed to be thinking, conniving, the way he always does. You don't get to be the best insurance salesman in the district by waiting for the phone to ring.

"You know, Larry, we could stop in and see Tadrick."

"For sex?"

"Want to flip a coin to see who goes first?" He winked at me.

"Ha. Ha. I don't want any part of that. I can't imagine getting anywhere near that loser."

"What would you do if we went there?"

"To his room?"

"What do you think? Of course to his room. You're starting to annoy me. You're acting like a little lapdog now."

"Sorry." He was right. I sat back in my chair and crossed my arms. "I'd like to beat the shit out of him…kill him. That's what I'd like to do if we went there."

"For coming on to your girl? You don't want to do that. I

mean that thing up in the Sault with Scott was an accident, right? Seriously injure someone and there's no calling it an accident. Plus, there's no way he'll go hunting with you. You don't want to really maim him for just coming on to your girl." He took another bite of lettuce, then cut his sandwich in three or four pieces.

"No, you're right. It was an accident up north—you know that. Even the police know it was. I don't want to kill Tadrick, but it seems that he's got to pay for all the anguish he's put us through. For all the arrogance he has. For the way he threatened Jamie, and said that he could help us out if he really wanted to."

"Sure. Don't get me wrong, I'm mad too…" He took another bite, and chewed with conviction. I got the feeling that he was weighing his options, and as he did it, he waved his fork around as if it was a baton. I felt like I was on the edge of my seat, waiting for some kernel of wisdom from the Apostle Jack. "Ah, forget it."

"Forget what?"

"If we do nothing with the tape, and use it later, it could really help us. Tadrick will eventually find out about Michigan Miners, and they'll fire us all. You never know though, that tape could help us."

"Yeah, we could keep the tape and I can still pound him into oblivion."

"No. Quit saying that, will you? That would be stupid, and then I'd have to send you letters in prison instead of calling you on the phone. Why don't we visit him and just rough him up a bit? Send him a little message."

"Okay…"

"You do the messing and I'll make sure everything goes our way."

"I'm going to beat him like a red-haired stepchild."

"No, no, no. You don't want to beat him; you want to deliver a message. Don't say a word. Just go in there and rough him up a bit—you know, punch him a few times. I'll watch the door. You ready?"

"Where are we going?" I asked, tossing a business card on the table. "He said 10 o'clock and it's only 8:45."

"We're going to K-Mart to buy a couple ski masks."

Thirty-Seven

We waited till 10:10 to knock on the door of room 240. Jack put his finger over the peephole. I was nervous and the ski mask made me sweat. We heard rustling inside, then footsteps that stopped at the door. I never heard a chain clink on the jamb inside. Don Tadrick swung the door wide wearing a cotton terry bathrobe. My shoulder hit him under the ribs, lifting him off his feet. We landed on the bed; he wailed like a newborn. I tossed a blanket over his head and neck. He flung his arms and threw his knees but I kneed him back until his entire body was under the blanket. He screamed, but the blanket muffled him, and Jack turned up the volume on the television. I was on top of him now, knees jammed under his arms. He squirmed free and I caught him with a right haymaker under the left eye. He squirmed again and I nailed him under the ribs. His wind left him and that's when I used plastic hardware strips to handcuff him to the bed. He coughed, once, twice in agony and we were gone.

We tossed our masks in the garbage can and ran down the side stairwell. No one saw us coming or going. We were soon in Jack's car, peeling out of the parking lot.

"Ha-ha—that was great. Nice job in there." Jack was huffing and puffing.

"Whew. Thanks, Jack…my heart is still racing. I haven't been that fired up since standing up to some bully in grade school. Whew!" My heart was still racing; my lungs heaved. Jack drove around the block to make sure no one was in the rearview mirror, and then went back to the bar where we had been only 90 minutes earlier.

"Let's go inside."

I followed him in, but didn't sit down. Instead I went to the men's room and ran the cold-water tap. My hands made a small bowl and I plunged my face into the cool water. I was still shaking. When I raised my hands, I noticed a swollen, red middle knuckle. Tadrick was hurting just as bad, I hoped; he had to be smarting, but I should have popped him a few more times. If I hit him once for Jamie and once for every crummy stunt he pulled over the years, he would have been in rough shape.

I found Jack at the booth, jacket off, and a cocktail at his fingertips. A brown manila envelope lay at his lap. Across the front of the envelope was a word, in bold red letters: CONFIDENTIAL.

"Where did you get *that*?" We looked at each other. Big trouble.

"I stole it."

"No you didn't."

"Yeah I did. While you were having your way with Tadrick, I grabbed this out of his briefcase sitting on the table next to the TV."

"Christ. If the police walk in here now, we're busted."

"We're okay...let's open it." He flipped over the envelope, unwrapping the red thread from its back. He reached in and pulled out a stack of papers. It appeared to be a memorandum—maybe from an e-mail—on the top with several pages of computer-generated printouts below. Jack put on his bifocals and read:

> *"Gentlemen, it has come to our attention that the accounting department has made two errors. The first involves commissions for the agency force between the period of October of last year and July of this year. It appears as if the accounting error has resulted in the shortage of commissions to agents. The problem is related to commissions paid at last year's renewal rates, not this year's. As you know, our pricing strategy has generated substantial increases in premiums that generated higher commissions. We contend that the agents have had little to do with the increased premiums, and therefore do not deserve this extra commission.*
>
> *The second error has to do with our long-standing accounting practices of withholding 20 percent of our profits for losses that have occurred, but have not yet been reported. Last year the accounting department withheld five percent of our profits instead of 20. This error has made our bottom line better than it actually is. Wall Street has taken notice of profits, and the 24-cent dividend per share. Regulators have agreed to postpone any formal investigation of this discrepancy until after the third quarter, and the sale of Surety Guarantee to an overseas investment group. We need your help in keeping both matters quiet until the start of the fourth quarter."*

Jack looked up at me like he just saw my mother naked or something—like he knew he shouldn't be looking.

> *"We understand that there may be agents in your territory who are not team players, and we encourage you to take swift and responsive action against them. Do not notify corporate offices in the event of terminating troublesome agents, but contact the corporate stewards in Newark... Sincerely* blah, blah, blah."

Jack looked at me in one long stare. "There now, aren't you glad I went with you?"

"Holy shit, Jack—this is huge! Now what do we do?"

"Wait a second. What's this other stuff?"

"Looks like some kind of report."

"I don't know. Hell, I don't want to know."

He put the papers back in the envelope and looked around the bar. Before he said a thing, he took a drink.

"Now what?"

"This is big. This is the kind of stuff that companies hate to see the press get a hold of. This is the kind of stuff that could really get us in trouble."

"Us," I backpedaled.

"We're in this together now."

"I'm not so sure I like our arrangement."

"Come on. Tadrick doesn't know who roughed him up—for all he knows, Jamie came to visit him, and who knows, maybe he invited someone another woman up to his room, and *her* husband beat him up. He acts like a jerk in his business life, and he definitely acts like it his personal life too."

"He's not that stupid. He knows it had something to do with Jamie. He knows it was me."

"But what the hell can he do to you?"

"I could lose my job, I suppose. Or worse—he could call the police."

"He won't call the police," Jack said emphatically. "And we're all going to lose our jobs. But more important, I'd be worried what he'll do if that memo ever sees the light of day."

"Maybe he didn't read the memo yet. What do we do now?"

"Let's just see what happens."

"You mean you'll go to the meeting tomorrow, and I'll go to the office."

"That's right. Nothing will change. Just another day in the life of two disgruntled Surety Guarantee agents."

"Yeah, but I suck at playing poker. I've never been good at bluffing."

"You'll have to learn quick."

"Jack..." I hesitated. "Isn't it quickly? You'll have to learn *quickly?*"

"Shut up!"

Thirty-Eight

JACK AND I had a few more beers that night.

The police never did show up to arrest us.

For all we knew, Tadrick was still handcuffed to the bedposts. The thought of him in that predicament made me feel like I got a little revenge, like I saved Jamie's honor. I wonder if he stayed there all night, only to be rescued by housekeeping in the morning.

Jack dropped me off at Jamie's close to midnight. The boys were in slumbering bliss when I tucked them in. She had fallen asleep with her bedside light on, a copy of *Cosmopolitan* draped across her flowered nightgown. I turned off her light, got undressed, and slid under the covers. She reached to me, placed her hand on my thigh, and whispered goodnight.

The following morning, I got up early, showered, and walked to the bakery for a peanut butter cookie and a cup of coffee. Summer is so nice—if for nothing other than hearing the birds chirp and smelling the flowers in bloom. Three blocks and 10 minutes later, I was at the office.

Tadrick was waiting for me, wearing a pair of dark sunglasses that barely covered the swollen shiner beneath. I invited him into the office but he refused. All he did was hand me a piece of paper that read: "*Your agent's licensing agreement has been hereby terminated. Because you broke the terms of your agreement, you have forfeited payment of your book value. In order to avoid legal action against you for damages resulting from your involvement in selling insurance for another carrier, kindly make arrangements for Surety Guarantee to take over the phone lines and pick up the computer located in your office.*"

"Just like that, huh, Tadrick?" I asked, folding the letter and depositing it in the breast pocket of my sport coat.

"I've been waiting for this day for a long time."

"Why's that, didn't I sell enough of your lousy overpriced policies? Wasn't I a good foot soldier when you crooks raised everyone's rates?"

"Has nothing to do with insurance, or rates."

"What is it then, or don't you have the stones to tell it to my face?"

"Oh, I don't mind telling it to your face." He took a step toward me. We were only inches apart, and I could smell the coffee on his breath. "You killed my friend, my colleague, last fall, and I'll never forgive you for it. You killed him—I know it. Oh sure, the cops called it an accident, but I know better. Scott was an experienced boater, and I know that you killed him."

"Is that right? You think I'm a murderer. Those are heavy charges, don't you think? Sounds like you're leading up to something, Donnie. Wanna do something about it? Wanna dance this morning, or are you afraid of falling down again and blackening your other eye?"

"Paybacks are hell, Johanson. I'd better get those phone

numbers and the computer or I'll hose you so bad you'll scream for mercy. I'll get even with you."

"Before you do," I said, loudly enough that only he'd hear me, "say goodbye to your dog and cat, your neighbors and all the honest businessmen in Newark, because if you try anything, I'll have you hanging from the buck pole like a 10-point on opening day."

He waddled away, got in his car and sped off without saying a word. Thank goodness. I didn't want any more trouble. I didn't think he had the guts to stand up to me the way he did. But at least it was over, and he was gone. I wouldn't have to watch out for that clown anymore. He wasn't going to come after me. He was a coward after all.

We wouldn't have to hide Michigan Miners policies, applications or manuals ever again. I had no idea how he found out, but it really didn't matter. We were legally separated now, and it felt like a burden was lifted off my shoulders. The albatross was gone from around my neck.

Before Jamie arrived, I was on-line with the computers, making one last printout of the policies that were up for renewal soon, and those that were up for renewal later. Tadrick should have pulled the plug on my access before firing me, but nobody ever said that he was the sharpest tool in the shed. While the printer was banging out sheets of paper, I was outside, taking down the two Surety Guarantee signs. The sign over the front door was a little tricky to remove from the brick facade. It had been there for three or four decades and the metal bolts that held it in place were rusted into the mortar. Symbolic after all—the sign that had stood for decades was removed in a matter of minutes. It was just like the company—it was once a great organization but had crumbled the same way.

I called Gerry and gave him the news. He couldn't believe it, but after all, we all knew that this day would come. We figured that somebody told Ted's camp and they in turn told Surety Guarantee. To avoid the appearance of unfairness when dealing with Ted's lawsuit, the company decided to fire us all. Gerry would get his notice by Federal Express the next day, so would Duck Hunter Dan and Allison. Jack didn't have to wait that long. He got his at the mutual fund training seminar and Tadrick seemed to take pride in doing it in front of everyone. We were cut loose—the heart and soul of the district that made up northern Michigan.

When Jamie arrived at the office we had a lot of catching up to do. She missed the melee the night before and all the excitement that morning. I think she was expecting just another day, but it didn't take long before she realized that the days of dealing with Surety Guarantee were over. She was beaming. "Really?" she asked me over and over.

"It's true."

"No more dealing with Don Tadrick?"

"No more Don Tadrick."

She came closer to me, "No more stupid underwriting rules, or memos about the latest and greatest Surety product?"

I put my hands on her waist, "We're through with them. All of them. They're not going to bother us any more."

"That's great, honey. This is great for everybody." She gave me an enormous hug, and it made me realize that this whole ordeal was hard on her too. But the burden was gone—the Wicked Witch was dead at last. For the rest of the morning she smiled while taking the printouts off the printer and organizing the data so we'd be able to access it later.

Michigan Miners embraced the change. They talked more about expanding into southern Michigan's more populated areas, and they still wanted us to head up the team. But we had unfinished business with Surety Guarantee. Somebody had to stop them. They needed to be stopped if nothing more than to combat their arrogance—if nothing more than to knock out the heavyweight that was past his prime. And we were ready for them.

Since the afternoon when Jack, Ted and I had steaks and a sailboat ride in Petoskey, we had been plotting this course. We had everyone fooled. Oh sure, I never plotted to kill Scott—I had a momentary loss of control in a perfect setting. I never planned on finding those incriminating documents in Tadrick's motel room. Finding them was a lucky break, but Surety Guarantee always taught their agents "the harder you work, the luckier you'll get."

Ted slapped his secretary on the caboose because he couldn't afford to give her a severance bonus. She was up for the stunt because she figured she could have netted a lot more by rolling the dice on a sexual harassment suit than taking a handshake and a $100 from Ted. It worked. Her cut of the $220,000 settlement after the lawyers were paid was $130,000. She didn't even tell her lawyer that it was all a setup.

And Ted, who was forced to pay a $90,000 judgment for soliciting his clients, actually won his countersuit against Surety Guarantee for breach of contract and defamation of character. He dinged them for $150,000 and my liability policy for $425,000. Surety was too stupid to realize that the whole thing was a charade. We never thought it would amount to that kind of dough, but we weren't complaining either. I later told Ted that I wanted a kickback of that settlement, because I played the part so well. He denied my request, citing that he earned that money fairly and squarely. "After all," he joked, "I suffered *defecation* of character." Ted was grinning ear to ear. After his case settled, I told him that I had tape-recorded statements of Tadrick acknowledging the letters, which proved he committed perjury. I told him that I had tape-recorded statements from Surety Guarantee's lawyer too, admitting that Surety Guarantee's rates were obscenely high. Ted loved it. He laughed and laughed; we both did. After getting screwed by the company for so long, it felt good to be on the other end of the shaft. But Ted wanted more. We all did. We wanted to see them squirm because they still had this swagger about them that humble people don't have. They needed to be stopped, plain and simple.

So with a couple bushels of Ted's "seed money," we hired the same law firm that scored big in the $80 million case against Surety Guarantee's employment practices in Pennsylvania. They had a chip on their shoulder for Surety Guarantee and that's exactly what our case needed. In reality, we didn't need much of a lawyer or law firm to make the case winnable. We had the tapes, we had the memo from the company, and we had proof of Tadrick accosting Jamie. Plus, we had affidavits from the policyholders we switched from Surety Guarantee to Michigan Miners stating that we had nothing to do with their decision. The damages were substantial, because we were terminated without cause. We were; after all, the best of the best in our district, and our income generated serious money when compounded over the remainder of our careers. So the lawyers were hired, the papers drawn, and the "wrongful termination/unfair business practices" lawsuit was served. I didn't see Tadrick until the first hearing. I never did give him the computer, the manuals or the phone numbers because they really never pursued it. Without a bargaining chip of my "book value," they had no incentive for me to cooperate. I kept both offices open and wrote tons of Michigan

Miners policies. By then we were hired as agents *and* recruiters for Michigan Miners. Eventually, the plan was to become Michigan Miners' version of Surety's District Coordinators.

So on a beautiful fall afternoon, I waltzed into the courthouse to hear our attorneys in action. As a witness, I sat in the hall and waited to testify. I had to rely on Duck Hunter Dan and his wife for the blow-by-blow of the case. Kyle Holbine was there, asking for an immediate dismissal of the case citing something about "just cause." The judge wouldn't hear anything of it. Rumor had it that His Honor came from a poor farming family in the community and made a name for himself in the legal profession by working hard and telling it like it is. Duck Hunter Dan had a brother who was arrested for drunk driving many years before. The same judge threw the book at him even though Dan's brother was the assistant principal at the high school and a very good football coach. The judge was tough, unswerving in his righteousness, and didn't like out-of-towners.

When the judge heard Holbine's pleas about "rolling over agents like this in courts downstate" the judge laughed, and reminded Holbine that the merits of this case would be determined on the facts. Our attorney was prepared. He argued our case as if he were pouring a glass of water—it flowed with ease. Surety Guarantee had unfair business practices, we alleged. Surety Guarantee terminated us without investigating what we had done wrong. The judge listened and nodded his head. Allison Kline was in the witness box answering questions from our lawyer and Holbine. Her testimony centered on Surety Guarantee's unfair business practices.

"Ms. Kline, while you were an agent with Surety Guarantee, how competitive were their rates?"

"They weren't."

"Can you explain that statement?"

"Surety Guarantee's prices were unbelievably uncompetitive. We were routinely twice the price of every other carrier in the state for the last year."

"Doesn't the insurance commissioner stipulate that the highest priced company can't be more than 50 percent more than the least expensive?"

"I don't know about that. All I can tell you is that Surety Guarantee is double or triple the other carriers." Allison sat on the edge of her seat, erect, wearing a dark blue suit to match her deep blue eyes. She was strong and confident as always.

"How did you sell insurance then?"

"We didn't sell much at all. I used to sell 40 or 50 policies in a month, but toward the end I only sold five or ten."

"Why only five or ten?"

"Our rates." She pawed at her hair, tucking it behind her ears. "There were hardly any new households; we mostly sold to existing clients who wanted to add a snowmobile or a new home. Most of our days were spent explaining to our customers why their rates went through the roof. We lost hundreds of clients in the last year, and it wasn't because they went with Michigan Miners."

"Why do you mention Michigan Miners?"

"Because I know that Surety Guarantee thinks that the reason our clients left our agencies was because we coerced them into leaving."

"Objection, your honor." Holbine was out of his seat, pointing a lead pencil at Allison. "Hearsay. My client is perfectly willing to explain their situation."

"The witness will answer the question."

"Did you?"

"No, we didn't coerce them. Not at all. When our clients said they were going to shop their insurance, we asked them if they wanted some referrals. Michigan Miners was just one of the companies that we endorsed."

"Tell me about midterm policy changes."

Kyle Holbine interrupted and pleaded to the judge about the relevancy of the question. Our lawyer said that he needed to establish that Surety Guarantee routinely ignored the Michigan insurance department's rule about changing the filed rate, midterm. The judge allowed the line of questioning, "The witness will answer the question."

"If clients make any change on their policies—a new car, a rider on their homeowner's policy, anything—Surety Guarantee makes the change, but also applies the rate that's in effect at that time. In other words, if a client calls in to make a change, there's a good chance that they will be getting a bill for the change."

"I still don't understand."

Allison moved up on her chair, and waved her hand at our attorney, like she was directing traffic. "Let's say you refinance your house in August. The new bank wants to be added to your policy and the old bank taken off. So you call your agent and make the change, but several weeks later you get a bill for $250."

"Why a bill, when there wasn't any coverage change?"

Allison's hands were spread at arm's length, "That's how Surety Guarantee operates. If your home policy renews in December, but a rate change went into effect in June, the change you made in August makes your policy eligible for the increase. Instead of honoring the December to December contract, Surety Guarantee plugged in the new rate because it made them more money."

"Is that legal?"

"I don't know. Seems like it shouldn't be. If Surety Guarantee filed a rate for a year or six months, they should honor it."

"And they didn't."

"Right. When we brought that up to the managers they didn't want to talk about it. They had the attitude that it would have been cheaper to pay a fine from the insurance commissioner than do the right..."

"Objection," Holbine shouted, "hearsay."

"Sorry." Allison sensed that she crossed the line. "They didn't offer to change their policy of charging midterm. They didn't apologize to the agents for all the irate customers that the practice caused."

"I see. Thank you, Ms. Kline."

Our attorney called me to the stand and began asking questions about my relationship with Surety Guarantee. I swore to tell the truth, so I had no other recourse but to tell everything I knew. Our attorney didn't mince any words, either. I had to tell the judge about those tapes of Tadrick regarding the letters to Ted's clients. I had to tell the judge about Kyle Holbine's tape-recorded statement about Surety Guarantee's pricing situation, and Tadrick not being the "sharpest tool in the shed." Of course the business with Jamie came up too, and I had to tell the judge about the tape of that. Tadrick squirmed in his chair, and his face turned red while his jaw muscle twitched nervously. Holbine was worse. He objected to almost everything I said—something about "hearsay" and "relevance," but the judge wouldn't hear anything of it. In fact, the judge was amused by Holbine's objections about relevance: "Mr. Holbine, if the testimony has to do with you, I think it's more than relevant." Duck Hunter

Dan's wife snickered in the gallery behind the wooden gate that separated the main courtroom from the rows of wooden benches. Jack's wife had to bite her tongue to keep from laughing out loud.

Then our attorney asked about any secrets that Surety Guarantee kept from the agents. I had no other choice in answering that—I had to tell the judge that Surety Guarantee routinely withheld the truth from the agents. And of course, I had to tell the judge about the memo that Tadrick had in his briefcase. I didn't tell the judge how we got the memo, but the judge was sure interested in its content after the bailiff handed it to him. Kyle Holbine whispered something to a burly, crooked-nosed guy in the front row of the gallery. He didn't make any facial expression; he only listened to whatever Holbine said.

"Have you ever received any money for the commissions that were allegedly withheld?" the judge asked.

"No, Your Honor."

"Have they ever acknowledged that they made this accounting error?"

"No, never."

"Do you know anything about the accounting principles of withholding five or 20 percent of profits for 'claims that have occurred but not yet reported'?"

"No, Your Honor, I'm just an agent trying to make a living."

"Who are the '*corporate stewards*'?"

"I have no idea."

"Have you heard anything about the sale of the company to an investment group, or the accounting error?"

"Never, Your Honor."

"What about these tapes you possess? Can I listen to them?"

"Your Honor, I don't have them with me today because my lawyer said that this was just a hearing."

"You do have the tapes, don't you?"

"Yes, sir."

"You'd better bring them Monday. We're going to meet right here at 10 a.m. and have the court reporter catalog everything on them. I'd like to hear exactly what they said."

Kyle Holbine raised his hand, got the judge's attention, and said that his client couldn't be there Monday because of a Surety Guarantee meeting that had been scheduled for several months. The judge looked over his horn-rimmed bifocals: "Mr. Holbine, is your client telling the truth this time?"

"Yes, Your Honor. My client has scheduled a meeting on Mackinac Island for Monday. They have an agent's seminar at the Grand Hotel."

"The Grand Hotel…Is that right? And how can Surety Guarantee pay for that kind of a meeting place when they're losing all this money? Never mind. We'll see everyone back here at 10 a.m. Tuesday, and Mr. Holbine, if this witness's statements are true, you've got some explaining to do. Tell your client that they don't break the insurance code and get away with it here, or they'll be looking at fines or punitive damages to go along with any judgments. Better yet, you tell your client to bring their checkbook with them; they've got some heavy checks to write. This court is adjourned." The judge picked up his gavel and slammed it artfully, as if he was swatting a fly.

I pushed open the witness-stand gate and walked back to our table. Our attorney was sifting through papers in our file, adjusting the metal tines that kept the stack organized. He told me that I did a good job, and that he wanted to talk to all of us in the conference room in 10 minutes.

Dan's hand reached over the wooden railing: "Mr. Holbine, is your client telling the truth this time?" He was mocking the judge. "Nice job up there, Hanson."

"Just telling the truth, pal." I laughed too.

"How can they argue with the truth?"

Holbine was rounding up his troops. They pushed through the swinging wooden doors and were gone. We wanted to gloat, but thought the better of it. It seemed that things were going our way, and there would be time for celebrating when the ink dried on our settlement.

Five minutes later we were in the conference room with our attorney, who looked like a taller version of H. Ross Perot. "Listen, gentlemen, Allison, this is just the first stage of a long process. You two were wonderful up there today. We fired the first blow, but you can bet that they'll come back at us hard. I'll tell you what though; the 14 million dollar demand that we filed with this suit may not be enough. We had a great day today. I wouldn't take a red cent less than that!" We all applauded.

"Tuesday, Hanson, you're on the stand first, then Jack, you go. Allison, we may need you here again. We'll get Gerry down here from up north.

"Really, though—we have a great case here. We're going to make them pay. I wouldn't doubt if Surety Guarantee offers us a mighty big number a week from now."

We were handshaking and backslapping all around. Ted lit up a smoke when we made it outside. Jack was in the mood to party, and so was Dan and his wife. Allison had already hopped into her Navigator and dashed away. They wanted to go to the Judge's Chambers for drinks, hors d'oeuvres, and more drinks. It would have been fun, but then I would have to drive home. It's no fun drinking when you know you have to drive. It takes all the fun out of it. Besides, I had my bags packed for Gerry's cabin up north. Opening day of duck season began the next morning.

Thirty-Nine

I SAID MY goodbyes to the gang in the parking lot of the courthouse, and pulled my truck to the side-door. The lot was almost empty and most of the sparse foot traffic was headed for home. I grabbed a change of clothes and a hanger for my suit. After opening the door of the courthouse, I turned left down the hallway to the men's room. It was dark and dingy, like the rest of the building. The bathroom was vacant when I got there, so I walked by the bank of sinks to one of the stalls down a small aisle. I took off my jacket, thinking that I should have left it the vehicle. Instead of hanging it over the door, I draped it over the back of the porcelain toilet. As I slipped off my loafers, my mind was already past my testimony and onto the drive ahead. I'd have an early dinner in Gaylord, and if I hurried, some fresh whitefish to take to the cabin from the fisheries in St. Ignace. I pulled on my tie knot until I had enough slack to pull it over my head. Then I unbuttoned my oxford, placing it on the hanger over the tie. Just then I heard the old door to the men's room swing open. I pulled on a sweatshirt when the voices started.

"Listen, I was justified in firing them. They were selling outside companies, and that's immediate grounds for termination. You know that."

"Why didn't you investigate their arrangement before you canned them? They were setting us up. Can't you see that?"

"What else should I have done? We've bagged agents for less, you know that."

"What the fuck are you, incompetent?" The voices were getting louder, more gruff with each exchange.

"You don't have to get personal now."

"You really are *stoopid* aren't you? Personal? You're done. If those tapes see the light of day the company will have your ass. We'll all be out of a job and those bean counters in New Jersey will have hell to pay. You understand me? We're not going to let those country bumpkin agents take us down."

"They won't. I know where he lives, his office, the girl in his office. I'll get those tapes somehow…this weekend."

"Think, you dumb ass! You've got that fucking meeting on Mackinac Island this weekend. How? Think?"

I froze, eyes peering through the crack of the stall door. One voice I recognized as Tadrick's, but the other one I'd never heard. Whoever he was, he paced back and forth, nervously. Tadrick just sat there, resting his backside on the sink with his arms crossed.

"I dunno yet. Lemme think about this for a second…Hey quit it—ah, ah…" Tadrick's head was in the sink, with a pair of clenched hands around his neck. The hands slammed his head into the bottom of the sink and up into the faucet. "Help, help. That's hot! Ahhhhh!" The hands kept smashing him, into the sink, then into the faucet.

"Can you think of something now, Donnie boy?" The hands lifted him out of the sink and dragged him my way in a headlock. Tadrick kicked and screamed with a mixture of blood and water dripping on his lapels. I froze, but recognized the face of the man seated behind Kyle Holbine at the hearing. “How about a little cold water now, you piece of shit.” The stall door next to mine blasted open and the place erupted with the sounds of scuffling feet and men fighting. “Think of something yet, Donnie? I’m gonna flush your brains down this fuckin’ toilet if you don’t some up with something quick.”

I held my breath as the toilet flushed. Tadrick screamed more but was muffled by the sounds of water filling up the bowl. “How ’bout another round of ‘bobbing for apples,’ Donnie boy?”

“Help me. Help.” His voice gurgled again and again, but I was busy scooping up my belongings. I opened the door and dashed out, running down the hallway, down the stairs, to my truck. I tossed my clothes onto the seat next to me and sped away. Nobody was chasing me, nobody saw me running. I had a brush with violence—a side of Surety Guarantee I never knew existed. I was scared.

A few minutes later I was headed north to Gaylord, St. Ignace, and the Sault. I reached behind the seat to the extended cab and moved my 12-gauge to the passenger side of the cab. I grabbed a pair of shot shells and set them in the console, just in case the bastards wanted to tango on the road. When I did, my clothes were in a heap. I moved them to the back seat. It quickly became apparent that I had left my suit coat on the back of the toilet. I was so mad at myself. It’s part of my marketing strategy to leave cards wherever I go, so it’s my practice to always have cards in my pocket. All I could see was Tadrick riffling through my pockets and realizing that I heard the entire conversation. What worried me even more was the guy who was having his way with Tadrick. He must have been part of that 'corporate stewards' group. If the marketing arm of Surety Guarantee was The Gestapo, then the 'corporate stewards' must have been the "SS." That guy was scary, and he wasn't the least bit afraid to throw his weight around. He was prone to violence—just how much violence was hard to say. What was worse, in my eyes, was the fact that he knew we were setting him up. They were on to us, but I had a few more tricks up my sleeve.

Ninety minutes later I was in Gaylord, where I drove through the drive-in at a Burger King, then slipped into Jay's Sporting Goods. Jay's is known throughout the Midwest for their huge inventory of fine firearms. I always wanted to shoot ducks with a double-barreled gun that the aristocracy used 100 years ago. The loads are different today than they were back then, but the craftsmanship they exhibited years ago is seldom matched in today's era of mechanized production. Thank goodness for Visa's liberal credit limits. I pushed my $10,000 limit to the max when I placed a 1912 Parker side by side shotgun on the counter. But you only live once.

When I got back on the road, I called my "new" Surety Guarantee agent and added the gun as a rider on my homeowner's policy. My agent now had inherited not only all my old policies, but Ted's too. Before this mess started he had 700 polices that generated $40,000 in annualized commission. After Ted and I left, he had 3,500 polices that netted $120,000. Suddenly he had more than he bargained for, more than he could chew.

Jamie was next on my phone list. She was just wrapping up the week, and dying to hear from me. "Hello, Jamie, sell any Michigan Miners today?"

"You know you have to be 18 to buy insurance."

"I didn't mean that kind of minor...you're so cute. How's my girl?"

"Ready to close up the shop."

"Thank God it's Friday?"

"Oh yes, I'm ready for a nice relaxing weekend. This place was a zoo today. Let me see...we sold...three homeowner's, eight autos, three boats and two life policies today. But how did the court thing go?"

"You know, it went fairly well. I'm glad we hired this lawyer. He seems really sharp, and he made mincemeat of Surety Guarantee. I wish you could have been there; Jack and a few other people in the audience were laughing at Tadrick and his lawyer. The judge totally liked us and our case. Our lawyer thinks we should win no problem. We should win big."

"Great, great. So where are you now?"

"On the other side of Gaylord, headed for Mackinaw City. Beautiful weather, but not much for duck hunting."

"Gerry Buchanan called, said to bring suntan oil and bug spray."

"I know—this weather is horrible for duck hunting."

"Be careful what you wish for."

"I know, I know. Hey listen, couple things. The first is that I bought another gun. I figured that you could use my old one and I'll use the new one. It's a really expensive gun, though."

"What? You did? Have you won the lotto?"

"Almost, sweetheart. We're going to be rich when this lawsuit is through, besides, I got a really good deal on it. And one other thing—Jaim, you need to take the boys and spend the weekend at your mother's."

"What? I haven't done that in years! Have you lost your marbles?"

"No, I haven't. Listen, I wouldn't ask it if I wasn't serious."

"Larry, come on, why?"

"I'm sorry, Jamie, we've really done some things that hurt the company and I think they may come after me. They may come after us."

"You're scaring me. Why are you still going up north with all this going on?"

"You know, I'll be as safe up here as I'll be down there."

"I don't like this at all, honey. I'm scared already."

"Hey, hey, we'll get through this in flying colors. They can't hurt us—you know that. Before you know it, Monday will be here and it'll all be over. Keep your cell phone on, just in case, okay?"

"Okay."

"One other thing."

"What."

"I love you."

"I love you too."

I hung up the phone and stared into the I-75 oblivion. I should have had my eyes peeled. Dusk is a good time to spot elk or deer crossing the expressway, but really I could have cared less about them. My mind was back in Mt. Pleasant with Jamie and the boys. It felt weird, loving someone the way I did. It was hard to acknowledge, hard to say, but it felt so right. There was no denying it now—I really did love her.

Forty

ANOTHER HOUR LATER I pulled into the cabin's long driveway. For the last 15 minutes I watched the rearview mirror to make sure nobody was following me. Gerry met me at the threshold as usual and Mess gave me a sniff or two, tail wagging like mad. We exchanged pleasantries, like old times, and he helped me toss my overnight bag into the spare bedroom.

"Let me show you something." I walked out to the truck and came back carrying two gun cases.

"Holy cow, man. Are you nuts? Wow, it's beautiful. Look at that gold inlay! That must have cost a small fortune."

"Sure it was a lot, but what the heck, it's insured and the way the lawyer is talking, we're going to be rich."

"What happened? I've been dying to hear about it."

"Aw, Christ, Gerry, we slaughtered them. It wasn't even close."

"What happened?"

"When I got there, Allison Kline was on the stand, telling the world about the way changes to policies generate earned premium. Plus she told the judge about their pricing strategy." Gerry raised the gun to his shoulder over and over again, turning it on its side to admire the gold English pointer on the receiver and its sleek, checkered forearm. "The judge almost laughed at Surety Guarantee's lawyer and the way he came prepared for the case. Check that—how he *didn't* come prepared."

"Ha! That's great. It's about time somebody stood up to those bastards."

"Then I get on the stand and really let them have it with both barrels. I told them about the tapes of Tadrick and the letters to Ted's clients, Tadrick and Jamie, Holbine and Surety Guarantee, the whole ball of wax. Man, was Tadrick livid. His face was beet red. I think he felt betrayed when I turned on him."

"Now what?"

"The judge wants to hear the tapes and see the evidence on Tuesday."

"Why Tuesday?"

"Cause Surety Guarantee has that agent's convention Monday on Mackinac Island."

"Oh yeah, I remember that now. Boy, aren't you glad you don't have to listen to that all over again? One lie after another. One pompous jerk after another. I'm glad we're out of there. We're in a better place."

"Hey, how 'bout a cocktail? It's the night before opening day. Can you believe it?"

"I know. The last 12 months have flown by."

"Looks like we won't have the good weather we did a year ago."

"Probably not as good hunting, either." Gerry put my gun back in the case and walked into the kitchen.

"Yeah, but at least at the end of the day we won't have to worry about someone falling overboard."

"What a mess that was." An instant later Gerry had a highball glass in one hand and dribbled a handful of ice into it.

"I know it. I forgot to tell you about what happened after the hearing while I was changing my clothes at the courthouse…" I told Gerry all about the goon at the hearing and the way he beat the snot out of Tadrick afterwards. Gerry seemed concerned, but figured that we were safe up in the wilds of the eastern Upper Peninsula.

"Here's your drink, cheers," he raised his glass next to mine. "Let 'em come here and tangle with us—right, Mess?" patting him on the head. Mess's tail wagged against the side of the old, threadbare couch, sending plumes of dust billowing into the smoke-filled cabin. "We've got enough shotguns and duck loads here to thwart the best of what those chumps can throw at us."

Gerry reached up and turned on the weather radio, then sat down and jingled the ice in his drink. I picked up my prized shotgun and laid it in my bed, then went to the kitchen to make sandwiches. "Here we go…."

The strange voice became louder now, *"For the eastern U.P. and Algoma Region, tonight's forecast unseasonably warm with mild temperatures and variable winds. Sunrise tomorrow morning will be at 6:17 a.m. Expect partly cloudy skies, a southwest wind at five to ten miles per hour. High temperatures will reach 65 degrees. Saturday morning mostly clear, with patchy fog developing after midnight."*

"Geez, that's horrible," Gerry said, taking an extra pull on his cocktail. As he reached up to turn off the radio, I told him to wait.

"Water temperature at Whitefish Point 63 degrees."

"Thank you… Looks bad. Where should we hunt?"

"Miami Beach."

"I think we should try the upper river again. That was good last year, other than the outcome."

"Other than the outcome."

"What do you say? Should we go up there again?"

"I don't care. If we go up there, I need to swing by the house and pick up the tarps."

"Okay. I'll hook the boat up to my vehicle, drop you off at your house, and then meet you at the launch."

"Great. Let me get some baggies for those sandwiches."

Forty-One

GERRY DIDN'T NEED a jacket when he went outside with Mess, but remarked that there were a lot of lights on at the neighboring cabins. It was 10:30 when he turned out the lights and set the alarms. Mess collapsed on the linoleum between the two bedrooms and I could hear him snoring. As is always the case, I could hardly sleep. No matter how poor the forecast, how tired I am, it is always hard to sleep the night before opening day. Anticipation is a powerful emotion—strong enough to keep hunters up at night. It's always easy to sleep the night of opening day because anticipation has changed to reflection. You remember the hunt; you remember the day and everything that went into it. You don't care about remembering the stuff you need on the opener, because the opener has come and gone.

Strangely enough, I couldn't sleep because I kept hearing Tadrick scream over and over. I heard his cries and saw his face, with a trickle of blood streaming down one cheek and his lapels spattered with water...I heard that thug in the brown suit cursing "I'm gonna flush your brains down this fuckin' toilet, you piece of shit." These guys could be capable of anything. "You're nothing but shit for brains, how 'bout a game of bobbing for apples?" Then Jamie came to mind, and I wondered how she was doing with her mom. "They set you up, man. It was a setup. They're on to us; now scrub that porcelain throne with your nose." I thought about getting up and checking my phone for messages.

Then the thought hit me again: they knew that I listened to the fight. "That's his suit jacket. He heard everything, and he knows what we're up to. We've got to stop him. We've got to stop him. We've got to stop him..."

Somewhere after 1 a.m. I heard the noise and saw the lights. Mess was still fast asleep, but I knew better. The lights dashed across my bedroom ceiling. I jumped out of bed and pulled on a sweatshirt. I crawled to the living room and unzipped my shotgun case. Gerry kept a box of shells on the ledge behind the door next to the weather radio, and I reached up and pulled out a handful. I eased the action back on the forearm and stuffed one in the chamber, then two in the magazine. Duck loads would make a mess of a man at 10 yards, but if Tadrick and his goons wanted to tango, I'd dance with them. If they charged in the door right now they'd get a hell of a surprise.

The voices were loud enough that I could hear them, but not loud enough that I could understand what they were saying. I crouched behind the recliner, my 12-gauge propped on the arm, pointed at the door. A flashlight hit the neighbor's cabin, then the trees above ours. I couldn't sit there all night; I had to see what was going on. Slowly, I opened the door, voices only 20 yards away. I crawled on my belly and used the picnic table for cover.

"Shhhhut up!" The voices said. "You're going to wake them up."

"No, you shut up and keep that bucket under it."

I stood up, flicked on the flashlight and said good evening to my unexpected guests. They squinted at the light and after I realized that they weren't Tadrick and his goons, I put the flashlight down. I never pointed the business end of the gun their way; they were just a couple of our neighbors filling up their buckets from the artesian well. They obviously had too much to drink.

While I was up, I unlocked the truck and checked my phone for messages. Jamie called, just make sure things were okay. She said that the boys were fine and that her mother wanted to meet me soon. *Lovely,* I thought. Jack called me from the road, stating: "I hope your client is telling the truth this time. Ha-ha-ha."

I laughed. Jack, Jamie, Gerry. All good friends, one my lover. What a great life. Surety Guarantee wasn't going to get the better of me—I was going to get the better of them. What the hell was I doing up at two in the morning? This was stupid. In three hours the alarm would sound and begin the most holy of days in a duck hunter's world. I closed the truck door and walked toward the cabin.

Just then I heard commotion on the porch. I raised the gun, holding the flashlight under my forearm. "Come on outta there. I got a gun on you, man. Tadrick! I'm going to use this!"

The commotion stopped, but I stepped closer and closer to the screened porch. I moved around the side, to where it met the edge of the house. My heart was racing again, "Come on, Tadrick, show me your face. I'll blow it off."

Up and down the flashlight panned over the clutter of an

avid sportsman: the plastic and wood duck decoys, the waders, the fishing poles, and tackle boxes. Then I saw him, crouched low, ready to pounce. I saw his deadly little eyes and squat nose—that worthless little shit. I found the front bead on my gun in the flashlight's beam, and lined it up between his eyes. "Now put your hands up slowly or I'll smear your brains all over the cabin wall."

Damn skunks.

Forty-Two

At 5:15 the following morning we closed the cabin and headed north to the Sault. I dropped Gerry off at his house to round up the canvas tarps and bags of decoys, then proceeded to the boat ramp. By the time I launched the boat, Gerry would show up with our blind.

Launching a boat by yourself isn't the easiest thing in the world to pull off, especially in the dark with unfamiliar equipment. I backed my truck down the ramp till the big boat's propeller was nearly kissing the water of Mosquito Bay. I put the truck in park, reached behind the seat and grabbed Gerry's gun, my old gun, and the cooler of sandwiches and soft drinks. I left Mess in his kennel in the back. Gerry could take care of the old boy when he arrived.

After I threw our gear in the boat, I untied the straps at the stern, and the one that stretches across the beam. I popped the back window and tossed them inside, then turned and unhooked the rope that connects the boat to the trailer's winch. Finally, I tied the bowline to the dock post over deeper water so when I backed the boat down the ramp it wouldn't drift away.

Done.

I hopped back into the driver's seat and Mess growled. "All right, Mess, we're almost ready."

"We are ready." I turned slightly, and there was a gun barrel jabbing me in the temple. "Put your hands on the steering wheel or this will be your last duck hunt." The voice came from the back seat, and it smelled of coffee and cheap cologne. It was Tadrick's sparring partner. Mess growled again, and I really regretted not letting him out of his kennel. He would have tipped me off. I put my hands on the steering wheel and watched as a Lincoln slammed on the brakes three feet in front of my vehicle. Another man jumped out of the driver's side and rushed toward me, roughly putting plastic straps around my wrists. He punched me in the face and dragged me out of the seat, then tossed me in the open trunk. I saw the license plate and memorized it, *UN 3646... UN 3646... UN 3646...*

I heard them yelling, "Come on, back it up. Good. Now go!" Gerry's boat whined as whoever was at the helm tried to start it. They didn't have enough gas or not enough choke. "Start that thing, will you, and light that son of a bitch!"

They'll never start it, I thought. Only Gerry has the touch when it comes to that motor. I kicked the trunk as hard as I could. I screamed till my lungs roared. The plastic straps hurt my wrists, but I was determined to get out of there. I fumbled in the dark until I found a sharp metal edge. I sawed at the edge—pleading, hoping, and praying that it would sever my shackles.

Gerry's motor started. *Damn,* I thought. A few seconds later I heard the motor roar, then gradually fade away. *UN 3646... UN 3646...*

"Let's go." The car dipped slightly when the driver got in

and slammed the door, and then lunged as it sent bits of gravel against the rocker panels. After a hundred yards it stopped. I heard the rattle of Gerry's trailer speed up then stop next to us. The passenger side door opened, and then closed. "All right, now let's throw the corpse over the edge!"

I sawed at the cuffs like mad. *Come on, come on, I'm not even dead yet and they're calling me a corpse,* I thought. *Please God, help me, help me. I don't want to die this way.* They were going to throw me over the rock pile and into the power canal. "Let me outta here! Help! Help!" It was useless to scream. I should keep sawing. *Think, think.* The trunk swung open and someone hit me in the face. I kicked like mad, but they punched me again. It hurt, but adrenaline was flowing like a geyser.

"Shit. Let him go, here comes a car." They slammed the trunk again, and sped away. They were flying. I tried to saw the cuffs but it was impossible. "Now what?"

"There's another bridge upstream of the power house. The fall alone will kill him."

"Okay. All right. Hurry."

I sawed at the cuffs, and then held them to my lips. They were notched. It was working. Finally, a ray of hope. I sawed and sawed. The bridge upstream of the powerhouse is high above the water, but not too high. For Sault Ste. Marie, the road was a fairly busy one. Maybe a man on his way to work would foil their plans again. But if there was no car I could survive the fall. The trick was getting to the edge before the current swept me into the turbines. I sawed and sawed, knowing that it wouldn't take long to get to the bridge. *Useless,* I thought. It wasn't working. So instead, I went to Plan B; I unsnapped my waders and wiggled out of them. If I was going swimming, I could do it faster and better without the encumbrance. Next, I reached in my shirt pocket and found my money clip and hid it in the wheel-well. If nothing else, the police would have something to go on when Gerry's brother-in-law investigated the case. *Jamie, Jamie, my Jaim. I'll never see her again*, I regretted. I sawed some more; the notch was bigger now, more than halfway through. I twisted until my wrists burned.

"Turn left here...There's the bridge."

I sawed, and sawed, as best I could. This was it, the big finale. I knew the bridge and the eddies on either side of the main current. If I could flounder to them I might have a chance. Without my arms, I couldn't swim. With my arms, I'd have a hell of a swim ahead of me. *What was that water temperature? What was the license? Come on...UN36... UN3646!!* The car came to a screeching halt and they popped the trunk. I kicked the lid open and tried to climb out before they could get there. I had one leg out and my cuffs in the trunk's locking mechanism when they yanked me free. The cuffs caught on the lock and broke—they yanked me free.

A second later I was over the metal railing and falling, falling toward the swirling oblivion. The powerhouse, only a quarter mile away, stood ominously over the mighty river. I'd have to hurry or the current would sweep me into the teeth of the monster. The water felt like concrete when I hit it, but it wasn't that cold. I stroked to the east end because it was closer. I cursed my warm clothes now. They held me up, but still I stroked like mad. I stroked like mad, but the powerhouse was drawing ever closer. I could hear the hum of the turbines. I could see the reflection of the lights inside. The eddy was only a few yards away, but for every stroke I took to the eddy, the current carried me two toward the powerhouse. This was it. The eddy was too far away. The hum of the turbines roared.

I was drifting now, planning my last move, my Hail Mary.

I spotted a cement pillar—one of four-dozen that slices the water into manageable columns on the backside of the house. I straddled it with my arms and my legs on either side, current pushing relentlessly. It pushed so hard I thought my lungs would collapse. It pulled my socks from my feet, ripped buttons from my shirt. Finally though, I looked up and found two metal handles built into the cement fascia. I reached and grabbed the closest. I reached again, and got the second. It took everything I had, but I was safe. I climbed onto the grass raceway above the river, above the turbines, at the foot of the old block building, and lay there for 10 minutes. It took forever to catch my breath. It took forever to realize that I was still alive. I was alive. I was alive.

Now what?

Forty-Three

THE POWERHOUSE USED to employ hundreds of people once upon a time, before computers and automation made deckhands obsolete. Computers program the turbines to produce as much or as little electricity as the customers demand. Hardly anyone works at the powerhouse now, except for a few programmers and a handful of maintenance personnel. I walked down the grass raceway to the east end, where the biology department from the university had their own aquatics lab. The students would be along any time now to feed the salmon fingerlings held in huge vats. I had to act fast.

I found a window that had been boarded up and kicked it in. It hardly made a noise, compared to the hum of the turbines. I snuck inside and jumped between the vats of salmon, then up the metal stairs to the aquatics lab, which was locked. I heard police sirens headed for the upper river, the boat launch. Gerry must have been a wreck—two years in a row, and two deaths. I climbed onto the handle of the door, and, using a pipe nearby, pushed up a ceiling tile. The pipe made a horizontal turn, which was all I needed. I climbed up, up and over, to the inside of the lab. I reached down and pulled another ceiling tile. Somehow I finagled my way inside to the phone and called Jack.

"Jack, wake up."

"Hanson—what the hell are you doing calling me at this hour of the morning? Do you know what time it is?" His voice was groggy.

"Hey, shut up, it's after 7 a.m. I need your help. I'm in some big trouble."

"We didn't get home till after one last night. What do you need?"

"Are you listening?"

"Sure, sure. I'm listening."

"Surety Guarantee has tried to kill me, but they couldn't do that right, either."

"What? Holy shit!" He paused for a second. "You're bullshitting me."

"I'm not; I'm up here in the Sault and I need you to pick me up."

"What? It's Saturday morning…"

"Come on, you said we were in this together!"

"Okay, where? Now?"

"Jack, listen—I don't have time to talk. I'm at the east end of the Edison Sault Power Plant. *The east end of the power plant.* The police think that I'm dead, so don't say anything to anybody. Tell your wife there's been an accident and you're coming up to help out. Got it? The east end of the powerhouse! I'll see you in two hours!"

I hung up the phone and made my way to the door, grabbing a chair in the process. I stood on my tiptoes, fixed the ceiling tiles, unlocked the door, and slipped down the stairs. The police swarmed the building shortly after, dressed in orange life jackets. They stretched a dragnet of giant hooks and nets across the quarter mile face of the powerhouse, looking, hoping for some sign of a corpse. They were serious, too—

the captain was barking orders and shouting commands through a bullhorn: "All right you guys, pay attention. We still don't have a body yet, but it won't take long until Mosquito spills its guts, and he drifts down here."

Shortly after dispersing, one of the cops shouted, "I got him. Give me a hand." They bunched together, throwing a giant snagging hook into the current. The hook found my waders. It wouldn't have been the end of the world if the police found me. I could have fingered the thugs who damn near killed me. I would have taken great joy in seeing them squirm. The lawyer we hired to handle the civil case would have loved to have my testimony; surely it would have bolstered our case. But then there were all the police reports that had to be done, and then Surety's lawyers would grill me. No, it would be better if the police and everyone else thought I was dead. Then we could carry out the rest of our plan.

I'm sure Don Tadrick and his bands of goons were smiling at the prospect of my demise. They must have figured that they pulled off the ultimate murder. They started Gerry's boat, lit a rag stuffed in the end of a jar of kerosene, and drove it into Mosquito Bay. Since there was no body, it looked like it could have been an accident. No witnesses, no evidence, no smoking gun. In a year the police would rule my disappearance an accident. In a month the evidence I had stockpiled against Surety Guarantee would be nothing but a memory. They were in the clear, and would have smooth sailing to defeat our case against them.

I wondered if Jamie had gotten the call yet. Or Caroline. Gerry probably called Caroline to get Jamie's number, maybe my parents' too. How hard would Caroline take it? She'd be strong and confident under pressure, just like she was when the chips were down at the office. And Jamie, my Jaim. She would be a mess, and wouldn't forgive me for continuing my journey to the Sault. She would have to explain to her boys that I wouldn't be around anymore, that momma didn't want to cry but couldn't help it. She would be out of a job with more questions than answers.

And all my old policyholders...they trusted me to insure their biggest investments. They were my friends, and I was theirs. How many of them would remember me for being the best agent they ever had? How many of them would think of me as just another salesman? I did my best for them, and that's all they could expect.

The policemen's posture went from intense, to relaxed, to downright bored. After a half-hour they brought out some bloodhounds that walked to the place where I jumped out of the river. I was busted. I saw the dogs and knew their body language—the quickened pace, the deliberate track, the wagging tail. The dogs led the cops to the boarded up window, in between vats of salmon, then up the flight of metal stairs. The dog was good.

The police knocked on the door, "open up in there. This is the police..."

It seemed like minutes before the door slowly opened, and two students backed away. They looked awfully young. They looked naïve. They were guilty.

"I'm sorry, officer," he said.

"Please, officer, everything is okay. We had a key, but the door was open when we got here," she said.

"Are you okay, Miss?" the officer asked. His dog still pulled at its leash, sniffing at her thighs.

"Oh yes, officer. We were just studying up here," fumbling with the buttons on her blouse.

"Okay, miss, what is your name?" One officer opened his

pocket notepad and scribbled information. The other officer escorted the dog to the truck waiting on the curb, where Jack would hopefully meet me in a few minutes. There were police vehicles everywhere. This was going to be tricky.

"And you, sir?"

"Andrew Frett, from Westland. I'm not a fisheries biologist, but I do like to fish. She's my girlfriend, and we came up here to…study."

"Biology?"

"That's right, biology."

"You're claiming the door was open, is that right?"

"Oh yes, it was open."

"Have you seen anything suspicious?"

"Just that hound up here snooping around."

The cop became agitated and stormed down the stairs. If he had looked over his head to where the false ceiling met one of the girders, he would have seen me standing there, water dripping off my pant legs, arms crossed in shivering stupefaction. I had a view of the parking lot, the entrance to the aquatics lab, and the raceway outside. I watched the cop put his dog in the kennel and drive away. He should have been more patient. Any avid bird hunter knows to trust his dog. The dog knew where I was, but the police gave up too soon.

I looked down at the raceway; the police were huddled together in groups of three or four. They were smoking cigarettes and laughing. Hardly any of them were watching the river; they were just killing time until the guys in charge called off the search. It was a beautiful morning; the sun shone on the east end of the powerhouse, through the wavy windows, against my skin. It felt warm and good. I looked down the long drive that ran adjacent to the fenced canal and saw Jack's black Thunderbird.

I moved the ceiling tile again, used the girder as a launching pad, and gracefully landed on the top metal step. It stung my bare feet, but I kept moving, down the stairs to the main floor. All I had to do was walk 20 yards and I'd be free, but when I reached the bottom stair, I saw two cops coming right at me. Instead of bolting, I turned right toward a large box of life preservers. I pulled several out of the box, but the two policemen stopped, not three feet behind me.

"Who's in charge on this one, the Coast Guard, or the Department of Natural Resources?"

"You know, I think the Guard's on this one."

"How much longer, you think?"

"Hour, tops. If he hasn't shown up yet, the whitefish and seagulls are having a meal of him by now." I reached in the box and found a pair of big yellow boots. They fit. Rolling up my sleeves, I pulled a smelt dipping net off the wall. In no time I was headed for the giant rollaway door at the east end of the powerhouse.

"Hey," one of them shouted. I stopped and turned around slowly, thinking that they'd recognize me. "If you're going out there on the raceway, you'd better put this on." He tossed me a plump orange life jacket emblazoned with the letters, EDISON.

"Thanks." Jack's car was parked 30 yards away, but it seemed like it took me 15 minutes to get there. I walked behind the bumper, tossed the smelt net on the curb and hopped in. The heater was blaring, but it felt great. My feet were cold, and I was tired and weak from the whole ordeal. I couldn't believe that I pulled it off. Everyone except Jack thought that I was dead. What a great cover. What a great way to get even with Tadrick and his band of goons.

I couldn't wait to crash their party on Mackinac Island.

Forty-Four

"JACK, JACK. OH Jack. Thank you. Man, what have we done! Oh, man. I could be dead by now..." I felt like I was about to vomit. I felt like I had just cheated death. I was safe, but I couldn't believe it. It was hard for me maintain my composure. "Thanks for coming so soon. Come on, step on it. They may be watching out for me."

"Who?"

"Them!"

"Who's 'them'?"

"Surety Guarantee, man. They want me dead. They tried to kill me this morning, and they almost succeeded."

"Wait a second; I thought you came up here duck hunting. How did they almost kill you, and how did you get hung up in the bowels of that building?" He pulled out of the powerhouse's driveway, and onto the road that lead to the bridge over the river. When he neared the bridge, I told him to slow down.

"Here's where they tried to kill me. They threw me off this blasted bridge."

"What?" He slammed on the brakes, jumped the curb and put his Thunderbird in park.

"Yes! That's exactly what they did." I jumped out of the car, and stood on the sidewalk. Jack joined me. We looked down—some 60 feet—to the cement-lined, churning river, then a quarter mile downstream to the powerhouse, where policemen still sauntered on the grass raceway.

"Holy shit, Hanson. They mean business this time," Jack whistled, sending a toothpick spiraling to the water's surface. "Was it Tadrick?"

"No, no. Remember that clown at the courthouse? That big burly dude with the brown suit?"

"It was him? He must be part of that corporate stewards department that was in that memo. But how or why did they throw you off this bridge?"

"They threw me in their trunk at the boat launch, then hauled me up here in handcuffs—the same plastic straps we used on Tadrick. I sawed them apart on a piece of metal in the trunk just before they threw me over the railing.

"Let's go. They think that I'm dead. The police think that I'm dead. Gerry thinks that I'm dead too. Let's go. We've got some work to do."

Jack jumped in and drove away. "Where are we going?"

"To the cabin. I've got a gun to pick up." He pointed the car south toward the cabin downstream of the locks and Sault Ste. Marie.

"You know, I'm driving up here listening to the radio and I started hearing reports about a missing downstate hunter, and I figured that there is no way it could be you or Gerry. You guys are too experienced—it must have been some other hunter. And my wife! I made up some story about an accident that might have happened. She nearly blew a nut. I really should call her and tell her that you're okay and that I'll be home soon."

He picked up his phone and began pushing buttons, while keeping one eye on the road.

"Not so fast."

"What are you doing? I picked you up, you're okay, right?"

"I'm okay, but I could have let the police pick me up to make sure of that. We've got a golden opportunity here to screw over the company and really send a message. I'm talking about revenge. Besides, they *were* talking about me on the radio."

"What are you suggesting?"

"Let's go to the cabin, pick up my gun, then drive to St. Ignace and get a motel room. That'll give us time to think about our situation. We'll come up with a plan."

"Why St. Ignace?"

"Because Surety Guarantee is having their agent's convention on Mackinac Island the day after tomorrow. Surety Guarantee is having a party Monday and we're going to crash it. Us and all the ghosts of agents past." I fumbled through his glovebox.

"Now what are you looking for?"

"A piece of paper—I memorized the license plate of their vehicle and I don't want to forget it. They've got my wallet in the trunk of their car, and I want to get it back."

"You don't have any money?"

"Or credit cards."

"Lovely. Guess I'm buying."

Forty-Five

At noon Jack checked into a motel on the north end of St. Ignace. I stayed in the car with the doors locked, still paranoid that Surety Guarantee's goons would see me. I had to avoid everybody that might recognize me. If one of my buddies at Surety Guarantee saw me, our cover was blown.

When we got into our room I turned on the television. The evening news was just starting, and the lead story was about a missing hunter. We watched the reporter silently, on the edge of the bed: "*Police are investigating the disappearance of a downstate man who was supposed to meet a friend at this Sault Ste. Marie boat launch. When the friend arrived to go hunting, the boat was missing and so was the man. Thirty minutes ago, police found the charred remains of the missing hunter's boat, beached on the rocks across the expanse of Mosquito Bay, but the downstate man is still missing.*

"Police say that around this peninsula is swift current that last year claimed the life of another downstate man. He allegedly fell out of his duck boat during a storm that kicked up waves that were three feet high. But as you can see, today the weather is nice

and balmy, so police aren't ready to give up the search for the man. Here is an excerpt from a press conference held minutes ago by police chief Darren Whitefoot: 'The Sault Ste. Marie police department, in cooperation with the United States Coast Guard, continues to search for a downstate man who was reported missing at approximately 6:30 a.m. Saturday morning. The man is an experienced boater and sportsman, and his disappearance is still under investigation. This is the second year in a row of boating accidents during duck season. Last year's incident has been investigated, and only recently was ruled an accident. We will release the name of this individual pending notification of relatives.'

"That's the story from Sault Ste. Marie. To summarize, a downstate man is reported missing in an apparent boating accident. Police aren't willing to give up the search yet and are asking anyone with information about the case to call the number listed on the bottom of your screen. Reporting live from Sault Ste. Marie…"

Jack flipped off the television and laughed. "I've got some information. Ha-ha-ha. I've got the downstate man in my motel room and he doesn't want me to say anything. Ha-ha-ha."

"Hey, shut up; someone might hear you, and then we'll both be dead."

"Well, what the hell? We can't stay here for the rest of our lives. What do you want to do?"

"The first thing I'd like to do is get out of these hunting clothes and take a warm shower. I'll think of something. Hand me that bag of dry clothes will you?"

Fifteen minutes later we were in business.

Forty-Six

WHEN I CALLED Jamie, she was hysterical. Gerry had already called to give her the news. She was distraught. So was Gerry. They were already talking about a memorial service and who would make the arrangements. Ghastly.

"I thought you were dead!"

"Shhhh, Jaim. Don't say anything. Promise me that. Shhh."

"What do you mean don't say anything? You're alive! You're alive!"

"Jamie, please. Be quiet. Don't let your mother hear anything."

"Why? You're alive! What happened?"

"Jamie, please. Come on—don't say anything. I can explain. Leave the boys at your mother's and come up to St. Ignace. I'll explain then. But don't say anything to anybody. Tell your mother that you need to come up here right away." She calmed down slightly, and I gave her the name of the motel and a list of things we'd need.

"Oh, I almost forgot. The neighbors called and said that someone broke into my house last night," she sobbed again.

"What! Are you okay?"

"Yes, I'm okay, that was the least of my worries until you called. The police are looking into it, and I'm going over there to see what's missing or damaged."

"Did the police say anything else?"

"No, other than it must have been a robbery…everything in my house is trashed…something random."

"Okay, the most important thing is that you're okay, right?"

"No, the most important thing is that *you're not dead* or missing!"

"Right. I'm alive, and I can't wait to see you. Call me from the road so I know what time to expect you."

"It'll probably be awhile. I've got a lot of things to round up, and the police might keep me for awhile too."

"Drive safe."

"Safely."

"I love you."

"Love you too."

Jack rolled his eyes at me. "You're really caught up with her, aren't you?"

"You know, I've never met anyone like her. She doesn't try to control me or twist things around. No head games. She's just great, and I really love being close to her."

"Look out. She'll try to get her hooks into you. All women do that."

"You mean marry me?"

"That's what they all want," Jack said.

"What's wrong with that?"

"Haven't you heard the old saying? 'When a woman gets married she spends the rest of her days hoping he'll change, while the man hopes she never does.'"

"Is that how it works, Jack? You old married man?"

"Just offering you a little advice." Jack was gathering his wallet, a small pile of coins, and his watch off the motel's countertop. He had been married for a dozen years or more, and I could see that he wasn't putting much effort into the relationship.

"Anything else?"

"No, let's go."

"Wait." Jack paused, slid his arm into the sleeve of his jacket and looked back at me. "I think you've got a great wife, and if there's anything I want more it's to be happily married like you. I think if you spent more time wooing your wife instead of cohabitating with her, you might look at marriage a little differently."

"Are you sure?" He had the door open and was getting antsy.

"Let's go eat."

Forty-Seven

On Monday morning Jamie and I woke up early. She went down to the lobby and picked up some coffee, rolls and fruit, wearing a blue jogging suit. She looked like a tourist, which is exactly what we were. Indian summer had its hold on northern Michigan; when I threw open the curtains of the motel room, seagulls swooped halfheartedly on mild breezes across the sunny sky. When I turned on the news, they had more details about *"missing downstate man Larry Johanson, Mt. Pleasant businessman, aspiring writer, and what neighbors called 'a nice man and neighbor—kept to himself and never caused much trouble.' The Coast Guard has all but given up the search for his body. Police fear that he may have been swept into the power canal and into the turbines at the powerhouse a mile downstream."* They showed a picture of me with the caption "Mt. Pleasant duck hunter, feared missing."

It was weird. Here I was, watching the news report of my death on television. Jamie laughed at their ignorance. She liked making love to the ghost of Larry Johanson, "Better than the real thing," she rejoiced with a snicker. "I've never had sex with a stiff before. All you do is lay there." And all the Surety

Guarantee people watching the same news reports—they must have thought that they had done a good job of getting rid of me. My old buddies in the district—they must have had a bit of remorse, for seeing me go at such a young age. I had friends who were Surety Guarantee agents outside the district too—they must have been shocked at my ill fortune. Poor Gerry; he must have been a wreck, having lost two hunting partners in two years. He wouldn't forgive me for quite some time.

The Surety Guarantee meeting was scheduled to take place at the Grand Hotel at 10 a.m. The Grand is one of the oldest hotels on the island, and without question the most prestigious. The hotel is surrounded by ivory pillars and lilac gardens. The famous Mackinac Bridge, which connects Michigan's Upper Peninsula to the Lower, stands guard in the background. The view is spectacular, the ambiance splendid, and the atmosphere steeped in tradition. What a great place for a meeting. It's a great place to rally the troops and tell them all about what's in store.

Mackinac Island doesn't have any motorized vehicles. Tourists rent bicycles, two-seater bikes, and horse-drawn carriages. The only way to get to the island is via ferries from the mainland at either St. Ignace or Mackinaw City. Surety Guarantee reserved a block of parking places on the St. Ignace side of the Mackinac Bridge. They placed a huge sign over the parking lot: "Welcome Surety Guarantee Agents."

Jamie, Jack, his wife and I took the 10:00 a.m. ferry across to the island. I felt kind of silly hiding from people by wearing a baseball cap and sunglasses with my suit. Jack let the wind blow through his hair on the upstairs balcony. It must have been the sailor in him. He didn't care who saw him. He didn't care if Surety Guarantee knew he was there. But then, he was only half the surprise.

After the ferry came to rest dockside, a horse-drawn carriage took our gear. Jack hopped aboard and shouted, "The Grand Hotel, sir, and shake a leg." The little man in the driver's seat tapped a pair of giant draft horses on the chops, pursed his lips and whispered, "Let's go." The cart lunged ahead and we were off—the giant hooves clip-clopping on the red brick road.

Several minutes later we strolled by the lilac gardens, now almost dormant in the swansong of the year. The carriage jerked to a halt as the driver threw the parking brake under the balcony. Jack hopped off and walked away, letting his wife fend for herself. I jumped off next and helped her down the steps, mumbling something about "who said chivalry was dead." She giggled, and so did Jamie. We checked in like we were tourists, directing the busboys to put our luggage in our rooms, and the other equipment in the conference room we rented.

When we walked into the room, Allison was waiting for us, still confused with what we had up our sleeves. "Don't worry, Allison," Jack directed. "Just listen to what Hanson tells you. Do exactly what he says and you'll be in good shape by the end of the day."

I asked Allison to give me a hand with the electronics. She seemed amused with our grand scheme. We heard voices behind the plastic divider wall, but we didn't pay much attention to them. When we were all ready I gave Allison a white cotton blazer to go along with her dark slacks. Jamie had one too. As we neared the front desk, I slipped into the phone booth and made a couple phone calls—one to detective Plouf in Sault Ste. Marie, the other to the constable on Mackinac Island. I then hid beneath the white linen tablecloth inscribed with the words "Microtel Inn."

Allison and Jamie rolled me through the closed doors of the meeting room, and along the aisle way. Over my head, I heard the coffee service jingle. The voice on the public address system kept rambling about the necessity to cut the agents' commission. It was pathetic. They were lying again when they said there was no other alternative. I heard grumbling from agents near and far as the cart moved slowly toward the front of the room. When the cart stopped, I watched Jamie's feet move to the side of the cart. The coffee service jingled again and then her feet walked away. The voice on the public address kept rambling until I heard yelling near the main table. "Hey, watch it. What's wrong with you? These are expensive suits!"

That was my signal, so I threw back the white linen, charged the podium, and seized the microphone. The crowd gasped. "Ladies and gentlemen, friends and colleagues, fellow insurance agents, frustrated professionals. I have come here today to save you from the ravages of the lies, deception, and bad faith this company has continually forced upon you." The crowd went from surprised to attentive.

"All right, mister, this isn't your meeting—get the hell outta here." I'm not sure who approached me in an expensive blue suit, but when he reached for the microphone, I caught him with a beautiful right haymaker that sent him sprawling toward the projection screen. Several cronies with fancy nametags caught him. It was then that I spotted Don Tadrick and the goon from the hearing with coffee spilled all over their jackets. They hid their faces in disbelief, and must have messed their pants when I popped out of the coffee cart. They must have thought I was a ghost. By then the crowd was getting restless.

"Listen to me, folks. These two men abducted me, threw

me in their trunk, then tossed me handcuffed into the St. Mary's River. They tried to kill me...Yes, constable, I believe you received a phone call about an attempted murder... Here are the two men responsible, and I am the man who they tried to kill." Mackinac Island's constable was in the rear of the meeting room, and as he approached the podium, Tadrick squirmed. "Officer, arrest that man too, for larceny and burglary. He has stolen property in his car."

Tadrick stood and shouted, "No! He's the only liar here. Officer, throw him out of here!"

"Ladies and gentlemen, please listen to me. I am here to offer you an excellent opportunity that Surety Guarantee only wishes they could. Please, settle down. I was a Surety Guarantee agent until last summer, and am now a recruiter, a District Coordinator if you will, for Michigan Miners. Unlike my former company, Michigan Miners has a reputation for honesty and integrity. We have enjoyed considerable success selling their products and I am here to make you all wealthy..." The words poured from my lips like I had practiced my speech for days. Maybe I was practicing it in my head. The police officer handcuffed one of the men at the table, then frisked the man seated next to him.

Tadrick's mouth was running nonstop, "Officer, we paid for this conference room, and he is stealing our agenda. This is absolute lunacy. I had nothing to do with larceny, with any robbery."

The cop didn't believe him: "Sit down and shut up."

"Before you hear any more lies, any more falsehoods, I want each and every one of you to have an alternative. We want the best that Surety Guarantee has—its agents. We know that you know how to sell insurance. Take a look at what we can do for you. Take a look at Michigan Miners, and how it can rejuvenate your career. The time has come to send Newark a message. Send these slimy crooks home to slither back under the rock that they crawled out from. Jamie, if you please…" Jamie pulled back the dividing curtain, looking a bit like a game show assistant in the process.

There, in front of a large screen of his own, stood Jack, the emcee of his grand business plan. The faces in the crowd turned and chuckled, not because Jack had said or done anything, but because of the ingenious way we stymied the company. "Thank you, Larry. Thank you, Jamie. How 'bout it folks? Wasn't that spectacular?" Jack put the microphone under his bicep and applauded. Everyone applauded, except for the big shots in suits at the front table. The cop led the three men away in handcuffs. "So long, Don, sorry you couldn't stay for the party. How do those handcuffs fit you? Hey, we know exactly how you feel. Agents, am I right? How long have we been handcuffed to a company that doesn't care about the agents? How long have you wondered about the integrity of the management?" Jack really knew how to work a crowd. He was drawing them in.

"What I'm about to show you the company wishes would never see the light of day. They want to keep this a secret. What a shame the cat is out of the bag." He clicked the remote and the screen went from a logo of Michigan Miners to the memo we grabbed from Tadrick's briefcase.

"And I quote: '*We contend that the agents have had little to do with the increased commissions and do not deserve this extra commission.*' Troublesome agents? Do not notify the corporate offices? Company stewards in Newark? I think the stewards aren't in Newark anymore, they just left for the jail on Mackinac Island."

The crowd roared approvingly, but I could tell that they

were truly surprised with the memo. *"Sincerely, Greg Gustoff...Is that your name, sir?"* Jack bellowed as he pointed the microphone at the podium, where the man I decked held a bloodstained handkerchief to his swollen lip.

"I can explain that!" He shouted, but no one could hear him because I still held his microphone.

Jack was quick to take up the fight. "Oh, sure you can. Who's going to believe you now? You cheated us. You cheated our families out of the money that was rightfully ours! You're pathetic. You don't deserve these agents! They can do better than Surety Guarantee! I suggest you take the first ferry back to the mainland before I show them the next graphic." Whatever his name was, he left. Jack showed everyone the filings from the state insurance department, which depicted the loss ratio for the company. The company was making money, despite their continual denials.

Then Jack clicked the machine and it showed everyone sample quotes from across the state. He picked nice cars in decent neighborhoods with average-aged drivers. From Grand Rapids, to Detroit suburbs, the results were similar—Surety Guarantee rates were almost twice as much. When he pulled out the home quotes, the results were the same—Surety Guarantee rates were more than twice as much as Michigan Miners.

"Do you think you could make some money with these products?" he asked. "We're just getting warmed up. Who sells commercial insurance here?" Jack raised his hand and about 30 hands in the crowd were held high. "How many of you would like to sell commercial but haven't been able to because Surety Guarantee software is so hard to figure out?" Almost everyone raised his or her hands. "Well, let me show you how easy this can be." The projector changed gears and brought up the software for the Michigan Miners rating system. In five minutes Jack rattled off a quote for a drycleaner in downtown Ann Arbor—not because he had it pre-programmed, but because that's what a member in the audience wanted to rate. "Look at that, we've got a drycleaner in Ann Arbor with property, liability, delivery coverage, and insurance to cover him if he ruins one of my $8 K-mart sport coats. All this for only $3,200! Is this competitive? Why don't you tell me?"

The man in the crowd shook his head, "Heck yes it is. I ran this one through Surety Guarantee and it was $4,900, but the guy said he was paying $3,750."

"Sounds good, doesn't it? Who wants to know more about Michigan Miners? Why don't we cut to the chase? How can you become Michigan Miners agents? Let me show you how we can get this done! Buckle up, ladies and gentlemen; we're going to change your career today. Today is the first step in the rest of your life." Jack went through each step of the process. He showed them how easy the change would be. He showed them all the things that Michigan Miners could do for them, and how Jack, Allison, and I would be their District Coordinators. He covered everything, and the agents loved it. He brought up the lawsuit, and how we were going to win, and win big. Soon we were conducting interviews, signing contracts and passing out the software packages.

Lunch came and we hardly missed a beat. After the agents signed up with us, they headed off to the only golf course in the island. Carts were allowed on the course, as long as they were electric powered and not gas. By 4 p.m. the boys were getting off the course and stopped by for a drink in the lounge. We were having a blast. There was lots and lots of laughter. Jamie was on my arm, and was inputting data into her laptop for the 73 new agents in my district, compared to Jack's 58 and Allison's 62. My old colleagues asked me questions about the future of Michigan Miners and its income potential. They also asked about how and why Surety Guarantee almost killed me, and found it hard to believe.

Jack and his wife were on their third vodka tonic when the six o'clock news came on the lounge television. "Hey, turn it up," they yelled. The bartender dropped his towel, reached for the remote control and turned up the volume. The lead story had all the sensationalism that news programs crave: *"Good evening. There has been a huge development in the missing downstate man feared drowned last weekend. This man, Larry Johanson, has been missing since Saturday morning, but police on Mackinac Island say that he is alive and doing well. In fact, Johanson was on Mackinac Island today, helping police apprehend the individuals responsible for his disappearance. Sault Ste. Marie police chief Darren Whitefoot has given this statement. 'Larry Johanson was abducted by these two men last Saturday morning at the boat launch on the west side of Sault Ste. Marie, then taken to the bridge on Portage Avenue and thrown over the railing. We know this is true because of Johanson's signed statement and the fact that his wallet was found in the wheel-well of the suspects' rented Lincoln Continental. Further, the suspects are employees of the insurance company that Johanson used to work for, and we allege that they were sent here from Newark as part of a major cover up.'*

"Police also have in custody Don Tadrick, who is the main suspect in a burglary at Johanson's acquaintance's house in Mt. Pleasant, Michigan. Whitefoot also said that Tadrick had one of Johanson's stolen shotguns strapped to the underside of his Mercury Sable.

"On a related note, Whitefoot added that the investigation

into the missing person Scott Husted has been closed. You'll recall that he showed up missing last duck season near the same place Johanson disappeared, and has been unheard of for almost 11 months. Whitefoot has officially closed the case, and deemed his disappearance 'an accident.'"

I couldn't believe it. There was Don Tadrick in handcuffs, getting shoved into a squad car in St. Ignace. My new shotgun somehow got strapped to the underside of his car's bumper. At least Tadrick had the good sense to leave the gun in the case so it wouldn't get beat up.

All the guys in the bar were laughing and carrying on—seeing the bully of the company getting carted off like a common criminal. What nobody noticed were the orange solicitation flyers that were still under everyone's windshield wipers. We put them there before we loaded the ferry—just in case any agents lost our information. And Chief Whitefoot, holding up my wallet as if it were the black leather gloves in the O.J. Simpson murder case. Gerry Buchanan knew about me now, Whitefoot was his brother-in-law.

Somebody needed to get me my wallet; I couldn't keep leaching off Jack and Jamie the rest of my life. I was sure that detective Plouf would be along any moment to take my statement and figure out what happened. He'd be mad about the way I dodged the police force inside the power plant, but that was okay. Whitefoot said that Scott's disappearance was an accident, that's all I cared about.

"What do you say, Jamie? Want to order some cheese and crackers, maybe something to drink, and go for a carriage ride?" I held up my drink, our glasses chinked and she smiled.

"Sure. Great idea, it's not too cold."

"Why don't you go up to the room and grab a blanket, and I'll get the goodies."

"Okay, see you in a few minutes." I gestured to the bartender and he ambled my way. I ordered a big spread, complete with fresh grapes, a bottle of wine, cheese and crackers. Jack tapped me on the shoulder and asked what I was up to. "We're going for a carriage ride. Jamie went up to the room to get a blanket."

"Sounds romantic."

"It does? Well, sure it does, that's why I suggested it. Women like that kind of stuff, even the married ones."

"Sure."

"Amazing, wasn't that? Man, the look on Tadrick's face when I stepped out of the coffee cart. He looked like he swallowed a goldfish. And the two clowns that tried to kill me…"

"They couldn't even do that right," Jack laughed again.

"Hey, you did a good job up there today. They loved you. Can you believe how many agents we enlisted? Man, that was awesome. We're going to make a ton of money with these guys."

"We're going to make big money on our lawsuit against Surety Guarantee."

"They'll never learn. They'll keep up their routine for years. They'll keep hosing every agent and their customers until there are none left."

"You know what, though, we've got a plan in place, and we're going to be successful in spite of Surety Guarantee. Who knows, maybe they'll come around and become an honest company again."

"Don't hold your breath."

"Oh, I won't. They need a complete overhaul, top to bottom. But why are we talking about them?"

Jamie was back in the bar, and she bumped Jack on the elbow.

"It's Vanna White. Behind curtain number one, we have…"

Jack was laughing, his wife was laughing. They were laughing together. It was nice to see them happy; it was nice to see them happy together. Maybe what I told him about his marriage made him think.

"Behind curtain number one is Jack Jenkins, a.k.a., Pat Sajack," she giggled. "You were awesome up there."

"I bet you say that to all the boys."

Jamie put her arm in mind, and bobbed her head my way, "No, I only say that to the boys that matter…" She winked at Jack, then asked me if I was ready to go.

"After you, Frau-line." I grabbed our care package off the bar and lead her to the front of the Grand. The concierge was bundled in a thigh-length, black cashmere topcoat and top hat. Beyond the grounds, the lighted spires of the Mackinac Bridge were beginning to glow. A band of a dozen Canada geese dropped over the town and into the safe harbor.

I ordered a carriage, and the concierge waved a man up from the bottom of the hill. I put my arm around Jamie as it approached. She looked up at me and said, "this is great, just look at that carriage. It's beautiful." It was too, with huge, frail wheels, white sides, and blue velvet interior. Two white horses were decked in polished brass and porcelain hardware. The coachman asked where we were going, as I took Jamie's hand and helped her aboard. She couldn't stop smiling.

"How about a tour of the island? Take your time."

"Yes, sir."

Jamie spread the blanket and draped it over our legs. "Burr," she said. "My little nose is cold."

"Would an Eskimo kiss help warm it up?" I turned to her and our noses brushed against each other, eyes caught in a momentary lover's stare.

"It is cold," I whispered. "You'll never make it as an Eskimo."

"I don't want to make it as an Eskimo—don't the women have to make candles out of whale blubber and stuff like that?"

"Blubber keeps you warm."

"What are you suggesting, Mr. Johanson? That I put on a few extra pounds to keep warm?"

"No, no. I like blonde-haired, green-eyed, thin Eskimo women like you. That way, I can keep you warm." I gave her arm an extra squeeze. "Besides, your career as a game show hostess demands that you maintain your svelte, sexy physique."

"You like my physique?"

"I *love* your physique."

"What about the rest of me?"

"I love the whole of you."

"How about pouring me a glass of that bubbly?"

"Sure. Maybe we should have packed a thermos of hot apple cider instead." I reached into the wicker picnic basket and pulled out the small bottle of chardonnay and two long-stemmed wineglasses. Our horses kept clopping on the brick pavement, our carriage lunging softly every few steps. We were in historic downtown Mackinac Island, where the fudge shops that attract tourists like bees to honey in the summertime were now barren. "So what did you think about today?"

"That was fun."

"You really think so?"

"Oh yes. The look on Tadrick's face when I spilled coffee all over the front of him…I wish you could have seen it. It was great. Serves him right too, for all he did to us."

"Jerk."

"You did a nice job too. The way you pummeled that guy from Newark; I didn't think you had the guts to do it."

"You liked that? This hasn't been the best year for my right hand," I said, kissing my knuckles like a heavyweight boxer. "The whole thing was gutsy, but it worked. Wait till Michigan Miners hears about this. They'll love us."

"Are you ready to be in charge of all those agents?"

"Most of them are really good people, really strong agents. All they wanted was the same thing I wanted—one good company to represent. I'll need lots of help, though, and I hope I can count on you."

"I might want a raise, first," she asked.

"How much?"

"I don't know. You want to make sure your employees are perfectly satisfied don't you?"

"Well, sure I do." She sipped the last of her wine, then reached in the basket and pulled out a handful of chocolate covered strawberries. The first of several melted in her mouth, and one or two in mine.

Our carriage had made the turn and was headed back to the hotel. I wanted the day to last. I wanted to feel Jamie on my hip for the rest of the night. She was amazing. "I'm not in a very strong bargaining position now, though."

"Why's that?"

"Because I've fallen in love with my best employee, and she's got me over a barrel."

"She sounds like a pretty shrewd negotiator, and just as good a schemer as you are."

"Think so?"

"Well, you're out of aces now, aren't you? Wasn't today the last part of your grand plan?"

"Don't bet on it. I still have one more trick up my sleeve."

"Come on. You're done. Isn't this the part when we ride off into the sunset, win the lawsuit, and collect millions of dollars from the big bad insurance company?"

"I think I'm getting misty," I said, dabbing a mock tear. She swatted me again, laughing, then tipping her head to my shoulder. We were climbing the hill to the entryway of the hotel. Our ride was over. Our big day had passed. I paid the coachman and helped Jamie out of the carriage. A few steps later we were back inside, near the front desk. "I've got a little business to take care of here; do you want to wait for me at the lounge?"

"No, I'll wait for you here."

I reached in my suit coat pocket and pulled out two documents, asking the blazer clad woman behind the counter if she'd fax them to the numbers on the coversheet. She asked if I wanted them back or placed in my room's mailbox. "I'll wait."

Jamie's elbows were on the countertops, attention turned to the bustle of the lobby. My eyes turned to the locket she wore over her turtleneck and how it rested in the valley of her chest. She mentioned something about getting some dinner. The wine and berries made a good appetizer, but we both were hungry. "How about some nice whitefish? The chef is famous for his planked whitefish and cherry pie."

"Sounds great, what are you faxing?" she asked.

"Oh, I have to report a couple of claims before I forget."

"Claims? Someone at the office?"

"Not exactly, it's not even for Michigan Miners."

Jamie looked confused. So instead of explaining what was going on, I handed her the "Report of Claim" documents that had just exited the fax machine.

One claim was against my homeowner's policy for $9,500 and it involved a stolen gun, and the other was for a $250,000 life insurance policy.

"Oh wow," Jamie said, with a confused look on her face. "Who's the beneficiary on that one?"

I smiled, almost embarrassingly so.

"Really…who died?"

I nodded toward the papers in her hand, watching her lovely eyes pan left and right, as they scrolled down the page. Suddenly her right hand covered her mouth in shock. She blinked, and blinked, seemingly unable to comprehend what was written on the page. "Scott Husted?" she asked, even more confused. "But that was a long time ago."

"I know, I know…I took out a policy on him before the accident."

"Yeah…but…that was."

"No…I don't understand. Jamie?"

"Why did you wait so long to turn in the claim? Did it have to do with the police calling his disappearance 'an accident'?" She looked like she could start crying at any second.

"No way. I forgot that I had the coverage…really. I took out the policy last year before this whole thing happened…when Scott bought our office building. I figured that I should have some sort of coverage on him since he was my landlord. The life application was just one of the many papers he signed that day. When I got the renewal notice it reminded me that I still had it, and I should turn in the claim."

"Is there more to this?"

"More to what, Jaim?"

"Please tell me." She cradled my hand in both of hers, eyes swelling with tears.

"That's it. It was an accident, and this whole thing is behind us now. We have our whole lives ahead of us, and I want you in mine. You believe me, don't you? Jaim…"

The world stood still. We were face to face, only inches

apart. I brushed a tear from her eye, and held her trembling hands. All I could do was ask her one more time. "You believe me, don't you?"